"When you sit with a nice girl for two hours, you think it's only a minute.
But when you sit on a hot stove for a minute, you think it's two hours.
That's relativity."
Albert Einstein

THE BENJAMIN CHRONICLES:

RELATIVITY

Matthew DiConti

Libby
Enjoy the Book!
Matt DiConti

To my best friend and the love of my life, Erin.

Acknowledgements

My editor, Casey Hynes, thank you for all your hard work and dedication.

My proofreader, formatter, and basically the person who gave my work the fine tuning it needed, Toni Rakestraw, thank you for helping me across the finish line.

Rachel Thompson, and Shawn Dusseault, thank you for your advice and support.

Thank you to the family and friends who supported my writing. Mom, Jenine, and Tracy: you read the entire first draft and smiled. You deserve a medal for that. Sherry and Allyson, thank you for your support.

My son Austin ~ Life is a gift, make the most out of the time you have been given, no matter how crazy people might think you are.

Thank you to my Lord and savior Jesus Christ for the strength and determination to follow my dream of writing.

One

It was an atypical storm, even for springtime in California. Rain had been pouring steadily all day and now it slashed angrily from the sky, slamming against windshields and windows like angry fists.

Conal Benjamin squinted through the downpour, nose inches from the dash as he tried to see beyond the wall of water. Headlights from the other cars slid toward him and a knot in his gut kept him tense. This was a bad one.

As a result of the storm, the shop had only seen two customers all day long. Customers were staying inside and that left the garage Conal worked at empty most of the day, giving him plenty of time on his own to think. That meant a bad day at work.

The other guys had learned pretty quickly Conal liked to be alone. Unlike the rest of them, who liked to sneak peeks at *Playboy* on the job, go for beers after work, and dreaded going home to their wives, Conal preferred solitude. At work, he liked to stay busy, his hands and mind covered in grease and car parts, no time for thinking about anything else. At home, he was alone. Conal had no wife to hate and didn't care to look at *Playboy*. There had been only one woman in his life, but she had disappeared and he missed her. Even if his heart had been able to get over her, his guilt wouldn't let him get near anyone else. After what he had done, he didn't deserve a wife. He deserved to be alone, spending his lifetime trying to fix this one mistake.

Thunder rolled across the sky, booming as though Thor's hammer was being slammed down on top of him. Conal wasn't ashamed to admit that part of him hoped there was a giant hammer that would turn out his lights permanently. An end to this monotony and grief would have been a gift. But he didn't deserve that, either. And again, his guilt forbade him from swiftly bringing that end. If there was anyone who had even a hope of making it right, it was Conal. No one else. So that had become his life.

He embraced the fury of his surroundings, daring the other drivers, the elements, the universe to come at him. The bad weather was his respite. Nature was affording him a distraction and he was going to relish it tonight.

The other people on the road were driving like frightened rats abandoning a sinking ship. Blasting their horns; swerving in and out of lanes without a thought to use turn signals; drivers nearly killing themselves just to get somewhere five minutes sooner. *The irony of five minutes saved.* Conal laughed. A little more care could save their lives, but what did they know about that? No one ever knows that until it's too late.

It had always been like this, Conal going one way, the rest of the world the other. He buried himself in his studies. Ever since he was a child, Conal had loved to read. He devoured every book, every newspaper article, every text that was put in front of him. What he read took him out of his mundane high school existence and opened his mind in ways his classmates' surely were not. By the time he was halfway through high

2

school, Conal had trained himself to more or less ignore the world around him. He often preferred the one inside his mind, anyway.

It was ironic, he often thought with a sardonic smile. He had built a world for himself inside his head so he could avoid much of what was around him, and the one person who had made him want to come out of his own head was the one who it seemed would keep him permanently inside it.

There's a woman on the road!

"What the—!" Conal slammed his brakes to avoid hitting her, hydroplaning for what seemed an eternity before smashing into a nearby tree. The squealing tires, his head smacking the window, the jerking of the car as it settled. The blood dripping down his face. This was all unimportant to Conal. He needed to see for himself if he had seen a ghost or some kind of hallucination.

He swung the door open, practically falling out of the truck's cab. He had to know if the woman was all right. The rain showered him, clothes and all. Rain mingled with the blood streaking his face as he stepped outside. The woman turned to him.

Her face was twisted by terror and agony but there was no mistaking it.

"Abby?"

Conal began to run toward her and suddenly the street was full of people. Running, screaming people in strange dress, horror in their cries.

Abby didn't move. She stood still in the pouring rain, white as a ghost, her gray and red floral dress clinging to her soaking body. Her hair was matted down to her shoulders. Conal pulled his eyes from Abby for just a moment and felt sick. The screams, the cannon fire, the explosions in the distance. Abby was standing in a warzone.

"What in the hell is happening?"

3

He tried to reach Abby, but the faster he ran, the slower he seemed to move. Time seemed to drag Abby backward, the entire scene was being sucked away from him as though by a vacuum. The realist inside him told him it was another 'damned hallucination' but all his remorse, anger, and more importantly, love, for Abby wouldn't let the realist get a word in.

Conal tried to yell but the words were stuck in his throat. A man grabbed Abby by the arm and dragged her away; she screamed and thrashed in his arms.

"Conal!" Her voice caught in the explosions and just like that, she was gone.

No war, no people, no screams. No Abby.

Conal sank to his knees in the rain, sobbing. He wished he was dead.

Two

The sound of a blaring horn and squealing tires dragged Conal from his stupor. He heard a car door slam and the shout of nearby voices.

"Hey! What the hell are you doing? Are you all right, man?"

A burly, middle-aged man in a plaid shirt and denim jacket ran toward him.

"Was there an accident?"

Conal turned to him, still kneeling in the street.

"I-I'm not sure. I thought I saw—I must have hit the tree."

"Yeah, man, can't see anything out here. You're lucky you're all right. Anyone else in the car with you?"

"No, no just me." Conal could feel his throat tightening and knew there were tears in his eyes. He was grateful that the rain hid them. "Thanks for stopping. I'm all right. I've got it from here."

"Hey man, you're bleeding. You shouldn't be driving like that."

Conal looked down at his hands. The headlights from the man's vehicle shining through the rain lit them up, they were smeared with the rainwater and blood. "Shit," Conal muttered. "I must have hit my head."

"It's all right, I'm fine. It's just a cut, nothing major. I live close by and this truck is a tank, it'll get me home. Nothing a hot shower and some aspirin won't fix!"

The man rubbed his brow, looking down at the ground for a second, then he looked around as if to see if anybody was watching. "If you're sure...I-I can go call for help," the man shouted. Eager to return to his car, he had backed away from Conal and kept one hand on his door.

"Yeah, yeah, I'm all right. Thanks, though. I appreciate you stopping."

A sigh of relief passed across the other driver's rain-spattered face. "Sure. Take care of yourself."

Conal managed his way back into the driver's seat and stared at the tree a few feet from his face. A crack ran down the windshield in front of the passenger's seat and he had already glimpsed the damage to the hood and the fender. He didn't care about any of it.

Nausea settled in his belly and his head began to swim. He rested his forehead on the steering wheel, closing his eyes and letting blackness slide over his consciousness. He stayed there for a minute.

He had about five seconds before Abby's horrified face appeared before him again, her body writhing as she struggled futilely to pull herself out of the man's grip. But this time she wasn't gone. This time the scene played over and over again.

Conal gasped, shaking himself, coming to. His hands pulled the door handle, shoved the car door open. At some point, he leaned out of the car. His stomach heaved and he vomited on the pavement. He saw it happening, but none of it registered.

"What the hell is happening?"

He sat there for a few more minutes until he was able to focus. Some rational part of his mind reached forward and seized control, instructing him to drive home.

As the storm was beginning to let up, he reached his driveway. The darkness began to lift for the first time that day. Still groggy, he got out of the car, moving from the driveway to the mailbox, then scanned the stack of bills and junk mail in his hand. As he was turning up the walkway to the front door, a voice called out his name.

Startled from his daze, Conal dropped his keys.

"Ah, didn't mean to frighten you, Conal." Edith Clauson, an eighty-nine year old British emigrant who lived across the street from Conal, was making her way across the street.

"It's all right, Edie, was just in my own world is all."

"My goodness, Conal, what happened to your head?" Edie came closer when she spotted the lump on his head and the leftover blood that hadn't washed away with the rain.

"Got into a bit of an accident in the storm. Nothing major. No one was hurt. I'm fine. Tree's still standing. Just shook me up a little."

"I would imagine so. Are you sure you're all right? You should get to a hospital."

Conal sucked in a breath of air and exhaled slowly. Edie meant well. He knew that. But this was the last thing he needed right now.

"Nah, no need for that. I'm fine. Just need a hot shower and a good night's rest."

Edie looked unconvinced.

"Well, if you say so. If I can't get you to go to the hospital, I'll come by tomorrow morning and check on you, make sure you're all right. There's something I wanted to talk to you about, anyway."

Conal preferred that she never come by. Edie was a nice enough old lady, but he wanted to be left alone. Maybe that made him cold, but he was averse to entertaining lonely old ladies. The only people he had time for was himself and the ghost of Abby. Still, what was he supposed to say? She was almost 90. She had probably been looking forward to this all day.

Cue the guilt. *Why can't you be more sociable? This is probably what you need. A visit from another human being will probably do you good.*

Conal sighed with resignation. The sad thing was, that part was probably right.

"Sure, Edie. Tomorrow morning's fine."

Conal walked into the house and began his nightly ritual, stripping out of his uniform and throwing the greasy clothes directly into the washer. His coveralls caught on a hook on the laundry door and he yanked hard, ripping a hole in the sleeve.

"Dammit!" he screamed, tugging it free then throwing it into the machine with a slam. He wanted to hit someone.

"WHY?" He repeated that question over and over, unaware of the tears filling his eyes.

His six foot two inch, two hundred pound frame lumbered into the shower, collapsing under the scalding water, determined to burn away his skin, his thoughts, his memories.

Why?

That was the key to all of it. Why was he being tortured with visions of Abby? Why was she in a warzone? Why wasn't she here with him, or at least somewhere she could have a chance at a normal life? Why was any of this happening? What had either of them ever done to deserve this?

The cold hard reality of everything that had happened sent shivers rippling over Conal's skin. Conal wrapped a black towel around his waist, his back bright red and burning. He examined his scruffy facial hair for a brief moment. No grays yet, maybe tomorrow. He ran his hand through his wavy wet brown hair and headed for the kitchen to heat up his standard frozen dinner.

Conal flipped through a few frozen dinners he had, glancing at each cover and then tossing them back in the freezer one by one.

Lasagna, or chicken and carrots? "Lasagna." *In another life, I might be eating lasagna out at some fancy restaurant, with a bottle of wine and...*

He snorted and went upstairs to change while he waited to hear the familiar ding from the microwave. After two years of the same routine, he had this down to a science.

In his room, he put on a pair of sweatpants and a clean undershirt. A picture on the dresser caught his eye. It was of his parents. Another lump caught in his throat. They reminded him of when life had been easier. Duller, perhaps, but easier, sane. He turned the frame around and looked at the photo he'd stuck in the back. A wallet-sized photo copied from a high school yearbook. Abigail Bradley, age 18. It was the only photograph he had of her.

We never even took a picture together.

Conal heard the ding of the microwave, put the frame back and headed downstairs.

He carried his dinner to the living room and sat down to read. Conal had spent every night of the past two years reading, ever since the loss of Abby. The house was covered top to bottom with books of every genre and on every subject: history, physics, language, anatomy. What had once been a favorite pastime had become an obsession, an only way out. Aside from the History Channel, the television was never on. Edie would stop by occasionally to nose around or drop off some baked goods. Conal would accept politely, then shoo her out as quickly as possible.

The library had a purpose, but he wasn't about to discuss it.

The storm had picked up again, so he lit a candle in case the lights went out. He opened a book to where he had left off, dissecting Einstein's theory of relativity, a subject he was beginning to know uncomfortably well. Reading helped ease his anxiety, it gave him a sense of productivity, the illusion of moving toward a solution. He often read for hours at a time. Tonight, though, his eyes began to droop under the weight of depression and exhaustion. It had been a terrible day.

"I promise I'm trying, Abby. I promise. I'm working on it. I just need to rest my eyes for a minute, Abby, just a little while."

He was asleep within seconds.

Three

E xplosions. Conal was surrounded by them. Black clouds of sulphur choked the atmosphere and screams pierced the air before being drowned by more explosions.

Conal struggled to see clearly. He was lying on the ground, wounded. His vision was blurry and his mouth was dry. His body jolted with every thud, every pound.

"Abby..." Conal murmured. The pounding intensified.

"Conal!" A woman's voice broke through the fog.

More pounding.

Gasping, Conal sat up on the couch. His shirt was soaked with sweat.

"Conal! Are you there? It's Edie."

"Edie. Shit." Conal jumped off the couch, breathing heavily. "I must have overslept." "He peeked through the living room curtains to see Edie standing there, revved up and ready to go. "Uh, Just a second!" he yelled.

He stripped out of his shirt, rushing to find something relatively clean. He was out of breath when he came to the door.

"Edie, hey! I'm sorry about that. I guessed I crashed early last night and didn't wake up until you knocked. Please, come in. Let me just get myself together here."

"You could have had a concussion from that accident you were in. You've got to take better care of yourself."

"Yeah, thanks, Edie. I'm all right. Please, make yourself at home."

Edie's white brows crinkled together and her lips pulled off to the side as she was quite unconvinced, but she passed a covered basket to Conal as she made her way into the house.

"I'd love some iced tea," she said.

"Of course, where are my manners? Why don't you have a seat, and I'll be right back with your tea."

Conal paused in the kitchen, gripping the edges of the sink to steady himself. *That was a dream. This is reality.* Conal could hear Edie nosing through papers and books in the living room. *And there is an old lady in your house who will never leave you alone again if she thinks you don't have it together.*

Conal brought out some plates and the iced tea. He sat down across from Edie.

"This iced tea is delicious, Conal," she said after a few sips.

"Thanks. My mom used to make some pretty good tea when I was a kid."

"Well, my compliments to her. She taught you well. Conal, I'm going to get right to the point. You and I don't chat very often." Edie, tilted her head and paused for a brief moment as if she were searching for the right words." "No, no of course we don't why would we? I'm an old woman and you're a young man, so I won't pretend like we're close friends. However, we're still neighbors and we have been for sometime. I'm worried about you."

Conal began to fidget around in his seat, anxiously tapping his thumb on the arm of his recliner. *This is all I need.* "You don't need to worry about me, Edie. I'm a safe guy. I just go to work and come home, read for a little, and go to sleep. Wake up and do it all over again. Nothing to worry about."

Edie scanned the walls of the room, taking notice that the walls were completely bare. Outside of the mountains of books and bookshelves, there was no decor. "I watch you sometimes, Conal. I see you come and go, and no one else. No friends. No girlfriends. Not even a pet. It's just you here, and you don't appear to have much of a life. It's not healthy for a man your age to be so isolated. You don't even have any pictures out."

Conal sighed. "Edie..."

"Let me stop you there. You can tell me that everything is fine, but I suspect something is weighing heavy on your heart. You don't get to be my age without learning a thing or two about when someone's pulling your leg. Now, are you going to tell me what's troubling you?"

Conal's mind flashed back to his dream. Beads of sweat immediately formed on his brow. The explosions, the smoke, the screams. His heart began to race and his mouth went dry. Edie's words became unrecognizable as they echoed in the back of his mind. *Just tell her. Wouldn't it be nice to tell someone?*

"Conal...Conal!"

Conal quickly shook his head, snapping out of his flashback. "Huh? Oh! I'm sorry."

Conal sat there processing everything Edie was saying. What she said coupled with an oddly familiar feeling he had just being around her, allowed him for the first time in over two years to lower his guard. "All right, Edie. I'll be straight with you. You're right. It's not normal. It's not healthy. And it's exhausting. But there's a reason for it, a reason I keep to

13

myself. Most people are happy to assume that I'm a loner, a weirdo. If their lives are so dull they want to tell stories about why I keep to myself, that's fine by me. I couldn't care less. I have more important things to worry about."

"I'm not most people, Conal. I've lived across the street from you for the past two years and a sadder existence I've never seen."

Conal laughed bitterly. "Fair enough. All right, What do you want to know?"

"Everything. Whatever you want to tell me. I assume that somewhere along the way, this is about a girl?"

"What makes you say that?"

Edie shrugged, smirking to herself.

Conal paused, not knowing how to start this story. *Damn! She's good. Hmm, maybe it's safe to tell her? What's wrong with me? Why am I even considering this? She's a million years old, why not? Maybe it'll do some good. Maybe I could just come right out with it. You see, it's like this, Edie. I got cocky, made the biggest mistake ever and the love of my life paid the ultimate price for it. Probably not.* For a moment, Conal wandered, lost in his memories. *How had all of this begun?*

"Conal?" Edie prompted."

"Sorry, Edie, was just trying to figure out where to begin." Until everything had happened, Conal had lived a pretty normal life. He wasn't exactly an average child, although he was something of a loner in high school. He just kinda preferred books to friends, He wanted to hurry and finish high school and get to college.

He had a plan. He was going to do his working-class parents proud by being the first in the family to graduate from college. UC Santa Barbara. A good state school that allowed him to be close to home while pursuing his degree.

Looking back, Conal could see that his obsession with books and learning might have been an escape. He was the first to admit he was a little different from other people. He had never been able to put his finger on it, but when others wanted to go out to ball games and parties, he felt drawn to numbers and science. Some might consider it his calling, but it just felt like something more. Like there was some kind of an unexplained purpose for his passion.

After college, he landed a position teaching at a local high school, a job he loved. He was single and a little lonely sometimes, but he was optimistic. Women had never paid much attention to him, or at least if they had, he didn't notice it. Had he lived a little less outside of his own head, he might have noticed classmates and acquaintances who were trying to shake him back to reality. But he only ever stepped back into the real world for one woman. And now she was gone."

"This whole mess started about two years ago, just before I moved here. I was still teaching high school physics back then, and heard about a new exhibit going up at my alma mater.

"Edie, you should have seen this exhibit. It was incredible. In honor of National Science Month, the school showcased some amazing work.

"There was one exhibit in particular that I was looking forward to checking out: Einstein's never-before-seen "time travel machine." It was a recent discovery that had been made by the Albert Einstein Institute for Gravitational Physics. The institute built the machine based on some designs of Einstein's they recovered a few years ago. If it was real, it would be groundbreaking, a secret the great Albert Einstein had kept even beyond the grave. I was spellbound by the very idea, and humbled to know I'd be among the first to see it publicly.

"Most people still think of time travel as science fiction, the kind of thing you only see in movies or read about in books. What the majority of people fail to realize is, time travel is a reality. I admit, even I was skeptical about the possibilities, despite having been fascinated by it for most of my life. This exhibit was going to change everything."

"Conal, I was beginning to think you had nearly gone dead inside. It's nice to see you so passionate about something. Looks like I've found what makes you tick."

Conal grinned sheepishly. "It's been awhile since I've been able to talk about this with anyone."

"Well, go on. I didn't mean to interrupt. It's just nice to see you so open and lively."

"There I was, at the entrance to the exhibit. I hadn't been this excited about anything in a long time. I made my way through, checking out so many brilliant displays. They were fascinating. There were experiments utilizing various mediums for optical illusions, star wars military applications, life science genetics experiments, DNA mapping—literally rows of experiments.

"As I examined the exhibits, an old friend spotted me. Her name was Colleen Jackson. She was a beauty. Platinum blond hair, emerald green eyes, athletic. Physically, she was perfect. For some reason, Colleen always seemed to be into me but I never gave her a shot. I was always too wrapped up in my studies and..." Conal's voice trailed off. Even now, it hurt him to say it.

"And there was someone else, wasn't there?"

"Yes, there was someone else. It was silly, really. She was a girl I knew in high school. We had never even dated, just had a couple of classes together. She was beautiful. There always seemed to be a sadness about her, though. Maybe that's what I liked about her. Anyway, I never could quite get over her, and for years, I measured every other woman I met against her."

16

"What was her name?"

"Abby." Conal briefly fidgeted around in his chair. "Can we get back to the story? We're getting ahead of ourselves."

"Abby, what a lovely name. Oh yes, of course. I'm sorry. Go on."

"Colleen was excited to see me, way more than she should have been. Every time she had attempted to get together with me, I'd blown her off for one reason or another. This time, though, it was going to be different.

"I can still catch the scent of Colleen's sharp perfume, lingering around us as she reached up to hug me. The subtle twinge of electricity I felt when she touched me.

Maybe I should give it a try? I had asked myself. *This is getting ridiculous. I'm a grown man, I don't want to be alone forever. So Colleen's not the most intellectual woman I've ever met, maybe it's time I give her the benefit of the doubt. Besides she's hot, and she's into me. Why shouldn't I give her a shot?*

"And I was going to give it a shot, Edie. I really was. Contrary to the way I live now, there was a time when I wanted to find someone I could have a serious relationship with, maybe get married one day, or at the very least, go on a date.

"The way I saw it was, here I am in my mid-twenties, good career, nice home, and still single. So what if she doesn't make me nervous and tongue-tied the way Abby did. That had been high school and it was just a stupid crush. It was time to grow up and stop living in the past. Besides, what were the odds of running into Abby all these years later? These were all the things I told myself as Colleen hugged me, playfully teasing me for never being available to spend time with her, and resting her arms on my shoulders, her fingers locked as though we were slow-dancing.

"As it turned out, she was an event planner at the university, and had helped organize the event. 'Actually, Colleen, there is something I want to ask you.' Colleen's eyes lit up. I was about to go for it, about to ask her to dinner, when something behind her caught my eye as Colleen was pulling her hair back. I couldn't help but look behind her for a split second. 'That was odd,' I mumbled. I tried to brush it off and continue on. 'Well, Colleen, I was thinking that maybe...' Colleen tilted her head to the side, probably anticipating some kind of invite to a date. 'There it is again! Colleen, can you give me one second?' I systematically nudged Colleen out of the way.'"

"What? What was it, Conal?"

"My heart started pounding, curious about a blurry figure some thirty yards away from me before my thoughts could catch up. Edie, I thought I was going crazy, that I was broken. Every time I try to move on, I think of Abby and ruin something real for myself.

"If Colleen was offended, she had every right to be. I was shoving people out of my way to get closer. I was borderline desperate. I remember that I felt I could barely breathe. To be honest, I wasn't sure if I could handle it if it wasn't her.

"The closer I got, the more the figure took the shape of a five foot three inch, petite brunette. She was like a vision. My heart was like a jackhammer, beating uncontrollably, thrashing against my ribcage.

"The crowd and all the exhibits were now a blur around me. My vision became a tunnel. Standing in a gymnasium filled with hundreds of people, exhibits, booster club banners, and concession stands, all I could see against this palette of life, was a single being. And there it was —the nervous feeling I had been missing moments before with Colleen.

"I watched her pull her long beautiful dark brown hair just behind her ear, tracing her soft flawless complexion. Her hair was dark, the color of a rare Arabian smoky quartz gemstone with hints of amber in just the right light. Her smile was warm and inviting. The world came to a standstill around this woman.

"It was Abby."

Four

Conal shook his head, and wiped a small bead of sweat that had begun to form on the left side of his brow with the back of his hand, forcing himself to focus. *Nerves. Get it together, man. I'm not a teenage schoolboy anymore. I'm a grown man. I have a life. A small, routine one, but a good one. I'm more than capable of saying hello to an old classmate.*

The nerves and excitement dancing in his stomach said otherwise, but Conal forged ahead.

"Ahem, excuse me. Abby?"

For one heart-stopping moment, she stared at him, searching his face for something familiar.

Great! She doesn't remember me. Way to go, genius, she's going to think you're a stalker. Ought to be calling for security any second now.

"Oh my goodness! Conal Benjamin. Wow. How are you? What are you doing here?"

She sounded as flustered as Conal felt. Her friendly smile and eager to please attitude belied her cool, professional appearance.

"I went to school here and heard they were showing this exhibit. I've always been kind of a science nerd, couldn't resist checking it out. How about you? Do you work here?"

"Oh, no, I'm just helping out with the exhibit, actually. Conal, it's been so long. The last time I saw you was in high school, wasn't it?"

"Yeah, yeah, I think we were outside in the student parking lot. Weren't you crying or something?"

She looked at him quizzically.

Nice one. Come across as a stalker, and now we can add tactless and utterly socially inept to the list. You're batting a thousand, Benjamin.

"Well, how've you been? You kind of disappeared after the last time I saw you. I was worried about you, actually."

Before Conal could answer, a booming voice cut in.

"Abigail! What're you doing? You're supposed to be backstage. We're on in ten."

Seven years evaporated in that moment. Conal watched as once again, Abby went rigid at the sound of that voice, a look of sheer panic flickering across her face.

"Tristan, this is Conal. I'm not sure you two have ever met. Conal and I went to high school together."

Tristan clasped a huge paw on Conal's shoulder. The two were similar in height, but that's where it ended. Tristan had to be at least thirty pounds heavier than Conal, chiseled, and was built like some kind of demigod. "Nice to meet you, buddy, but the lady and I have work to do. You should come check it out. This shit will blow your mind."

"Yeah, maybe," Conal said, dismissing the thought immediately. "Which exhibit are you showing?"

"You ever heard of Einstein's theory of relativity? The guy thought it was possible to travel through time. Pretty cool, even for a weirdo. Well,

21

apparently he even built himself a time machine and we're going to reveal it today. I'm the spokesperson for the exhibit." Tristan mistook the dumbfounded look on Conal's face for being impressed. "I know, it's cool, right?"

You gotta be shitting me! This tool has my dream girl and my dream job.

He looked almost exactly the way Conal remembered; only now his hair was pulled back into a slick black pony tail, and he was obviously spending upward of the national debt at his local tanning salon. There was a faint line around his eyes from where his tanning goggles sat.

"So, Tristan, you're a scientist?"

"Nah, man. My father runs the company sponsoring the exhibit, said it'd be good for their corporate social responsibility reputation, or something like that. He suggested I present the exhibit, since, let's face it, I'm a lot more appealing than some nerdy scientist.

Abby caught the look on Conal's face as it twisted into contempt and disbelief.

"It's a really interesting exhibit, Conal. We should probably get going, the opening presentation is soon, but you should check it out. I think you'd be really interested in it."

"Yeah, I've heard a thing or two about it. Maybe I'll see you there."

How could she have not learned after all of this time? It felt as though someone had sucked the life directly from Conal's soul. Of all the cruel tricks of fate. Let him come within an inch of what it feels like to have everything you've ever wanted, only to watch it be snatched away by some Fabio wannabe with a greasy hairdo.

Someone slid an arm around Conal's waist, holding him tightly. The sharp scent of her perfume announced her before he even saw her face.

"Hey, you took off kind of quick. Not trying to sneak away from me again, are you?" Colleen grinned at him, a look of teasing merriment in her eyes.

"No, sorry, Coll. I ran into an old classmate from high school."

"Oh? He or she?"

"She."

Colleen's quickly put her hands on her hips in a pouting manner. "Dammit, Conal, just when I think I've got you pinned down, another woman swoops in to grab you away from me." Colleen stuck out her index finger, poked Conal in the chest, widened her eyes, and emphasized the next three words: "Not...this...time! We've got a lot of catching up to do." Colleen grabbed Conal's arm, squeezing his bicep like a child hanging on to a new toy. "But first, the opening presentation for the big Einstein exhibit is about to begin. I know that's right up your alley and I don't want you to miss it."

Conal's heart sank again. Here was a woman who actually wanted to be with him, a beautiful woman who knew his interests and actually cared what he thought, and all he could do was act like a petulant schoolboy, pouting because a girl, who had until a few minutes ago forgotten he existed, was here with another man.

He let Colleen muscle her way through the crowd to the exhibit so they were sitting close to the front of the stage, vaguely wondering if Abby would notice the gorgeous blonde at his side, and more importantly, if she'd be jealous. Not that it mattered.

Tristan was already speaking, gesticulating grandly as he described the many achievements of his father's company while grinning toothily at the audience. He was a good corporate spokesman, Conal admitted, but there was no way he was going to pull off acting like he understood anything about this exhibit.

Relativity was far, far beyond this guy's ken.

Abby was on hand to field audience questions, but had a tough time interjecting in the Tristan Show.

"Tristan..."

"Not now, Abby."

She turned back to the audience. "Those who have questions can line up behind the mic in the center aisle, and I'm sure Tristan will be happy to answer your questions before the unveiling. Tristan, I think we have a question over here."

Visibly agitated, Tristan covered his mic, lowered his voice and turned to Abby with a smile on his face but coldness in his eyes.

"No, I won't, Abby, dear. People can wait until after the presentation. Besides, I'm sure I'll have answered all of their questions by then. I'll call you back up when I need you.

"So what was the point of even asking me to volunteer and help out if you're not going to let me?"

"Oh believe me, Abby, you're helping."

Abby looked at Tristan, puzzled.

"You're eye candy for the audience, Abby. Come on, babe! Did you honestly think I needed your help with anything else? Look, let's not make this a big deal, okay? If you really want to be useful, why don't you fetch me a bottle of water? I'm parched up here." He shooed Abby away with his hand.

Anger and disappointment flooded Conal's system. He'd had enough. His entire life had been neat, orderly, and above all things, lonely. For years, he had dulled this pain with memories, doped up on his dream of Abby, and in the cruelest, sickest play at dark humor, life had given him this. The woman he thought was the love of his life was still with this...worthless jerk-off who talked to her like she was nothing more

24

than a damn trophy wife. He would have loved to go up there and throw Tristan offstage by the seat of his pants, but that would make him no better than Tristan.

Conal pulled a dollar out of his wallet, dropping it on the kid's lap sitting next to him, grabbed an unopened bottle of water from his hand, and stood up. "Actually, Abby, there's no need for that. Here you go, Tristan, I have an extra bottle of water."

"Hey!" the guy started to speak.

Conal ignored him and stepped up to the edge of the stage as Tristan reached down for the bottle of water. "Let's hope you know more about time travel than you do about manners." Eyes blazing, he stared hard at Tristan.

Colleen, who had been sitting with her arm linked through his, had sensed his tension and was staring at him with a look between bewilderment and concern.

Conal slowly released the water bottle to Tristan. Losing his mind over his high school crush wouldn't play well with this crowd. Besides, he already felt guilty enough about Colleen. There was no reason to terrify her with his misplaced anger.

Tristan looked as though he was struggling with a similar battle, clenching his lips together, and noticeably hiding the tightened fist he had just made behind his back.

He stared at Conal for a long moment before he turned his toothy, stomach-churningly sweet grin back to the audience. "Forgive me, ladies and gentlemen. I forgot myself. That was totally inappropriate on my part. It's no excuse, but this is the first time I've ever spoken in front of such a distinguished audience. Abby, my apologies."

The look on Abby's face made it plain she didn't believe a word dripping from his tongue, but she held hers, out of fear or for the sake of propriety, Conal couldn't tell.

"Moving on," Tristan said, giving a pointed look in Conal's direction.

Colleen gave Conal's side a little pinch and grinned at him.

"I like that you stood up for her," Colleen whispered.

Conal nodded, a twinge of guilt slicing through him.

"Ladies and gentlemen, let me add that light really is not a factor in time travel," Tristan said. "In fact, it is my opinion that this idea has gone so far as to actually misguide some of Einstein's experiments."

Conal shook his head, fury giving way to astonishment. *Who the hell is this guy? Where does he come up with this stuff?* Conal chuckled out loud. "Tristan, if Einstein were here today, he would be the first to tell you the opposite of what you just said," he called out. "Light is far more effective at twisting space and time than anything else."

Tristan was losing his patience. "My friends, we appear to have a scholar among us. Please, Mr. Benjamin, do tell, why would Einstein say that?"

Glancing over at Abby, I could see she was absolutely stunned at the interplay between Tristan and me. She looked curious.

"Well," Conal powered on, "If you were to use a very powerful beam of light and moved it in a circular motion fast enough, it could twist space, and close time into a loop. You just need a source of light that would be strong enough. This would create a wormhole. In Einstein's theory, a wormhole is kind of like a black hole, only far smaller, and on earth rather than in space. I'm guessing by the looks of your machine here, that he may have been trying to do just that."

"A wormhole; light—are you serious?" laughed Tristan. "Listen, little man, why don't you sit back and let the experts explain this?"

"Space and time are connected," Conal forged on, his vision blurring around Tristan. "A very powerful source would do it. It would have to be extreme light, like a star, or a bolt of lightning, something of that nature.

"Think about it like this, Tristan. Say you're traveling through space at exactly half the speed of light. Now imagine that I stayed here and fired a powerful beam of light past you. How fast do you think you would see the beam of light pass you? You're probably thinking, half the speed of light, right?"

"Obviously," Tristan replied, his eyes rolled.

"Wrong! It would pass you at the same speed it left me, the full speed of light. Your speed through space would make no difference whatsoever to the beam of light. Even if you turned around and traveled back into the direction of the oncoming light, you and I would both be seeing the light traveling at the same speed. So if both you and I see the light traveling at the same speed, then something else must be changing."

"Time?" one of the observers called out, emboldened by Conal's assertiveness.

"EXACTLY!" Conal called out. "It's pretty simple when you think about it. So, by this example, it proves that time can be manipulated, which is the basis for time travel."

A murmur of conversation sprung up among the crowd.

"Well, well, well. It looks as though we have ourselves a bit of an expert," Tristan said snidely. "Since you know so much about the subject, please illuminate us with your expertise. Why don't you come up and give us a demonstration?"

Conal and Tristan stared at each other, tension boring between them. From the corner of his eye, Conal could see Abby looking on, wide eyed, and uncertain.

"No, really, Mr. Benjamin," Tristan said. "Why don't you go ahead and take the floor? Please, a demonstration, if you would?"

Conal was fully aware Tristan was pining for him to make even the smallest mistake.

"Conal, get up there!" Colleen hissed. She shoved him out of his seat toward the stage. "Come on, Conal, do it."

Conal glanced back over his shoulder as he moved forward. "Thanks, Colleen!"

He could hear his inner voices swirling. This is your opportunity to do something big, something she'll really remember—The time is now. Fate is giving you a second chance.

"All right, Tristan, if you're sure it's okay?"

"Really, Mr. Benjamin, do you need a written invitation?"

Someone had to have Abby's back; Conal took a deep breath. *If shutting you up on stage is what it takes, then so be it...* He trotted up the steps to the stage, like a new contestant on some kind of game show.

"Thank you, Tristan," he said facetiously. "I don't mind if I do."

Conal felt his confidence grow as he spoke on parallel universes, and the dangers of going back in time and changing events of today by small changes we make to the past.

In defiance of Tristan, Conal had taken center stage.

"Ladies and gentlemen, I must admit to having been an avid follower of the great Albert Einstein, having read all of his published works again and again, and being a physics teacher myself. I have never attempted to travel through time before, but I'll safely demonstrate how to turn the machine on and walk you through what I believe the great Einstein would do to time travel."

Thoughts were swirling in Conal's mind as he turned to look at Abby.

"And now, ladies and gentlemen, I can't do this alone, so I would like to call up the lovely and extremely intelligent ABBY! Abby, if you don't mind, I could use your help."

Abby looked at Conal, shocked, then for a split second, glanced at the audience applauding her. She gave Conal a playful smirk. "Yes, of course."

Conal watched her gracefully walk up to the stage.

"Is this safe?" she whispered.

"Yeah. Everything should be fine. I'll shut it off if it starts getting weird."

For a moment, Conal felt like a Las Vegas magician with Abby as his assistant. He could see it so clearly: Abby in a sequined dress that showed off her ballerina-like legs, her smile wide and beautiful, only for him. His heart ached for a moment, the muscles tightening in his chest. He needed to concentrate on the task at hand *Focus! Watch what you're doing.*

He tried to work by instinct, trying to identify the switches and their functions by what he had read in Einstein's books and where he would have put them if he had built the time machine. *Funny, this thing looks like a stereotypical time machine. It's almost like what I read in the Wells novel. I would have thought Einstein would come up with something better than this.* Conal scratched his head in slight disappointment.

It was kind of like a small space-aged sleigh. Two six-foot-long curved metal rods protruded from a power source. Electrical charges shot back and forth between them. They were welded to the machine.

Abby sat with uncertainty in what appeared to be the passenger seat. She grabbed two nearby handles. The time machine had an energy meter on the side with about forty bars lit up and in big green letters the word 'CHARGED' was blinking. The machine was glowing like a small float in

29

a Disney Electrical Parade, and the drumming of its engine was drowning out the sarcastic comments Tristan was making to the audience.

"This one's shaking!" Abby shouted nervously, her hand wrapped around one of the handles.

The time machine sounded like jet engines firing up and it was vibrating rapidly, the entire control board shook. People in the audience began to back away." Shut it off!" someone cried.

Still, Conal was determined to make this a success. "Let me just make sure nothing is coming loose here!" He was standing outside the machine and delicately reached across Abby's lap to check the opposite handle, finding himself nose to nose with Abby. It was impossible not to catch her scent, a warm perfume and shampoo smell that made his heart ring in his ears. She was looking at him anxiously.

Conal tried to avoid looking directly in her eyes, hoping she wouldn't see through him, not thinking twice about his hands, and wrists that were once again a glowing bright red up to his elbows. Hell, his leg could have been on fire and he wouldn't have noticed it, and for a very brief moment, he imagined what it would've been like to kiss her. He knew this was unequivocally the best moment of his life.

Conal reached for the handle to pull himself back up. At that same moment, he felt a spark shoot through his fingertips.

"Ouch, dammit!" His fingers throbbed from the shock and Conal fell awkwardly on Abby's lap, slipping to the floor, and coming face to face with Abby's legs. For a split second, he looked right up Abby's skirt. *Awkward.* Realizing this, he instinctively grabbed onto her legs. His head was beginning to swirl with embarrassment and confusion. *For the love of God, let go of her legs! Holy shit! My hands are actually on Abby's legs!*

Before he could get his feet underneath him again, a sudden sound thundered, like a sonic boom, only stronger. Winds were swirling, lights were flashing erratically. Abby grabbed Conal's hand.

"What's going on? This isn't supposed to be happening! Turn it off!" Abby yelled through the hurricane-like winds. "We have to get off!"

"We can't! It's too dangerous!" Conal yelled. Abby was already buckled in. Conal glanced at the other safety belt, but instead wrapped his glowing red arms across her, holding her to the seat. The lights were flashing faster now, so bright Conal and Abby had to shield their eyes. She buried her head in Conal's chest, her screams muffled.

The scene was nothing more than blur now. Whatever was going on, the audience, the gymnasium, everything had disappeared, and the only thing below them was space and lights. With another massive jolt the machine bucked Conal right off Abby, forcing him to cling to the rail.

Conal glimpsed the light turning into many, stretching and bending; it had formed itself into a huge funnel.

Conal understood, but couldn't accept what was going on. Somehow he knew what was happening, however improbable it seemed. Years of studying and imagining this very thing were coming together now, and the knowledge gave him a sense of calm. He and Abby were hurling through a wormhole.

Five

Death had always seemed such a far-off thing to Conal. That's where he had imagined he would experience a wormhole. At least, he had hoped for it, that in his last moments of consciousness, he would at least hallucinate this one experience that was so alluring and yet so out of reach of man.

Perhaps he was dying now. But it didn't feel like he was dying, since his every instinct was telling him what he needed to do in order to live, and for Abby to live as well.

Abby clung to him and he clung to the machine.

"We just need to hold on!" It might have been true, but in truth Conal had no idea what to do. "I'm traveling through a wormhole." He began to laugh maniacally. Dead, unconscious, or in the most improbable situation imagined in human existence, Conal had to take this in. Panic and fear surged through his body alongside adrenaline, ecstasy, and a wonder he had not known since he was a child.

Then he looked at Abby and saw the terror written across her face as she screamed. The gravity of what was happening sunk in, socking him in the pit of his stomach. His palms were sweating, slipping on the rail he had been holding.

What the hell have I done?

Six

There was a brightness in front of Conal's eyes, a white light, almost as though he was staring directly into the sun. But his eyes were closed, squeezed tightly shut against the pain throbbing in the back of his head.

He heard someone screaming in the distance, it sounded as if the voice he heard was coming from under water. He opened his eyes slowly, and his head began to spin. He was nauseous from the pain.

"Conal! Conal!"

The voice was hysterical.

His head rolled in the direction of the sound. His vision was blurred; he could only see blobs of shapes and colors. What was the one moving toward him? The voice got louder as the blob moved.

"Conal!"

A familiar face, a pretty face floated above him.

I know her. The face was a comfort, an image he had seen many times before. *She seems worried. Why?*

It all came back to him as his vision began to clear. The tunnel of light, the shock as he grabbed the handle, the shaking levers, Abby.

"Abby." Relief shone in her eyes as he wheezed her name.

"Oh, thank God. Conal, I need you to wake up. I don't know what's happening. Where are we? I don't know what to do." She convulsed in tears, her sobs wracking her entire body.

Conal struggled to sit up, fighting off waves of nausea and the overwhelming desire for sleep. "It'll be all right, Abby. It will be okay." He swallowed his words as he surveyed his surroundings.

In truth, he fully expected to wake up on the floor of the gymnasium, humiliated from having hallucinated the entire thing and passing out.

He could not have guessed where he had ended up. His heart was pounding at the possibilities.

And then he was vomiting, his head exploding as his stomach retched and he clutched onto cobblestone in a futile attempt at finding stability.

Clearly he had been knocked out when they landed, or whatever it is that you do in a time machine.

Even a concussion could not keep at bay the sarcastic chuckle under his breath. He hardly dared to let himself imagine that this had actually happened.

The scent of horse manure carried lightly to him on a chilly breeze and he began to gag again. "Oh my God, okay, that's disgusting." *Don't worry about me. I'm fine,* he thought to himself

Abby cringed bitterly as she helped him to his feet. "I'm sorry, I just don't do well with throwing up. Are you going to be okay?"

"I'll be fine." *I don't have a choice.* "Just shaking the cobwebs loose."

"So do you have any idea where we are?"

He stared at the road, then looked all around in amazement and disbelief, reluctant to speculate until he had further confirmation. "I have no idea, Abby."

"Well, what happened? I don't understand. That machine wasn't supposed to work. It's never worked. It was just supposed to be some gimmicky thing that Tristan's dad's company was willing to sponsor as part of a PR stunt—'look how wonderful we are! We're bringing Einstein's treasures to life!' What happened to us?"

Conal heard what sounded like horse clatter in the distance. "All right, look, if that thing, that...machine, actually did what it was supposed to do, and given that we're not on the stage being harassed by Tristan anymore, I'm going to say that it did, then I'm going to go out on a limb and say that maybe... we just traveled through time?"

Abby's eyes widened. "That's crazy! This can't be happening." Her face went blank, and she looked unnaturally pale, almost colorless. "How could that possibly have happened? I know we were at a time travel exhibit, but this can't really be happening, can it? There's no such thing as time travel actually working. This doesn't happen to people. It's impossible. Okay, I just need to relax. We're going to be okay. I mean, at least were both alive, right?" Abby did her best to reassure herself.

"To tell you the truth, it sounds like a far likelier scenario that we have somehow died and both ended up in some sort of purgatory, than us traveling through time. However, we're still conscious and speaking. Either way, afterlife or another place in time, we've got to figure this out."

She nodded, biting her lip. "You're right. So can't we just get back on the machine and go home, and forget that this ever happened?"

"You can forget it if you want, but I'm not going to."

"You aren't terrified?"

"I'm a little scared, sure. But Abby, if we really traveled through time—if that machine actually worked...do you know what that means? Do you know what we've done? We're the first people in the history of the world to have traveled through time. Don't you get how incredible that is?"

From the frigid look on Abby's face she didn't have it in her to share Conal's enthusiasm. Her shoulders drooped as she summoned up the energy to rub her arms till they began turning pink. Then she began to rave. "So many things I haven't done yet. Why is this happening? I've never even been to an opera, or flown in a hot air balloon or, or—" Abby was thinking so quickly now her words couldn't keep up. "—or seen the Golden Gate Bridge, or children, I don't have any children. That's because I've never even been married! Ugh! There so much I wanted to do and now I...I'll never get to do it."

"Take it easy, Abby. Breathe." Conal motioned his hand in a circular breathing motion. "You'll get to do all of that. I promise. Hang in there. Look at this as, sort of a vacation. Take a couple breaths and keep thinking vacation, vacation."

Conal could see Abby taking the breaths and silently repeating "I'm on vacation." She opened her eyes, a little more relaxed. "I'm okay, I'm okay."

"You'll be back home before you know it." Conal had no idea if they would or wouldn't make it back home from wherever they were, but he didn't have much experience in comforting women, and that was the best he could do at that moment.

She walked over to where Conal was examining the machine.

"So you think we can get back?"

Conal evaded that question. "I don't know how it worked the first time, but my guess is that it's on some kind of power source and we drained that during our little road trip."

"What does that mean?"

"There is a meter on the side of the machine. When I was up on stage, it was completely full, there were about forty bars lit up on this meter. Now look." Conal tapped his finger against the meter. "It's empty. Not even a single bar lit up, and from the looks of it, it's not going to be charged any time soon."

Abby glared at him. "Maybe we should try to find someone who can help us."

"Maybe. But first, we need to hide this thing. There are some stables over there. We can put it there for now."

The stables looked abandoned and reeked of dried manure, mildew, and rotting wood. Whoever had used it had left behind saddles, horse blankets, and more than a few bales of hay, all of which were put to use concealing the contraption Conal had come to accept as a functioning time machine and their ticket home.

"Listen, even if that thing recharges itself, it's probably going to be awhile before it's up and running again," Conal said. "Wherever—whenever—we are, we're probably going to have to spend the night here, so we should probably try to go figure some things out."

Abby was staring at him with narrowed eyes. "You're excited about this."

Conal laughed nervously. "Yeah, a little bit. If we actually traveled through time, I would at least like to know when I traveled to and what's going on."

Abby nodded, more intrigued than she wanted to let on. Her responsible nature took over, the part of her that had always had to plan

38

ahead for everyone else. She never had been able to trust anyone around her that easily. She liked Conal, but sighed in resignation. She wasn't going to get anything different here. He was so excited about having possibly traveled through time, he'd probably like to stay weeks investigating this utterly bizarre and most unfortunate situation. Abby was going to have to keep him on track if she ever wanted to get home.

Still, it was getting dark and she was cold. They had to do something. "All right, Conal, let's go check this place out and find out where we are."

"And when." Conal grinned.

Abby couldn't help but smile back. "Yes, and when. Do you think we're still in Santa Barbara, just...in another time?"

"No clue," Conal said. "But we need to stick together. Who knows what or who we're going to find."

They walked along the cobblestone road in silence for a few minutes, heading in the direction of the faint sound of voices. The scent of burning leaves mingled with the pungent odor or rotting garbage. Fog began to roll in, and somewhere between all the gloom and fog, the sun was beginning to set. Sounds of chattering, some belligerent yelling, and more horse clatter in what appeared to be a livelier part of town lay ahead.

"Abby, listen, before we go any further, you remember what I was saying about if time can be changed?"

"Yeah, anything we do could change some major part of history, and even our own existence. I got it. We'll just try to blend in." Abby shivered as the road behind them was disappearing in the growing fog.

She hugged her arms around her torso and clamped her lips shut to keep her teeth from chattering. Whether it was from the chill in the air or her own nerves, she was beginning to shiver. "And don't forget the way back to the time machine," she continued.

39

"Sheesh, you're starting to sound like my mom." Conal smiled at her.

Abby wasn't smiling back; she was visibly cold and concerned. "I'm making a note of it too, but just in case we get separated, I think it'd be best if we both knew how to get back."

"Relax, I'll remember," Conal assured her quickly. "But let's make sure we don't get separated."

Darkness was falling quickly, and the thickening fog made it difficult to see far down the road. Many of the facades were fading with patches of overgrown moss and ivy covering them. Loose shingles flapped quietly on every other roof.

"Recognize anything?" Abby asked.

"No, not yet. No newspapers lying around or anything. It looks like there's a street sign up ahead at that intersection."

They were approaching an intersection: Commercial and Church Street.

"Neither of those sound familiar to me," Abby said. "Maybe we're in another part of town?"

"I don't think so. This definitely doesn't feel like home."

Abby tugged at her own tank top and then motioned at Conal's shirt. "Conal, we're going to look ridiculous to these people. How are we going to explain our clothes? "

"Yeah, I've thought about that. We're just going to have to try to lay low at first, try to figure out what kind of place we've landed in."

For so-called civilization, their surroundings were quite disenchanting. The area was poorly lit. Almost anything that could be contaminated with filth was, and everything was pervaded by a horrid stench. There were drunks passed out on the sidewalks and the ones who were still conscious were covering themselves, appearing to be settling in for the night. A smattering of children ran barefoot and laughing through the alleys in ragged clothes. Covered horse-drawn carriages lined the streets. Conal approached one small building, peering into a window only to be startled by an angry rooster. Everything looked like a scene from a Dickens novel.

There was a couple, probably in their late sixties, closing up a large fruit and vegetable stand across the way. Buildings were built with brick and mortar and had old-fashioned galvanized plumbing lining up the sides.

"Abby, look at these buildings. It probably doesn't mean anything, but they definitely don't build them like this anymore. I would imagine these buildings were built somewhere in the early 1900's. Possibly on the East coast; maybe New York or Pennsylvania. And their transportation—horse drawn carriages?"

"Great! So basically you're saying we really did travel through time. Vacation, vacation, vacation," Abby whispered under her breath.

They both paused, looking at one another almost as if there were an unspoken acceptance. Up until that point, there was still the chance that there was some other explanation. Now it was time to worry, it was real.

Everyone aside from the drunks and the children scurried like rats to wherever they were going, as though they wanted to spend as little time on the streets as possible. Uneasiness grew in Conal's stomach. Abby clutched his arm, a subconscious move for reassurance.

Despite their best efforts to hide, people had begun to notice them, shooting either nervous or mean glances at them.

The women wore long dresses that reached from their chins to their ankles, a strange type of straw top hat on their heads, and boots. Most wore shawls, and one old woman was even carrying a parasol, despite the late evening hour. The men wore velvet top hats, bugle caps, and long jackets.

41

Abby's outfit was attracting unwanted attention. Her denim skirt, laced tank top, and cowboy boots looked hopelessly brazen in comparison with these modestly dressed women. Conal wasn't much better in a button up shirt, faded jeans, and Wolverine work boots his mother had given him for Christmas, but he was at least somewhat less conspicuous than Abby.

"Disgusting whore!" A woman in a long navy dress spat at Abby's feet, glaring at her before hurrying on.

Abby turned and headed straight for the woman. "Excuse me! What did you just call me?"

The offender didn't even turn back.

"Conal, did you see that? That—"

We need to get off these streets. "Let it go, Abby." Conal pulled Abby closer to him, hoping his presence would ward off more unwanted attention, or at least keep randy drunks at bay. If this apparently respectable woman thought Abby was a whore, no doubt the lower classes would make that assumption as well.

Most shops seemed to be closing for the night. Conal scanned the street, looking for a place to get some shelter from this harsh crowd, and some information.

"Hey, I think that's a bar up ahead," Abby said. "Someone in there should be able to tell us something, don't you think?"

"I guess so. I don't know if you going into a bar dressed like this is such a good idea. Wherever we are, I'm guessing the crowd in that joint is going to be rough."

"I'll be fine. We need to get some answers. Let's go."

Conal had been searching for a scrap of newspaper, a discarded delivery box, anything that would give him a clue, but had come up with nothing. He had picked up that people spoke English with an accent. He hadn't been able to make out from where.

He sighed. "All right, we'll go. But stay close to me. I don't like the way people are looking at you. Let's get in, find out what we need to know, and get out."

Seven

I say, excuse me!" a man called to Abby and Conal as they crossed the street. Abby clenched Conal's arm tight. He could feel her body stiffen.

"Just act natural," Conal said, "and stay calm."

The man trotted in their direction. He wore a bowler hat, tweed suit and a matching brown bow tie.

"Good day." He extended his hand to Conal. "I won't take more than a minute of your time. The name is Maybrick; James Maybrick, of the Maybrick Cotton Exchange. I'm sorry, I was over at Spitalfields when I saw you two walking up." He pointed to a shop about twenty yards away. "I couldn't help but take notice of the two of you, and frankly, I'm not the only one." Maybrick glanced over toward the bar, where two men stood in the doorway, smoking cigars.

"I thought you might be looking to invest in some, shall we say, more appropriate attire? With all due respect, Miss, you might as well be walking around here without a stitch, dressed like that. Why, there's not enough material there for a full set of knickers. I won't ask too many questions, but I will warn you, you should be careful walking around here dressed as you are, some unsavory characters might peg you for a dollymop."

"Dollymop?" Abby mouthed. Conal shrugged.

"My shop is closed for the night, but if you come by tomorrow, I'm sure we have some trousers for you, sir, and perhaps something more suitable, Miss. My Bunny has quite refined taste, so I'm certain there will be something to your liking, Miss."

"Bunny?" Conal said.

"Oh, yes, that's my wife. Her Christian name is Florence, but with affection, I call her Bunny. We have two children, Bobo and Gladys."

"James!" a woman called to him from a nearby market.

"Is that Bunny?" Abby asked.

"I must be off now. Remember, the West End—Maybrick Cotton." Maybrick scampered off before Abby could get an answer to her question.

"Wait!" Abby shouted but he didn't turn back. "Dammit. I was hoping we could at least find out what year we're in. Looks like we're heading to the bar after all."

"I don't know what to make of that guy, Abby. Don't you think it's a little strange, running up to people on the street like that?"

"I wouldn't say that. I mean, at least he didn't call me a whore, that's gotta be a step up, right?"

"But he did call you a dollymop. I'm pretty sure that means the same thing around here."

To his surprise, she laughed. "Good point. At least he was friendly."

The sign above of the bar read: The Ten Bells.

"The Ten Bells. Why does that seem familiar to me?" Conal was puzzled. He shivered as he took a last glance around before entering the bar. The light from the street lamps cast a sickening glow across the fog. *Something doesn't feel right.*

45

He grabbed Abby's hand and led her into a dark corner of the bar, where she sat with her back to the wall in an attempt to blend into the scenery.

The pungent smell of musty cigars and alcohol filled the fairly crowded bar, still, it was warmer than outside. Conal looked over at Abby, who was darting nervous glances around the room. He laughed to himself. Grabbing a drink with Abby at a little hole in the wall bar, probably in England. *How many times had I hoped for a drink with her, and this is how it happens?*

"You know, there's something oddly familiar about this place," he said.

"What do you mean? You know where we are?"

"Not exactly," he said. "But I recognized the Spitalfields Market sign when Maybrick pointed it out to us. And the name of this pub, 'The Ten Bells.' I know both of these from somewhere. I'm positive I've heard of them before."

"Ordinarily, I'd say that's a weird déjà vu thing, but considering how we came to be here in the first place, I'm guessing there's a little more to it than that."

"I'm not sure. It's something, though, I know it is." Of all the times to forget something.

"You know what?" Abby said. "Let's try and relax a little. Maybe you're trying too hard to remember. I'm sure it will come back to you."

"Yeah, maybe," Conal said. "So, what? Do you wanna talk about something else? Wormholes? Astrophysics? After all, we're pretty much experts by now."

Abby laughed, shaking her head. "Intriguing as our situation is, I think I need to take a break from that just for a few minutes. Tell me about you, Conal."

"Me?" Conal's eyes nervously squinted.

"Yeah, you!" Abby laughed. "We never really got to know each other back in school."

Just like that, there they were again. *Damn butterflies. I've got to be the only heel in the universe who would travel through time, only to be flustered by a pretty girl trying to reminisce about our teenage years.*

"Yeah," he replied. "As I recall, you and I didn't exactly run in the same social circles."

"I always wondered why we didn't get to know each other better. I remember you kept to yourself a lot. Why was that?"

"Maybe it had something to do with the fact that you were dating Mr. Personality, a.k.a Tristan. You were kind of off limits."

Abby smirked. "Fair enough. I did have a boyfriend, that's true, but he didn't even go to our school. His name was Barry, not Tristan." Abby laughed, a full throaty sound. "Once he saw *Legends of the Fall*, yeah, that was it, he had an instant man crush on Brad Pitt. He hated being called Barry, so he figured he'd reinvent himself.

"Ohhh, so that's why the..." Conal motioned to Abby's hair.

"He has better hair than I do?" Abby finished his sentence. "Yep." She smirked.

"Well you have to admire the guy's commitment." Conal laughed.

"You know, Conal, I used to see you all the time in the halls. I even tried talking to you one day, but you always seemed to blow me off. You didn't even try to get to know me."

"Yeah, you know what? Maybe this trip down memory lane isn't such a hot idea. Let's just find someone who doesn't look like a complete sleazeball and try to get some information."

47

Abby crossed her arms and instinctively moved back in her chair. Conal could sense a shift in her mood, as though in that one instant, she had begun to withdraw.

"Look, Abby, I'm sorry. I didn't mean to cut you off. High school wasn't exactly one of my shining moments. As you pointed out, it was more about my studies, and I was a bit of a loner. I was okay with that. I just don't like talking about it."

"Conal, high school is hard for everyone. You don't have to be embarrassed."

"I'm not embarrassed!"

"Okay, so you're not embarrassed. Bad choice of words. Well, I'm sorry you felt like you were alone, but if it makes you feel any better, your lone wolf persona always gave you a mysterious appeal."

"You're kidding," he snorted. "Too bad I didn't know that then."

Conal looked at Abby for a couple of seconds that seemed like forever. Wondering about the what ifs and the woulda, coulda, shoulda's.

"You okay, Conal?"

"Yeah, I'm good. So what about you? What's your story? Tell me about your family. Wait, wait, let me guess. White picket fence in the middle of suburbia, with a chocolate lab, a swimming pool, and a mom and dad that went to your dance recitals? Am I getting warm?" Conal laughed

Abby suddenly began avoiding eye contact. She was visibly uncomfortable.

"What? Something I said? Oh come on, how bad could it be?"

"There's really not all that much to tell about my family. I mean, I know I brought it up, but..." Abby paused for a moment and then gave a large, nervous sigh. "I'd love to be able to say we had one of those perfect families you see on television, but it wasn't. Conal...I don't speak to my parents, and I wouldn't be exaggerating by saying that my parents would honestly be thrilled if I never make it back. My parents were young, young and careless, when they had me. They didn't plan on having me. They made it more than clear throughout my childhood that if they hadn't had gotten pregnant with me, their lives would have been so much easier. They'd have been able to travel, have careers, success, better lives, the whole nine yards. Mom and dear old Dad have never been shy about letting me know. Especially my dad." Abby's eyes were drifting as if she was connecting to the bad memories.

I looked at Abby in complete shock, embarrassed that I had pushed the issue. "I...I'm sorry. I would have never—You just seemed so—You know, good. I just assumed."

She took a deep breath and refocused on Conal. "So what? I can't be good now?"

"No, that's not what I meant." Conal sighed, considering how much the conversation seemed to unsettle her, he wanted to at least try to console her, but he didn't get the chance.

From the corner of his eye, Conal could see three men sitting at a nearby table eyeing Abby closely. They almost looked more out of place than Conal and Abby. All three of them were dressed in what appeared to be expensive suits, looking far too wealthy to be in this seedy little bar. They wore gloves, black velvet top hats, and some kind of capes or cloaks. Two looked as if they were in their late twenties, early thirties, and the third looked much older, possibly in his sixties.

None of them made any attempt to disguise that they were staring shamelessly at Abby. Conal noticed they would frequently turn to talk with each other, then look back to continue appraising Abby.

Might as well take advantage of their attention and see if they can tell me what the hell is going on around here. He didn't relish the idea of leaving Abby alone in this place, but bringing her along dressed as she was would likely prove to be distracting.

"You see those men looking over here?" Conal whispered.

Abby glanced over at them. "Yeah. They're staring, and they aren't being shy about it. Okay, Conal, they're totally giving me the creeps. Maybe we should leave?"

"No, it's okay. I don't think they want to draw any attention to themselves. They don't exactly fit in here, either. I'm going to walk over and see if maybe I can get some information about where we are. Will you be okay sitting here for a minute?"

"Yeah, I'll be fine." Abby looked unconvinced but resigned. "Just be careful, Conal. Good luck."

Conal stood and walked over to where the three men were sitting. They picked up on his intentions right away, and eyed him coolly.

The oldest one spoke first. Conal guessed the man was short, no more than five foot nine or so, though it was hard to tell while he was sitting down. He was heavy set, husky, the folds of his neck just threatening to spill over the edges of his collar and necktie. He seemed to have a peculiar attachment to a gold pocket watch that he kept opening and examining, then shutting again after a time. For a few moments, he stared at Conal, observing him as the watch dangled from his sausage-like fingers, like a trophy of wealth he wanted everyone else in the bar to see. Maybe they didn't care about attracting attention after all.

At last, he addressed Conal. "Who might you be, my strange friend?"

Conal swallowed hard. He wanted to tell himself there was nothing to be nervous about, but he knew that wasn't true. The two younger men were still darting glances in Abby's direction, and the expressions on their faces suggested they were just barely holding back from licking their chops. He wouldn't have put it past them to bolt for her while he talked to their geriatric pal.

"Hey guys, sorry to interrupt, but my, uh, fiancée and I, well, we're visiting some relatives and have gotten a bit lost. We're not from around here, and well, we were wondering if you could help us out."

The old man threw his head back and chuckled loudly. "What do you take me for, boy? Your fiancée? That's a good one. The way that girl's dressed, there is no mistaking what she's about."

One of the younger men smirked as he chimed in, "No doubt that one's a whore. But I give you credit, she's undeniably the most fetching I've seen in these parts in a long while."

Conal could feel his blood pressure rise and his fingertips began to tingle. "Whoa! Careful who you're calling a whore. Let's keep it friendly. I'm just trying to get some directions."

All three of the men guffawed. The older one, who seemed to be the ringleader, responded. "Now, let me tell you something, young fellow. The only way I'm going to believe that woman is your fiancée is if you own up to being her john. Men don't marry women like that. And be honest with me. Saying you're not from around these parts seems to be a bit of an understatement, because wherever that accent is from, it is certainly not from around here. Why don't you stop trying to pull something over on me and let's talk like gentlemen?"

The younger man who had called Abby a whore cut to the chase. "Listen, my friend, I understand what your concern is. Your, shall we say, companion, is quite enticing and you're worried about a couple of gentlemen of our stature and their driver acquiring her services in your stead. Well, as a gentleman, I'd think of a better lie next time you try to keep her, because this fiancée story is clearly false. Now tell me, what are

51

your intentions toward her? Perhaps we can work on a deal, she can double up tonight."

"Or triple," the third man chimed in. He and the elderly crony tipped their glasses toward each other and laughed.

"Yes, yes, Walter! Netley has been a good driver for many years. Think of it as a show of gratitude for his loyalty."

Conal looked back at Abby, angered by the thought of these men approaching her. She seemed even smaller than before, retreating into herself as she rubbed her arms to protect herself from the cold and the men ogling her. He didn't have much time. These guys weren't the only ones who thought Abby was open for business, and he was already running a risk by leaving her alone.

"Three pence if you let me have her right now," the man they called Walter said, dragging Conal's attention away from Abby.

"Look, pal, I'm really trying to be nice here, but you're not listening. She's not a prostitute. Now maybe you guys have had a little too much to drink. Out on the town, having a little bit of fun. I know how it is sometimes. Three well-dressed guys like you. I'm sure you'll find some women more suitable for what you're looking for as soon as you step back onto the street. This place seems to be crawling with them."

"Looks like you'll need to do the same. Someone else has already obtained her services. Bloody hell!" Walter slammed his fist onto the grimy table.

Conal heard Abby's scream before he saw her, a burly drunk was wrenching her arm and trying to drag her from the table.

Conal lunged forward, shoving at the man while Abby tried to pry his fingers off her arm. The drunk released Abby and grabbed Conal by the throat. Conal's face began to turn purple as he tried to pry the man's grip from his throat. Glancing at Abby, then back at the man, he jammed one of his thumbs in the man's left eye, causing him to release his grip. Conal gasped, trying to catch his breath. He reached out to grab Abby so they could leave. The drunk had one hand covering his eye, using the other hand to grab a chair. He raised the chair and attempted to smash it onto Conal's back, but he missed, a chair leg scraping painfully across Conal's shoulder.

The man who had first called Abby a whore joined the fray and began tugging at her. "Come on, darling. You'll be spending the night with me."

Abby clawed at him, resisting with every ounce of her strength. Conal punched the man in the eye and then the jaw with more force than he knew was in him, bloodying the man's face. He sent the man staggering backward, rubbing his bloody jaw.

Somewhere in the chaos, Conal heard the sounds of a whistle blowing, but it didn't register until he realized that Abby's cries to stop were directed at him, and a man in a constable's uniform was delivering blows to his body with a billy club. A hit to the back of his knees brought him to the ground.

"You're under arrest!" the man shouted.

The face of the man he had punched, dripping with blood, loomed over him.

"You stupid fool. Do you know who I am?"

Conal struggled to free himself of the constable's grip but he couldn't get away. The man was like a grizzly bear. He looked for Abby. The fear and confusion on her face told him he had just taken their situation from complicated to nearly impossible.

"This man works for the royal family, are you mad?" the constable said.

"Take him away," another officer ordered.

Conal attempted to calm his breathing, to think clearly. Abby and the drunk were both thrown out of the pub for causing trouble. The constable who had been restraining him was dragging him outside and putting him in shackles.

The rich man stood outside as well, wiping his face while he watched Conal being chained. His white handkerchief was soaked bright red.

"You all right, Mr. Sickert?" the constable asked. "Rest assured, sir, this ruffian won't be going anywhere but jail. We'll see who's doing the hitting then."

Sickert nodded wordlessly. The constable touched the rim of his hat.

A crowd of curious drunks had gathered in the doorway, and Conal found himself getting splashed by the drinks they threw at him. The scent of stale gin and cigars would cling to him for days.

"Get the bloomin' bugger outta 'ere! Whore lova!" they screamed.

Before he was shoved into the dark hold of the constable's wagon, Conal caught a last glimpse of Abby. A woman had approached her and was helping her off the ground. Perhaps she had been pushed down in all the commotion. Conal watched as the woman brushed Abby off and put a comforting arm around her, and his heart ached. If he hadn't screwed all of this up, he would be there protecting her. Still, better a woman than one of these filthy men. He couldn't hear what they were saying, but with a tilt of her head, a smile, and a sincere look in the woman's eyes, she appeared to be speaking kindly to Abby.

That's when it hit him. The street, The Ten Bells, Spitalfields, Sickert. It was all coming back to him.

"Did you say Sickert, as in Walter Sickert?" he asked the constables as they dragged him to the wagon.

"Yes, you fool! That there was Sir William Gull and Walter Sickert. The gentleman you just hit was Walter Sickert. Brilliantly done. You'll be lucky if they don't have your head."

Abby was screaming to him. "Conal! Where are they taking you? What do I do? Stop it! You can't take him away." Abby tried to make for the wagon, but the woman held her back. Conal was grateful for the woman's sense. If this was the kind of reaction Abby drew in a crowded pub, the last place she should be right now was a police station, surrounded by criminals and street scum.

He decided to give it one more try. Throwing all of his body weight against one of the constables, he shoved him hard into the carriage then turned to kick the other in the groin. It would be a futile attempt, but he had to try something, had to have some outlet for his rage.

Within an instant, what felt like a shower of clubs rained down on him and he could feel the welts forming across the back of his legs. One of the men grabbed him by the hair and dragged him the rest of the way to the carriage.

"Don't worry, Abby, we're going to be all right," he yelled through the bars at the back of the wooden carriage. "Find shelter for the night, and in the morning, come to the jail. Stay safe tonight, Abby; get off these streets."

He didn't hear her response as the carriage jerked away. He had wanted to tell her what he remembered, but hadn't the time, and he didn't want the crowd to think they were any stranger than they already seemed. Besides, he didn't want to drop something like this on Abby without being there to comfort or explain it to her.

The Ten Bells, Spitalfields, Sickert, Gull. He repeated the words to himself again and again until they matched the rhythm of the horses' hoofs hitting the cobblestones.

The Ten Bells, Spitalfields, Sickert, Gull. They were in the Whitechapel District in the East End of London. The time was between 1885 and 1889. And more importantly, they had landed in the time of Jack the Ripper.

PRESENT DAY:

"Oh dear, I've heard some unusual things, but this, without question, takes the cake. This can't possibly be."

"I know what you're thinking, Edie. Crazy, right? Impossible, I know." Just let me finish. I'll explain everything."

"Well, how can this be possible? What about Abby? I'm sorry, I'm just having a hard time..."

"We have a long way to go, Edie, try to let me finish."

Eight

WHITECHAPEL, LONDON: *sometime between 1885 and 1889:*

The carriage pulled away and the thudding of the horses' hooves rang in Abby's ears, mingling with her pounding heart. She took a steadying breath. This was not a time for panic. Conal had been arrested and she was outside a seedy bar where, to everyone within, she was dressed like a whore.

She felt a small, warm hand on her shoulder and turned to see the face of the woman who had helped her up when the drunken oafs from The Ten Bells had pushed her outside.

The barkeep scowled in the doorway, fists clenched and shouting.

"Go on! Get the hell out of here, ya bloody dollymop!" He thrust his index finger toward the woman standing with Abby. "I've told you time and again, Mary, I don't want you or none of your friends hanging about. Bloody 'ores!"

Abby braced herself to turn and walk away, but Mary halted her steps and defiantly turned around.

"You really ought to watch your tongue, little man, complaining about the whores hanging 'round your doorstep. You bellow loud enough when these so called respectable people can hear, but we'll be fine enough for all of you when you're cold and your wives are keeping their legs shut to ya!"

It was not lost on Abby that everyone within earshot was getting certain confirmation that she was also a prostitute, but she didn't care. If the only way to make a decent friend in this town was to be thought of as a whore, then perhaps she should embrace it.

"I'm not planning to be here long enough for my reputation to matter anyway," she mumbled to herself.

"I wonder what your wives would say if they knew what you gents been up to behind their backs, whose names you're screaming out while you've got another girl's knees in the air." The hecklers who had come out of the bar to watch the fray quieted down; most shuffled back inside. The odds of Mary divulging their dark secret to their wives were slim, since secrecy was a trick of the whoring trade, but there was always the chance if they were to anger her any further.

The barkeep didn't move. Mary sauntered up to him, circling him, tracing her fingers playfully, seductively across his lips. She didn't look like any ordinary kind of prostitute. Mary was neither used nor hardened. She looked to be in her mid-twenties, with pale, smooth skin, strawberry blonde hair, and striking blue eyes.

She faced the barkeep boldly, antagonizing him, and then gently dragging her finger across his chin. The barkeep nervously swallowed.

"What about you, Henry? You've got a few dirty little secrets you'd like to keep hidden, wouldn't you?" The barkeep lowered his head an inch or two in anger, touching his already hanging jowls to his chest. His face was turning a red orange color, but he said nothing.

Mary paused an inch from his face, the scent of gin on her breath. "Now you listen to me. You know full well this girl did nothing wrong.

58

Look at her. She's like a scared kitten. How many of us gals working the streets do you see entering bars looking like that? None. They'd be eaten alive. Abner Cowzy is a pig and has been causing problems in your pub since he started coming here. You can't seriously blame her without first turning an eye to him."

The barkeep grabbed her arm and held it tightly. "Get out of here, Mary, and keep your new cat on a leash or I swear to all that is good I will—"

He gave her a small shove into the street, bit his tongue giving Abby one last vindictive glance, and headed back into the pub. Abby nervously swallowed and her heart was racing, his aggression had triggered memories of how her own father once treated her, but not Mary, Mary was laughing when she returned. She linked her arm through Abby's and led her away.

"Bunch of lousy, piss-proud drunks they are," Mary said. "Sorry they gave you such a fright. You all right, love? I'm Mary, by the way."

"I'm all right, thanks, Mary," Abby said. "Thank you so much for helping me. I'm not sure what just happened, it was over so fast. Do you know where the prison is? I need to go find my uh...my brother."

Abby hoped the lie sounded plausible. She and Conal looked nothing alike, that she knew, but then there were plenty of siblings who looked nothing like one another. Never mind the decidedly un-brotherly attraction she had been feeling toward him.

"That bloke was your brother? Ah, no wonder he was defending you so ardently. Poor chap. I can take you to the jail, but not tonight. He was right to warn you off. That's not a place you'll want to be going after dark, and, sorry to say it, but certainly not like that."

Abby gnawed on the fingernail of her thumb. It was a habit she had been trying to break since she was a toddler, but she still fell back on it when she was worried or feeling helpless.

"I can't just leave him there all night."

"You'll have to, love. I know you're scared, but if you go down there, you'll just cause more trouble for him. Those constables who carried him off think you're one of mine as it is, they won't take the word of a whore. Your brother will likely just catch more of a beating if you go down there making a scene. We'll go tomorrow and figure something out. I promise you."

Mary was telling the truth. Even in 19th century London, prostitutes were the lowest of the low, the saddest, most depraved members of society. Some might pay for a look at their ladyhood, but most didn't acknowledge them as human outside of the bedroom.

"You're going to freeze dressed like that. Come with me, I'll get you some proper clothes and you can tell me how you ended up at a place like The Ten Bells. You don't seem like someone who would be much of a regular there."

Abby grinned in spite of herself. "I'm not much of a regular anywhere around here."

"I thought as much. Dollymop or not, you don't exactly look the part of a Whitechapel lady."

Abby snapped to attention.

"Where did you say we were?" Her heart began pounding again.

"Whitechapel." Mary looked perplexed. She put a hand on Abby's shoulder, her eyes filled with concern. "Do you really not know where we are?"

"It's a bit complicated, but no. My brother and I, we got a bit turned around. Well, it's a long story. But if you humor me just a little longer and tell me what country we're in. I wish I could explain —"

"No need, love. You've got secrets, so have I. We're in Whitechapel, in the east end of London, England."

"And...the date?"

Mary gave her a stranger look at that, but asked no questions.

"August 28, 1888, of course." Mary laughed and walked ahead.

Abby's hands flew to her stomach. *Oh my God! Ohh God, don't throw up! Breathe, just breathe! I have to be strong. I have to be strong.*

"Time to move," Mary said. "We don't need any more drunken louts bothering you tonight. Forgive me for saying so, but you're a rather strange one."

"It would seem that way," Abby managed. Her mind was racing. Mary was her only ally now. Conal was in prison, they had flown through a wormhole to more than 100 years in the past and they were in London. She wasn't sure whether to laugh or cry, but she pressed her lips together and regained her composure. Mary, at the very least, was kind, and would help her get to Conal tomorrow.

"That's all right," Mary was saying. "I've met stranger, I can assure you, and so will you soon enough. My girls are a hoot but there are some characters in our lot."

I'm going to spend the night in a brothel, Abby thought wryly. *Things just keep looking up.*

And yet, she was finding herself strangely enjoying this, or at least exhilarated by it. Traveling through time, being tossed out of a bar for looking like a prostitute, spending the night in a brothel with her new prostitute friend. Another surprising feeling crept to the surface. Relief. Abby wondered, what about this could possibly be a relief? *Oh, I don't*

know, maybe that you weren't given the luxury of caring parents and you
still run to your arrogant prick of an ex-boyfriend and I'm too cowardly to
tell all of them to go to hell?

It was true that Abby had been miserable up until the moment she flew through that wormhole. Seeing Conal again had been the brightest thing that had happened in years. She vaguely remembered him from high school but it wasn't that she had liked him. Conal was kind to her. When he looked at her, he seemed to see her, not just calculate the next thing he could get from her. *God,* she thought. *I really need a friend.*

"I'm guessing you're in need of a place to stay tonight?" Mary was saying. "Someone who doesn't even know what city she's in must not have lodging sorted, I'd imagine."

"Er, well, I spotted a stable nearby. I thought I'd just tuck up there until it's light out, then go look for my brother."

Abby hated the idea of wandering these streets alone again, and being cold and vulnerable in the stables, but maybe being alone would be better.

"A stable? No. It's a lot warmer over at my place and a whole lot safer, so long as you don't mind staying with me and the girls. They can be a bit boisterous at times, shall we say."

"Are you sure it's all right? I don't want to cause trouble for you. Maybe I should go on my own." Abby was thinking of the time machine now. What if some vagabond or drunk stumbled across it? Or one of the street children she had seen running around earlier? *It won't matter what happens to it if I don't make it through this night alive.*

"No trouble at all. The girls will love you. By the way, I don't think I ever got your name."

Abby sighed. "I didn't give it. Mary, I know that everything that comes out of my mouth is stranger than the last, and I really appreciate you not asking any questions. I hate to do this, but I'm going to have to ask you to do that once more. I just can't give you my name."

"Are you in some kind of trouble with the law? Is someone looking for you? Whatever it is, your secret is safe with me."

"No, it's nothing like that. It's complicated. Please don't ask."

Mary sighed. "I won't ask for your real name if you don't want to give it," she said. "But I'll need something to call you, and the girls might be suspicious of my new friend with no name. I'll come up with something for you, would that be all right?"

"Sure." Abby couldn't see the harm in it, and a new name seemed appropriate, given the circumstances.

"Let's see, what can we call you? Margaret? No, no you're definitely not a Margaret. How about Ruth? No, that reminds me of Sister Ruth, and judging by your clothing, you're certainly not a nun." Mary seemed to be enjoying herself. "I know, I have the perfect name. I'm going to call you Julia."

"Why Julia?"

"That's my sister's name. She's back in Ireland, with me mam and da, and our six brothers. Julia and I were always close. She's the smartest, kindest person I know. I miss her terribly. I haven't seen her or heard from her in some time. So for now, I'm giving you her name."

"In that case, I would be honored to be called Julia."

"Good, then it's settled. Let's get moving."

As they walked toward the center of town, she told Abby about her housemates.

"They're a little much at times when they're all together, but they're all right once you get to know them. I should warn you about Annie, she lacks a little polishing, but if you can get along with her and put up with Liz's loud mouth every once in awhile, then you'll get on just fine."

The description wasn't encouraging, but Abby wasn't going to complain. Mary was nice enough, surely her friends would be, too.

"The first thing we need to do is get you some suitable clothes. You'll make us look like a bunch of nuns with what you've got on."

Abby blushed.

"Well, we met a man earlier who said he'd get us some appropriate things, but his shop is closed till tomorrow."

"Not to worry, we'll get you something. I know just the person who can help us, if we can find her." Abby and Mary continued walking.

Abby tried to take note of the area she was walking through so she didn't get lost. She had to be prepared for anything at this point and still considered the possibility of having to leave and find her way back.

"Can you tell me one thing?" Mary asked. "You and your brother, are you American? We've already established that you're not from around here. Your accent sounds American."

Abby couldn't ignore a twinge of guilt at putting her off again.

"That would be a good guess, I suppose. Mary, I know it sounds strange, believe me, it's even strange to me, and I know it doesn't make sense, but I just can't tell you anymore right now. I can tell you this much, once my brother is back, I'll have more answers for you. I promise. But I can't say anything more than that."

Mary shook her head. "Fine, Miss Mystery. Let's get on then."

Nine

Conal pressed his face against the bars at the back of his moving cage, gasping for a breath of fresh air. The stench of urine and vomit surrounded him and it was all he could do to keep from adding to the filth. Even the steady rhythm of the trotting horses was making him sick. Every clip-clop of their hooves brought him closer to jail and farther from Abby.

Between controlled gasps for air, he caught glimpses of the city, a place more poverty-stricken than anywhere he'd ever been. A family of four was taking refuge for the night in an alley, huddled close against the wall of a building. Beggars and drunks, often one and the same, stumbled down the streets, looking frozen and hungry, and an occasional rat scurried out of the carriage's path.

The ride was long and cold. The shackles the constable had slapped around Conal's wrists were digging his skin, rubbing it raw. The metal was unforgiving; he had already begun to bleed. Escape was impossible.

Conal considered his predicament. He needed to make his next move wisely. If he could take advantage of the situation, he might be able to turn things to his advantage. If nothing else, the constables could give

65

him some information that might be useful later on. He desperately needed to know if his prediction about the year was right—and if it was, he needed to get out of jail and find Abby immediately.

If they had landed in the era of Jack the Ripper, he needed to know if the killings had already begun, and when.

Conal had long harbored a fascination with the famous serial killer and the circumstances surrounding his reign of terror. While other kids were out at the beach partying, and going out on Saturday nights, Conal chose to read stories and watch documentaries about the likes of those such as Jack the Ripper. Researching the great stories in history was a lonely hobby, and few people wanted to spend hours contemplating the complicated mind of a murderer.

But Conal had never been able to let it go. He had often questioned the motivations of those he read about: Why didn't they do this? What was the reason for that? Now he might be able to get his answers, though it would be decidedly less romantic than it had seemed from the pages of library books.

"We'll be needin' some help over 'ere, this one's a bit of a fighter." The cart jerked to a stop. "Got me right in the bollocks."

"Oh, quit your yammering, ya coward! Just get them inside."

The door to the holding pen swung open. Four men waited outside, glaring, looking expectantly at Conal. He recognized two of them as the men he had fought at The Ten Bells.

"Goddammit," he muttered.

"Relax, boys, I'm not going to fight you." An idea was forming, and it didn't involve another scuffle with these two oafs. "I know when I've been beat."

The constables responded by yanking him out of the carriage. Out of nowhere came a flying elbow right across Conal's jaw, sending him to his knees, where he knelt on the steps of Scotland Yard for a few seconds watching the blood spewing from his nose and mouth onto the stone.

"Ow! You son of a—"

Another constable grabbed Conal from the ground and shoved him up the steps toward the station. Conal caught a glimpse of a name tag: P. C. William Smith. A name likely worth remembering.

Conal stumbled through the Scotland Yard headquarters.

"Inspector, sir," Smith said to a man sitting behind a desk. "This one's been giving us fits. He's new to these parts, it seems. No name, no nothing. What we do know is that he was conducting a piece of business with a prostitute at The Ten Bells—a pretty dame, she was, but more low-rent than most, if you catch me drift—and then this one here assaulted Walter Sickert and Abner Cowzy."

"Look, I told you she's not a prostitute." Conal all but hissed the words. "That's not what happened. I didn't know that was Sickert, and Abner, the drunk, he's the one responsible for the whole thing." The Inspector, being a reasonable man, was the only shot Conal had at the moment.

"Shut your bloody trap!" Smith's spittle splattered across Conal's face.

"Or what, you'll club me again? That would be just fine. Then you can just continue to drag me around in these shackles like a dog. I'm sure you'll love doing that."

"Calm down, Smith!" The Inspector looked as though he was familiar with the officer's antics.

"My apologies, sir. It's been a long night." Smith looked pointedly at Conal. "I'm not sure why he's dressed so funny. I've never seen trousers like those before. Perhaps he's a mad man. After all, you'd have to be crazy to strike Sickert. Are you mad, chap?"

Conal refused to look at Smith.

"He gave us a pretty good fight, Inspector, but a couple smacks with the old stick and he's fallen right in line." Smith tapped the end of his billy club in the palm of his hand.

"Are you Inspector Abberline?" It would be the first break Conal had gotten since the damn exhibition.

"I shall ask the questions," he responded, circling Conal slowly. *Great. Another asshole.*

"I must say, you have quite the costume. I'm quite interested in hearing the story behind your unusual attire. Are you some sort of performer? A play-actor, perhaps?"

"With all due respect, sir, I'm only speaking with Inspector Abberline. If you're not him, then I won't answer your questions. I need to speak with him before telling you anything."

"What makes you think I'm not Inspector Abberline?"

"I remember now what he looks like. Inspector Abberline is much shorter and has dark hair. Your hair is red and white, and you're much older than Abberline. Listen, I'm sorry for hitting your pal, Walter, and everything else, but I'm not saying another word until I speak directly with Inspector Frederick Abberline."

The man's face betrayed nothing, no hint of emotion behind his appraising gaze. "Very well. I'm not Inspector Abberline. I'm Inspector Chandlar. I'll relay your demand to Abberline, but I'm going to need a reason why he should see you."

"If you get Inspector Abberline, sir; he'll clear this whole thing up, I assure you. But I can't tell you anything beyond that."

"Is that so? You and Abberline have some kind of special friendship, do you? We'll see.

"Smith, put him back with the rest of them and send someone for Inspector Abberline straight away."

"Aye, sir."

A faint yelling was drawing closer as Smith's fingers dug into Conal's arm, leading him to his cell. The burly constable opened the door to the jail as the sounds of yelling reverberated through the line-up of cells. It was like wild jackals barking on a pitch black night.

"Welcome to hell!" Smith laughed. "I bet you're wishing you would've let that whore go now, eh, boy?"

Conal remained silent.

"All because you couldn't let go of your whore." Smith spat as Conal struggled against him. He sent Conal stumbling forward with a hard shove. "Make yourself comfortable. You won't be going anywhere for awhile." Before Conal could turn around, Smith whacked him in the ribs with the billy club. Conal doubled over, gasping in pain. "That's for trying to get me in trouble with the boss."

A blob of spit, blackened from tobacco chew, landed inches from Conal's face. "I'm beginning to think you don't like me, Smith," Conal groaned in retort.

"That there's your uniform." It was tattered and had a faded number 12 above the left shirt pocket. "You get two meals, breakfast and supper, and bathe Wednesdays and Sundays. Enjoy your stay, whore lover." Another officer removed his shackles. Smith was chuckling again. He slowly backed out of the cell, tapping his club in his hand, and not losing eye contact as Conal wiped blood from his lip.

"Oh, we have a new mate in the Scotland Yard, fellas!" an inmate shouted when Smith had gone.

Conal didn't respond to him, or to the others raising their voices in a chorus of threats and obscenities.

He peered through the bars of his cell. Another cage. A few hours ago, I'm doing a surprise presentation on time travel. Now I'm a punching bag, locked up in Victorian England, surrounded by the dregs of British society. This just keeps getting better and better.

There were no walls between cells, only more bars. No privacy at all. The man in the cell directly next to Conal's was on the ground, crawling and sniffing at the hard stone. Greasy strands of dull brown hair fell in front of his eyes, and he shook the thin locks from his face as he crawled. His raggedy clothes hung off his gaunt frame. The man didn't look like much more than a walking skeleton. He pounced, like a cat chasing a string. When the man looked under his hands, there was nothing there. He pounced again. Conal watched the man clamber about his cell until he became frustrated by his lack of prey, and began banging his tin cup against the bars. He was screaming gibberish.

"Shut ya mouth, you crazy bugger!" another inmate shouted.

The hooting shifted from Conal to the other man; and a smattering of laughter rose up from the other cells.

"I won't shut up! I won't, I won't!"

Smith came swinging his billy club into the room shortly, and slammed his club against the cell bars. "Shut your mouth, Kosminski, or you're losing meals!"

Kosminski spat at the guard.

"Quiet down, you son of a bitch!" the constable growled through gritted teeth.

"You're the son of a bitch!" Kosminski screamed. "To hell with you, Smith. I don't want your meals, anyway! They won't allow it!" He was pointing upward.

"Just keep it down," Smith said. "This is your last warning."

"Do you hear them?" Kosminski said, seeing Conal for the first time. "I can hear them, the voices. I think they're coming from out there. Can you hear them, too?"

Conal ignored the man, he had already drawn too much unfavorable attention to himself. The plan for he and Abby to go unnoticed was a wash. He was going to have to come up with another plan, and given his current circumstances, he was going to have plenty of time to think about one.

There was a man directly across from him, in a cell marked thirteen. He looked to be about fifty years old. Unlike the rest of the prisoners, he was dressed in a threadbare suit that might have been a respectable get-up a long time ago. The gold pinstripes were faded but visible, and the man wore a tie and vest beneath the jacket. Conal noticed the man's shoes had been shined, a stark contrast to everything else he was wearing. He had oily hair that lay flat on his head as if he had been wearing a hat. His skin was sweaty and pale. A long handlebar mustache drooped over his lips, curling at the end. There appeared to be more hair on his face than there was on his head. If he had to guess, Conal would have said the man was once a middle to upper class gentleman. He wondered what the man had done to end up in this hell hole.

The man stared at Conal. "Son, what kind of clothes are you wearing? You in some kind of circus?" The man's accent was familiar; he wasn't from around here, either.

"Something like that," Conal replied. "What about you? Why aren't you wearing a uniform?"

"You think they give a rat's ass if we wear their uniform?"

"I see, so where are you from, sir? Your accent doesn't sound British."

71

"Born in Ireland, moved to the States as a child. I take it you're American."

"What gave it away?"

The American in thirteen laughed. "Whereabouts in America? I lived all over the East Coast before I ended up in London."

"I'm not sure where I was born. My parents moved around a lot, and died before I could ask any questions. I had to keep moving after they passed on, and haven't ever settled in a place I could call home yet."

The man nodded, smirking.

"That's charming," sniped the man in the cell on the other side of Conal, "Two Yankees, destined to find one another in the jails of Scotland Yard."

The American paid his fellow inmate no attention. Conal followed his lead. "Was she worth it?" the American asked.

"Excuse me?" Conal was perplexed.

"The girl," the man replied impatiently. He stroked his mustache thoughtfully. "Come on, there's no reason to play dumb down here, boy. Was the girl worth it?"

How did he know? Had Smith put in the word that Conal had been busted fighting over a woman?

"I'm sorry, I don't know what you are talking about."

The man laughed.

"Son, you ain't foolin' nobody down here. I know a poisoned seed when I see one. The man next to you, he's a wicked soul." Kosminski looked up from the floor where he had been hunting again, his eyes wild. The man held his gaze.

"You shut your hole!" Kosminski yelled. "They tell me to do it. I don't want to do bad things, but they make me. They're going to come and get you, you'll see, and you're going to be right off!" Foam formed at the corners of his mouth as he screamed, clinging to the bars of his cell, convinced he could shake them loose. It had been about thirty minutes, and already Conal had seen enough to dread this man's escape. A pitiful soul, that was certain, but dangerous as well.

The American moved to his bed, shaking out his rough horsehair blanket as he spoke. "You're not one of them. You look funnier than the others in here, but you're not a bad man. Only reason a man like you ends up in a place like this is over a woman. So unless you prefer the company of men—and I doubt that, 'cuz I know a man like that, too, it ain't you—I will ask you again, was the girl worth it?"

Kosminski perked up. "A woman? She's a whore, isn't she? The young lad fell in love with a whore!" He chuckled and walked up to the bars dividing their cells. "I hate whores; they do nothing but infest this place like rats! They're a disease, a plague, I tell you, they all need to be dealt with. You wait and see... wait and see! They will all be dealt with!" He was pointing above him again "You wait and see!"

That is one sick son of a bitch, Conal thought. "Thank God you're locked up, and far from Abby," he said quietly. *This place is no joke. I'm going to need to do better here than I did at The Ten Bells if I'm going to survive, let alone get out and find Abby and get the hell back to the present day.*

Conal winced in pain as he tried to get comfortable. "Hey, what's your name, pal?" he called to the man across the way.

No response. The man was awake, lying on his bed, staring at the cold gray ceiling.

"All right, if you're not going to give me your name, can you at least tell me the date?"

The American snickered. "It's the twenty-eighth of August, stranger. What's the matter? Too many beatings from Smith and you lost your memory?"

That wasn't a bad excuse. Conal rubbed his head for effect.

"Yeah, he roughed me up a little. It's still 1888, right?" he guessed nervously as he threw in a chuckle to play off he really didn't know.

"It's 1888, all right. Boy, he must've gotten you pretty good. Why do you want to know the date? Is it them? Do you know something?" Kosminski was back at the bars, foam bubbling as he spit questions at Conal rapid-fire.

"Hey, do you mind getting your face off my bars?"

Kosminski stared, letting a stream of drool dribble down his chin. He was disgusting.

"So, my fellow American," Conal called. "You gonna tell me what you did to get stuck in this joint?"

The American shifted up to his elbows, eyeing Conal.

"Stuck in here? You know, it always fascinates me when people fixate on how you've ended up in a place, rather than on how they plan to get themselves out. After all, what difference does it make how you got in if you don't know how to get back out again?" He sat up, swinging his legs over the edge of the bed and draping his right leg over his left. "My turn to ask a question. How long were you in your mother's womb?"

Wonderful. Not this guy, too. "Are you serious? What kind of question is that?" Apparently the American was also psycho.

"Really, I want to know." When Conal said nothing, he nodded in understanding. "She must have had you early. I bet she was a good girl, too, was she not? No, she wasn't like the cattle around here. I'd be willing to gamble that your father was the only one she'd ever spread her legs for."

"Okay, I think we better change the subject. My mother was a good woman, What happened between her and my father is not on the table for whatever sick fantasy you got going up there, okay?"

"Pure of heart, was she? Yes, it's easy to see, just look at you, boy— all indignant, locked up though you're innocent of any crime. You're a product of your mother's life, the sum of her virtues and transgressions. If she had been a filthy whore, her womb would have been rotten, and you would have ended up like him." He waved a hand toward Kosminski and shook his head. "His mother was a bad woman, as well you can see. Just look at what she produced. You're a nice boy. Your mother's uterus must have been, well, lovely."

Conal was beginning to wonder if perhaps the American was more dangerous than Kosminski. Silence seemed the best approach with this guy; he was turning out to be not much help, after all.

Conal unrolled his mattress onto the bedspring. His mind wandered to Abby. The nerves returned to his stomach as he wondered if she had found some place safe to get through the night. He tried not to consider the possibilities if she hadn't, but it was too fresh in his mind and there was too much to think about. *I can't get these damn images out of my head! What if that guy at the pub caught up with her or maybe there are other men that think she's a prostitute. They could grab her and pull her into one of these God-awful alleys. She could easily be overpowered. Dammit! Where is that inspector?*

He laid down on the bed. The springs poked through the thin mattress, and it stunk of sweat. Conal gagged, sitting up. He was beginning to feel claustrophobic. When he stood, his body ached from Smith's beatings and the shackles.

Kosminski watched him limp the length of the cell. Conal lifted his shirt to examine the black and blue welts that had already begun to form near his ribcage. It hurt to breathe in quickly.

"They're good at that, you know. The best, if you ask me."

Conal raised wary eyes to see Kosminski's face pressed against the dividing bars. His eyes were glassy but focused; drool still dripped down his chin. Conal turned his head to disguise the disgust on his face.

"Kosminski knows all about it," the American called. "Let him show you his scars. But be careful, those things'll give you nightmares, friend."

"Is that true?" Conal didn't like Kosminski, but crazy or not, no one deserved Smith's attacks.

"See for yourself." Kosminski turned his back to Conal. Marks of black and blue covered his skin, some surrounded by patches of yellow. It looked like fresh blows had been delivered as soon as the old wounds had begun to heal.

Conal shuddered.

"I'm sorry, man. Those look painful."

Kosminski glared at him. "What would you know about it?"

"Never mind him," the American said. "Everything that comes out of his mouth is nonsense. He has no idea what he's saying."

"Lights out!" a harsh voice called into the room. The lantern that had been casting a dim light into the dingy room was turned out, casting all of the cells into darkness.

Conal felt his way back to bed and covered himself with his own rough blanket. The coarse material scratched his face. Particles of dust rose from the material, sending him into a coughing fit.

"Knock it off!" a voice screamed in the darkness. Conal ignored it. He'd had more than his fill of these people. He closed his eyes and exhaustion finally settled in. His sleep was tortured, though. His mind took him through dark alleys, searching for Abby. She was nearby, he could hear her screaming his name. There were footsteps. Someone was just ahead of him. "Abby!" He called her name but the person kept running. He closed in on the person, adrenaline pulsing as he grabbed a shoulder and turned her around. But the face wasn't Abby's. It was Kosminski's, beaten almost beyond recognition except for his wild eyes.

Conal woke with a jolt, sweating. He gasped for air, trying to suck in oxygen as if he'd been holding his breath, clenching the side of the bed with his head leaning over his legs. There would be no more sleeping tonight if he could help it.

Facts surfaced in his mind, and he focused on them. In all his research on Jack the Ripper, he'd never read the name Abigail Bradley among the killer's victims. But that didn't mean anything. He and Abby had traveled through time but no one knew exactly how that was supposed to work. It had never been done before. Could they change the past? Could they be killed?

A light broke through the darkness. Startled by the interruption, he broke out of his reverie and noticed his knuckles were raw. He touched one. It was covered in something warm and sticky.

The door to the prison blocks opened wider and Conal saw the sticky substance was blood. He had been dragging his knuckles along the exposed springs on the bed without even noticing.

The night constable walked toward him, stopping just before he reached Conal's cell. He banged his billy club against the bars.

"Get up, Kosminski, you're being released! You've got two minutes to get out of here or I'm locking the door up again. I'd better not see you crawling around, digging through trash, eating from the sewers, or hassling any more women, you hear? Next time you won't get such a quick release!"

This has gotta be a joke!

"Ha!" Kosminski scrambled to his feet, laughing wildly.

"Let's go, you freak," the constable said.

Kosminski paused before walking out and turned slowly to face Conal. With a furrowed brow and a chilling blank stare from his bloodshot eyes in the faint light, he looked even more maniacal. "I can't wait to meet your whore, brother."

Chills spread throughout Conal's body, the hairs on the back of his neck stood on end. *What if Kosminski was a suspect for the Ripper?* Conal didn't recognize the name, but it was possible he had missed it, especially if he'd been written off as some kind of quack and set free to roam the streets. Just then Conal noticed a small bulge in his back pocket, it was his tablet and pencil.

You gotta be kidding me. Smith never frisked me. I guess he got so worked up he forgot.

Conal quickly noted the information:

Suspects:

Kosminski

"Just keep it moving," the constable ordered. "And you, number twelve. You'd better get up, too. It seems you have a visitor." Without drawing attention, Conal slid the small tablet and pencil under his pillow.

Ten

Inspector Abberline was a proud man. His shrewd gaze was trained on Conal. His pipe puffed between his teeth; the smoke drifted into the cell. Abberline was almost a caricature of every Scotland Yard officer Conal had ever imagined. He was middle-aged, and his years were beginning to show. The hair at the crown of his head was thinning and his facial hair was carefully groomed into a neat set of mutton chops connected by a bushy mustache.

Conal sat up straight on his bed spring, breathing deeply. A middle of the night audience with the inspector was unexpected. He thought for sure he would be waking up to the fine company of the American mustache and the other pillars of society surrounding him.

"Well, if it isn't Inspector Abberline," the American called from his cell. "I wouldn't have expected to see you cavorting about near us dregs at this hour of the morning."

"Well, Tumblety, I guess you never know who you're going to find here," Abberline responded without turning around.

Tumblety. That was the American's name. Conal stored that tidbit away for future reference. "Looks like I learned your name after all, friend," he quipped.

Abberline glanced between the two men. "His name is Francis Tumblety," Abberline told Conal. "In here for gross indecency, isn't that right, Francis? Not the first time, either."

"I don't know what you're talking about," Tumblety grumbled. He slunk into a corner of his cell.

"Now that we've gotten the introductions out of the way, why don't you tell me what was so desperately urgent that I had to be dragged to this cesspool of humanity at this godforsaken hour?"

"I apologize for the inconvenience, Inspector, and I don't want to waste any more of your time, but I must insist that we speak alone."

Abberline guffawed. "Alone? Who do you think you are, boy? You're in jail, in case you haven't noticed, and my patience is running extremely thin. What makes you think I would meet with you privately? No, I'm afraid this is as private as you're going to get."

"Inspector, I swear to you, I'll explain everything as soon as we're alone. I'm begging you, only a few moments of your time." Conal lowered his voice to a whisper, speaking to Abberline through the bars of his cell, hoping no one else would hear. "I have information that could be vital to you, involving a murder case."

"Oh? You looking to cut a deal, boy?"

"Maybe. But I want you to hear me out first, then you can decide. Look, Inspector Abberline, I know you're an honest man, and that you take your position in society seriously. You want to get criminals off the streets, bring them to justice, and keep people safe. I was an idiot for getting into a fight at The Ten Bells, but I'm not a criminal. I think I can help you find one, though."

80

Abberline eyed Conal warily, then sighed. "You better not be wasting my time," he warned, then signaled for the guard. "Constable, shackle this one and bring him to a private room. Smith's, perhaps. He should be gone by now."

In Smith's office, the constable shackled Conal's hands to an old wooden chair. Splinters pricked his skin, but by then, his wrists were too raw to feel much sensation.

Inspector Abberline lit two lanterns and placed them on the table, one beside a small stack of papers, a quill, and an ink bottle, and one in front of Conal.

Conal had the overwhelming feeling this day was never going to end. He summoned his energy. This was the only chance he was going to get at this conversation, and even if he gave a flawless performance, there were no guarantees. It would sound crazy, even in the present time, and he would be lucky if he wasn't burned at the stake for being some kind of warlock in this era.

"Well?" Abberline said, spreading his hands. He looked at Conal expectantly.

"Inspector, there's no easy way to say this, so I'm going to dive right in and you can stop me when you need."

"You can be sure of that, boy."

"Well, let me start by asking you this. What would you say if someone told you it was possible to travel through time or that they might know the future? Which scenario would you be more likely to believe?"

"I told you not to waste my time. I'm not in the mood for games. If I wanted to hear crazy talk, I'd bring Kosminski back in here."

"This isn't crazy, Inspector. I know how it sounds, but please let me finish."

Abberline waved his hand dismissively. "This is absurd. Neither scenario is possible, and anyone who thinks otherwise should be fitted for a strait jacket, not keeping me up in the middle of the night. Is this what you're telling me? You think you're some kind of witch? If that's the case, I believe we're finished."

"No, of course that's not what I'm saying. I'm a wrongly jailed man who is desperate to get out of this place, and I have information that can help you. Are you really going to walk away from that? From the possibility that you could prevent murders from happening? And not just any murders—the worst and most notorious that this city has ever seen."

"This conversation is over, sir. I warn you, there will be no more chances for you. Demanding to see me in the middle of the night, telling me fairy tales. I don't know who you think you are, but this will not go well for you."

"Think about it, Inspector. I dragged you out of bed—"

"Who do you think you're talking to? I never gave you permission to address me in such a way."

Conal pressed on. He was running out of time. "I dragged you out of bed in the middle of the night, and insisted on speaking with you privately for a reason. You must have known that whatever I had to say was going to be unusual, at the very least."

"I didn't realize I was going to be listening to the ravings of a madman."

"Do you really believe that I'm a madman? You're an inspector, you pay attention to detail. Think this through. I'm keeping my composure, and have not once tried to harm you or escape. If I were insane, it would be unlikely that I would want to speak with you in private, because in my lunacy, I would rant for all the world to hear. I'm no Kosminski, Inspector. I know you see that.

82

"Please, hear what I have to say. If I'm wrong, or you think I'm somehow duping you, then by all means, lock me away in a room with padded white walls and let me rot there." It was a bold claim, one Conal hoped he wouldn't have to make good on. "Inspector Abberline, there are lives at stake. If you don't believe me, you can go home and go back to sleep. Please, just listen, What can it hurt?"

"Very well! I'll hear your story. However, we'll do this my way. If you're serious and want to go through with this, then you do so, knowing that if I'm unconvinced, there will be serious repercussions. Furthermore, no more launching off into tales of witchcraft and sorcery. Let's start with your name. Smith said you wouldn't give anyone your name. Who are you?"

"My name doesn't matter, Inspector, not in comparison with the importance of what I have to share with you." Conal spoke fast; he could see Abberline opening his mouth to protest. "I'm here because you have something to fear far worse than anything you've yet to come across. There is no question in my mind; you can't do this alone and you're going to need my help. There's an evil man lurking in your city and he's going to make a mockery of your force. This repulsive town will seem like a day at the park, and your jail look will like a convent in comparison with what he has planned. These are going to be the worst crimes ever committed anywhere. This is what's coming."

"How about you stop with these vague threats about some crime that might happen at some point? I'm a first-class inspector for Scotland Yard; you must realize how many crimes I see every day. I'm not exactly in need of the expertise of some drunkard who gets tossed into jail for being in a barroom brawl."

"I'm sure you've seen things that would make normal men cringe, and I do not doubt your expertise. Because I know this, I have to believe

83

you'll listen to me when I say we're on the brink of what will be a bloody killing spree that will make the horrors you've seen look like child's play."

Conal's theory was an uncertain one, and he had no proof. He trusted his instinct and the years of accumulated knowledge, but Abberline wasn't going to care about that.

"There is a secret being kept from the people of this country, one so important that it literally could lead to an uproar. What the actual secret is, I cannot say, and it's not important at this time. Some powerful people will discover this truth and because of this secret, there's going to be a raid on Cleveland Street. I don't know the address, but I know a woman named Annie Crook will be taken. She knows this secret, and anyone who has knowledge of it is in grave danger. These people are going to want to silence anyone with this knowledge if they know they exist. It's highly likely this may have a direct link to the murders to come. This raid on Cleveland Street will mark the beginning of the murders."

Abberline chuckled. Conal didn't know whether to take this as a sign of his defenses weakening or if his own exhaustion was causing him to crack up.

"You have quite the imagination. If I were to believe your story—and believe me, I don't—but if I did, what do you think would happen? Kidnapping is quite illegal, but it's hardly the worst crime this city has ever seen. What do you propose I do, run off and start crying murder before anyone aside from a few drunken louts is even killed, and claim that some American cad who sees visions of the future is my source of information? You'd better start saying something worth my while or we're finished here."

Conal bowed his head with a sigh that sounded much more like a growl. He could no longer contain his frustration. He wrung his hands through the shackles, opening up fresh wounds. Raising his head, he looked around the room. *There's gotta be a way to get out of this damn place!*

"There's no way out of here, boy. You would be wasting your time, I assure you."

"Inspector Abberline, I'm trying to protect someone! She needs my help and I can't keep her safe if I'm locked up in here! Now, I'm telling you the truth. Bad things will start happening in this city and you don't want this kind of blood on your hands."

He reined in his temper. It would do no good to shout at Abberline, who was obviously a proud man. "Inspector, this woman is family. If anything were to happen to her ... I would never be able to forgive myself. Look, Inspector, if I'm wrong, then throw me in the Tower and never think about me again, but think about this, Inspector. What I'm telling you is at my own risk; if I'm wrong, it's my ass on the line and no one else's, because you'd have me committed indefinitely. Therefore, I would be leaving her alone in Whitechapel, which is something I will not risk. If it weren't so important for me to prevent the immediate future events, I would just quietly do my time, eat your slop, and tolerate being the victim of a self-absorbed aristocrat jerk-off getting away with whatever he wants just because he has connections. I'd be out in a month or two. So ask yourself what God-given reason would I have to make this up and risk a lifetime in this hell hole when I'm telling you in order to prevent it from happening?"

Abberline stood and began to pace the small office, hands clasped behind his back. "I'm sorry, son, but even if what you say is true, I can't simply let you out. It would be bad form, and not go well for me. Too many questions that are too difficult to answer. However, I will look into your story. If what you say holds up, then I'll consider your release conditional under my supervision."

Relief flooded through Conal. Finally, a break, albeit a small one. "Thank you, Inspector. You'll see that I'm right. I have no doubt in my mind that you will. But please consider my release in return. I'll help you, but please, I have to be able to look after my own."

"You have my word, boy, as a gentleman and honest member of Scotland Yard. I will take it into consideration. Is that all?"

"No, there's one more thing."

"There always is."

"You cannot reveal your source to anyone. Just as I cannot disclose my name; you cannot disclose your source. This has to remain your investigation of your own doing. It must be your hunches and suspicions. If anyone questions you, tell them it's your remarkable gift of intuition, or that you don't want to corrupt the investigation. I don't care what you say, just leave me out of it."

"Come now, what would I tell them, anyway? A convict hauled out of The Ten Bells has now become a major police source, leading me to prevent the greatest crime in British history? Be reasonable." Abberline opened the door and motioned for the constable to return Conal to his cell.

"I'll be in touch. There'll be no more for tonight. I've heard quite enough as it is." Conal heard Abberline's heavy footsteps falling as the constable slammed his cell door.

Eleven

A bby hated Whitechapel. She had come to that conclusion by the third dark alley she and Mary crossed, when yet another leering man that could barely stand and reeked of liquor stumbled his way in front of the girls. His face was sprinkled with a salt and pepper five o' clock shadow and his teeth were stained. "How much for ya?" Mary paused, leaning her head back to pull away from his scent, crinkling her eyes. "Well, how much?" His eyes were half closed as if he could fall asleep standing up at any moment. Before Mary could say a word, the silence was broken by the sound of what could have easily been running water . The man began to chuckle, exhausted. He looked down.

"You're pissing yourself! Ugh, sod off!" Mary pushed the man, easily knocking him off balance and sending him stumbling into some old crates. He fell to the ground. Mary's shoulders rose up to her ears with a shiver. "I swear! He's disgusting!"

Abby's eyes strained against the dark. There were no street lamps in these back alleys. She bit back the scream rising in her throat. She had never been the kind of girl who was afraid of mice and spiders and things that went bump in the night, but this place was beginning to get the best of her. The rancid scent of this city made it impossible to get a clean breath, and the sounds in the shadows terrified her, not knowing whether they were made by human or beast.

"Mary, please, are we almost there? I don't want to be difficult, but this place is freaking me out." There was no point in mincing words, and there was something about Mary that comforted Abby, made her feel she could be honest.

"Freaking you out? So it appears your attire is not the only thing odd about you. Your words are quite strange as well." Mary chuckled.

"I'm scared, Mary. It means I'm frightened."

"This ain't so bad once you're used to it," Mary replied. She reached out to take Abby's hand. "But I understand what it must seem like for a newcomer. Don't worry, love. We'll be there soon."

Abby wanted to believe Mary, but it was difficult to imagine this nightmare ever coming to an end. The night fog clung to the ground, wrapping them in its gray abyss.

Something—a cat perhaps, or an oversized rat—darted past Abby's feet. She screamed, heart leaping into her throat.

"Goodness, you're as skittish as a cat! I promise you, we're almost there."

At last they emerged from the alley near a corner. The street sign read Commercial Street and Wentworth. Lights cut through the fog and Abby saw people milling about. Top-hatted drivers drove horse-drawn carriages past them.

Abby sighed in relief. Mary laughed. "You see? I told you I knew what I was doing." She clapped a hand around Abby's shoulder and steered her across the street.

"Mary! Mary Kelly!" A voice rang out from somewhere in the haze. A small, broad figure waddled toward them. As she drew closer, Abby could see the voice was coming from a woman nearing middle age, her hair dark but graying, and faint lines showing at the corners of her eyes and mouth.

"Polly!" Mary called. "That's Polly," she explained to Abby. "Her Christian name is Mary Ann Nichols, but no one ever calls her that. Life hasn't been easy for Polly. She was married once, but her husband was a cheat. She had five little ones with him before she began to suspect that he wasn't hers and hers alone. Tragic, isn't it? She never caught him but she said she was certain, so when he wouldn't confess, she left him for good. William, the lout's name was. He sent her money for a time, for the children, but when he found out she was whoring to pay the bills, his payments stopped. But then, they always do. That was about three years ago, and she and the babes have been struggling ever since."

"That's awful," Abby said.

Mary smiled sadly. "That it is. Everyone has their story, and it usually comes out in their cups. Whitechapel is a drinking town. It's the only release we have from our troubles."

"I've noticed," Abby said.

"'Ello, Mary! Any luck tonight or the soddin' bastards tight to purse? Goodness, who've you got here? What's that you're wearing, lovie? This one'll put us all out of business!"

"This is our new friend, Julia," Mary said. "That prick Abner Cowzy gave her a bit of trouble over at The Ten Bells."

"Ah, Cowzy, that bloody pervert. He's no good, he is." Polly looked as though she had tasted something rotten. By the looks of her decaying teeth, it was likely she had a time or two. "You'd do well to stay away from the likes of him," she counseled Abby. "He'll be needing a fire-proof coffin, that one, mark my words."

"Yes, well, poor Julia found out the hard way," Mary said. "She was fortunate her brother was there to protect her, except now he's gotten himself detained at Her Majesty's pleasure."

"Shit, that's terrible, the poor sod. Didn't he know better than to mess with the Grand arse himself?"

"We're not from around here. This town is something else. How did it get so bad?"

"It's a city of immigrants, and immigrants are usually the poor. They're always fighting each other, no one giving each other a hand, just a constant battle. The Jews get the worst but the Russians, Poles, and Irish seem to come over by the boatload, and the Catholics are in the mix of it all. Everybody's got a personal problem that keeps them all down."

"Well, we weren't looking to cause any problems. It's just that guy wouldn't take no for an answer," Abby concluded.

"I'm not surprised, love. Dressed the way you are, your get up says otherwise. I've no doubt Cowzy went mad when you turned him down. Would have made you a pretty penny, but you made the right choice. Nothing good comes of getting mixed up with him."

Sensing Abby's discomfort, Mary cut in. "Ah Polly, Julia here isn't a working girl. She's just a long way from home, isn't that right?"

Abby could have kissed Mary then.

"Oh? That explains the get-up, I suppose. Those rags are a bit unrefined, even among the working women of Whitechapel. Where are you from then?"

Mary sensed where the conversation was going. "What say we head home and get out of the cold?" Mary said. "There'll be plenty of time for conversation later."

Abby smiled and Polly nodded in agreement. She continued chattering as they walked.

"What of Abner? What happened to him?"

"Free, of course." Mary said it as though it should have been more than obvious.

"Bloody wanker! My apologies, Julia, it's not like me to curse like this, but I can't help myself with people like him. I'm not the least bit surprised, I tell you. The police are useless."

Abby could feel the tension in her body start to relax ever so slightly with the help of Polly's colorful disposition. She was warm in a mothering way, something for which Abby had longed her whole life. Her own mother was only warm for strangers' benefit. Privately, she was cold and critical of Abby. Tears were a sign of weakness and laziness in her eyes, and Abby had learned early on that her mother would not be a source of comfort when she was afraid. Polly may be a prostitute, she mused, but she's a good woman.

"Polly, have you seen Crooksie?" Mary asked. "Has she gone home to Eddie?"

"Crooksie? No, she's still here. I just saw her over at the Alice with Liz and Dark Annie.

"Crooksie, Dark Annie; who are they?" Abby was just trying to keep up, with all the names and the slang. This was like learning a new language.

"Crooksie is the sweetest girl you can imagine, one of my dearest friends in the world," Mary said with a smile. "Annie is Annie Chapman. They're both named Annie, actually, but that'd be a bit confusing in our circle, so Annie Crook goes by Crooksie."

"And Annie Chapman, well, she's a bit more complicated. Like most of the women in our line of work, her marriage hit some troubles and she and her husband split up. She never breathed a word why, but he continued to send her money, even though she had started working as a florist to support herself. Then one day she got word he passed. She was able to keep working as a florist for a time, but money soon ran out and, like the rest of us, she had to take to the streets.

"She took his death quite hard, even though they weren't together when he died. She's mourned him for a long time. I know it hurts her to have to sell herself to other men when her heart is still so dark with grief. Life has not been kind to Annie, and she's always looking for someone to blame for that. She keeps her heart hidden now, and is quick to let her mean streak show. You'll want to tread lightly around her."

They had reached the door of a pub. The faded sign above said 'The Princess Alice.' Abby prayed this would be a safer place for her than The Ten Bells had been.

Polly pulled open the door. "Liz is probably pissed by now, God bless her!" she laughed.

Abby began to have second thoughts. What if some other jerk tries to buy something she wasn't selling? This time she wouldn't have Conal to fight them off, and as tough a game as Mary talked, she'd be no match for some drunken brute trying to get his kicks for the night.

"Maybe I should just wait out here, Mary." She gestured toward her clothes.

Mary nodded. "Perhaps you're right." She walked to a window through which Abby could see a group of women drinking and laughing heartily. With the exception of Crooksie, they all wore dresses that had faded and were more on the dingy side than colorful, most of them revealed ample bosoms. Abby murmured to herself, "There is no way I'm going to fit in here."

Mary tapped at the window, and motioned for them come out. Two women stood up from the table.

"What, the rest of them are too good to say hello to my new friend?"

"Oh Mary, don't be silly," one of them said. "We've got a good card game going, so the girls thought it best to send a messenger for all of us."

Mary rolled her eyes. "This is Julia," she said. Abby gave a nervous smile and a hesitant wave. "Julia is a new friend of mine, and she's in a bit of need. As you can see, she needs something to wear. She's already run into some trouble once, at The Ten Bells, and we're trying to avoid a repeat. Crooksie, do you think you can give us a hand?"

"Anything for you, Mary," Crooksie said. She eyed Abby. "You're a little smaller than I am, but I think I have something that will suit. Come on, you must be freezing."

"A little bit," Abby admitted. The treacherous alley walk and meeting with Polly had distracted her, but now that she was standing still, the chill was creeping into her bones again.

True to Mary's description, Crooksie was the opposite of everything that had been said about Dark Annie. She had a warm smile and kind eyes, and her energy was infectious. Or would have been, if the events of the day hadn't finally begun to wear on Abby.

She glanced at the other woman in the doorway. Mary caught the look. "Julia, this is Liz, another of our girls."

Liz peered curiously at Abby, as though she hadn't quite made up her mind about whether or not to share Crooksie's generous attitude.

"It's lucky you haven't caught your death of cold by now," she said sharply. "You're dressed like a—"

Abby's eyes widened, practically daring Liz to call her a whore.

Polly nudged Liz sharply in the side. "Liz! You're being rude. Don't be such a bitch." She scoffed, "You're not exactly the image of the Queen. Julia's a friend now, and she needs some proper clothes to wear."

"Shit, Polly! What'd ya elbow me for? Ya didn't let me finish what I was sayin." Liz shrugged. "For all your bloody costuming, though, you have a pure look about you. I was that way once."

The other girls groaned and laughed.

"You girls laugh, but it's true."

"She used to be the quiet one, too, until she started drinking," Mary quipped. "Now she's a regular drama queen. She's harmless, though. Don't take anything she says too seriously."

"Come on, then, Julia," Crooksie said. "I've plenty of clothes and you're welcome to your choice of them." She slipped an arm around Abby's shoulders. "You are a beautiful one. Better for you that you're not working. Beauty fades fast in our line of work."

"Who's staying and who's coming along?" Mary asked.

Liz had gone back inside and was standing beside a sullen looking woman who could only have been Dark Annie.

"We'll stay and have another drink, see if there's any work for us," Annie said. "We'll be back to your place later tonight."

"Suit yourselves, gentlewomen," Mary said with a laugh. "The rest of yous, let's be on our way."

"Eh, you know what? Maybe I'll give it another go before calling it a night, too. Wait up, Lizzie." Polly hurried into the bar after the other two women.

"Nice to meet all of you," Abby called after them, but they were already back at their cards.

"So you're also Annie?" Abby addressed Crooksie as they walked on.

"Well, yes," she answered.

Mary finished for her. "You've met Polly, Julia. That there was Liz Stride, also known around here as 'Long Liz,' and Annie Chapman, also known as 'Dark Annie.' I can't imagine anyone feeling good about being

94

called long or dark, so we usually just stick with Liz and Annie, unless we're giving them a good ribbing. This here is Annie Elizabeth Crook, but she's our Crooksie, and royalty; people just don't know it."

"Oh." Abby assumed the girls were kidding and laughed a little. "So you're royalty, but you're working, too?" Before the words were even out of her mouth, though, she had second thoughts. Crooksie didn't look like a prostitute. She wore a lovely perfume, and her clothes were neat and new.

"Oh no, Julia, not me, the girls are just my mates. I work at a store on Cleveland Street with Mary," Crooksie said.

"She's married to the Prince, so there's no need for her to do the dirty deeds we do." Mary suddenly stopped speaking as she caught Crooksie's eye. It was obvious Mary had spoken out of turn, and Abby had noticed.

"Mary, Crooksie, I don't know a soul in this town besides the two of you and the other girls. Even if I did, I have no reason to gossip about anyone, especially not after all you've done for me. I value trust and loyalty and you've been very good to me tonight."

Mary rolled her eyes. "Oh Crooksie, why should it even matter if people know? You love each other and have a child together. This country has much bigger problems than you, and it has for a long time."

"Mary, you know I wish it was that simple. But I'll tell you the truth, Julia, since you seem like a kind woman, and, like you said, you've got no one to tell. I am indeed married to the Prince, and we have a beautiful three year old daughter named Alice." Crooksie's eyes sparkled as she spoke.

"The Prince? Are you kidding? That's wonderful. I don't understand. Why would you hide such a thing? And why would a prince keep his wife a secret?"

"I'm Catholic."

"I'm still not following you, Crooksie. What's wrong with being Catholic? I'm Catholic as well," Abby asked.

"You see, Julia, if you're royalty and in particular; Anglican, as is His Royal Highness, Prince Albert Victor, Duke of Clarence, you don't wed a common girl, especially a Catholic one. The people would riot, and that'd be the end of his line of succession. And please don't take offense, Julia, but you'd better keep that piece of information to yourself. You'll be much better off. There are so many rumors of rebellion and anarchy that if the marriage of the Prince got out, it would inevitably lead to the toppling of the throne, especially regarding Ireland's desire for independence. With all the problems in England, the Royal Family is under a great deal of scrutiny. Word about this cannot get out."

"I had no idea. I promise, your secret is safe with me, Annie."

"Thank you, and please, call me Crooksie. All the girls do."

"All right, Crooksie," Abby said with a grin. Despite having gone through hell that day, she found these women a comfort.

"So where is home, Julia?" Crooksie asked.

"I'll tell you everything—"

"—once my brother is out of jail," Mary finished her sentence for her. "Yes, I can't wait. She is a very mysterious one, wouldn't you say, Crooksie?"

Crooksie raised her eyebrows. "Mysterious indeed. Let's hurry along then, girls. I'm catching a chill outside."

Twelve

The girls walked a few more minutes until they arrived outside of a surprisingly middle class apartment. They walked up the narrow stairway. Well 'ere we are. Welcome to my humble home," Crooksie said cheerfully as she opened the door.

The unassuming location was the perfect place to hide. It was a flat no different than thousands of other flats in the area. Inside, it was gorgeous. It was as if they were in the private quarters of Buckingham Palace. There was an oak floor and luxurious drapes. In the bedroom, Abby sat on a huge bed covered in immaculate satin linens. She watched as Crooksie and Mary went through trunks of clothes and pulled out two dresses. One was deep red with black satin trim, the other a lavender two piece with white lace trim.

"Which would you like to try on first?" Crooksie asked.

Abby marveled at the beauty of the dresses. She had always dressed modestly, more out of necessity than a desire for anonymity. But these were the finest pieces of material she had ever felt. She chose the lavender first; purple had always been her color, she thought. It fit her as though it had been tailor made for her.

The girls helped her into the two piece lavender and white floral dress and a pair of lace-up boots, and she was transformed. No longer having the appearance of a harlot, she looked to have as much of a lady's appearance as Crooksie. It was as if she belonged here.

"Please take the red one and the shawl, too. You can't be wearing the same one every day, and you need to keep warm." Crooksie smiled as she spoke, visibly happy to help.

"Oh, I couldn't," Abby protested. She didn't mention she was hoping to be out of this horrible place, and time, before she needed a change of clothes.

"Nonsense, I'm married to the Prince, remember? I may not be able to declare myself to the world, but I can get new dresses pretty handily. I insist."

"You are quite striking, Julia. That dress looks so regal on you," added Mary with a giggle.

"Thank you, Mary, and thank you so much, Crooksie. I don't know how I can ever repay you."

"Not at all, Julia. I do hope you'll get to meet Eddy and Alice soon."

"That would be wonderful. Do they...live here with you?"

"They do. It must seem strange, the Prince living in these parts, but we do what we must to keep our secret." During the next half hour, Crooksie did most of the talking, sharing her stories of the Royal Family, her daughter Alice, and the romance she shared with Eddy.

"It's so nice to see how happy you are, Crooksie. You're like a giddy school girl."

"You just like to make us girls jealous, don't ya, Crooksie?" Mary teased.

"Don't pay any attention to her, Julia. As beautiful as the two of you are, why, you'll both be kept women, too. By none other than royalty as well, I'm certain of it."

"Aw, Crooksie. I'm afraid there is but one princess in that fairy tale." Mary popped up off the bed and sneaked a peck on Crooksie's forehead " And there couldn't be a better one than thou, my lady." She gave a playful curtsy. "Now, Julia, I think it's time we best be going," Mary said at last. We'll need to get some sleep if we're going to get your brother in the morning."

Abby bid Crooksie a warm farewell, hoping sincerely to see her again.

The walk to Mary's was long and, for the first several minutes, quiet, until Abby looked up, with a curious look on her face.

"Julia, I'm going to take a guess and say you're a bit curious about me, too."

"Yes, I am wondering more about you, but..."

"But you're too polite to come out and say what you're thinking." Mary laughed. "You want to know why I've chosen to work the streets."

Abby sighed, "Was I that obvious? I mean, I don't want to be nosy but since you brought it up..." Abby wasn't used to someone being so up front, but she liked it. "Well, yeah. You and Crooksie work in the confectionery shop together. Isn't that enough for you to get by? Is there another way for you to survive instead of having to sell yourself?"

"A lot of questions from someone who can't answer any of mine?" Mary teased.

Abby rolled her eyes. "I know, and I'm sorry. It's just that you're so smart, and so pretty, it just doesn't make sense to me. You have a job."

"Some would say smart and pretty are just the things a woman working the streets needs to be."

"Are you one of those people?"

"In truth, nothing is that simple. Selling sweets doesn't pay much, but I've always tried to stretch my pounds as far as I could. As fate would have it, the confectionary shop is where I met Joseph. Joseph and I were together for a little while, but it just never seemed to feel right to me. We fell out awhile back. Still, the thought of me working on the street drives him mad. He has tried paying for my lodging, but I've already moved twice because he couldn't afford the rent, and we're already behind on rent for the current flat. I try to stay on good terms with him but that's no easy task. I go through bouts of needing to put myself back out with the other girls just to get by. Of course, I'd prefer never to be out there again, but sometimes it can't be helped."

Something about Mary felt more kindred and warm than anything she had experienced from her girlfriends in the past—or future, whatever it was she was supposed to call it. Having selfish, emotionally abusive parents only made Abby want to help others all the more. The fact that Mary had to live this way left Abby with a somber look on her face and a guilty feeling for accepting gifts, knowing what Mary had to do just to survive.

"I wish I could help you," she said softly, reaching out to touch Mary's shoulder.

Mary smiled. "I know you do, Julia, but I'm all right. Besides, you've got yourself and that brother of yours to help. You've got quite enough on your hands already."

Abby groaned. "Oh yes, that mess. How could I forget?"

As they walked the last few steps, Mary sang out cheerfully, "Here we are. Let's get inside and I'll start a fire."

Mary gasped, and stumbled backward when she opened the door. Over her shoulder, Abby could see a man looming over them.

"What in the bloody hell is this, Mary?" he roared. He gestured toward Abby.

"For Christ's sake, Joseph, you scared us! You can't just show up here whenever you like!"

"Who says I can't? I pay the rent on this place—

"Barely."

"Don't get cheeky, Mary. Who's this now? How many strays you going to pick up to bring home and raise?"

Mary seemed almost bored as she turned to Abby. "Julia, this is Joseph; this is exactly what I've been telling you about."

"Nice to—" Abby was unable to get in a word edgewise.

"Julia, huh? Well, Julia, if'n I see you walking the street and dragging Mary into your whorish world, I'll—"

"Rubbish! You'll do what, Joseph?" Mary interrupted. "You don't know her. Just because you pay the rent doesn't mean you own me and it don't be giving you the right to threaten my friends or tell me who I can and can't associate with. You have your own place. You should be getting on now."

Abby stood frozen in the doorway. There were voices behind her; Annie and Liz had followed closely after them after all. They were with a woman Abby didn't recognize.

"Look who we found, Mary!" Liz paused for a moment when she saw Joseph, and then flipped her hand as if to brush him from existence. The smell of gin was on her breath.

"Well, now all your tarts are here...EXCUSE ME!" Joseph pushed his way past the women.

"I swear, Julia; I keep telling Mary that man is mad." Liz plopped on the bed next to the door. "We picked up Kate. She be full as a goat, she be.

And Polly's gone off with a customer. She says she'll be staying at her place with Emily tonight."

"Oh, what a night this is!" Mary proclaimed. "Kate, this is Julia. Julia, this is Catherine Eddowes."

"A pleasure, Julia, please call me Kate." Kate was in the same boat as the others—separated with children. She had tried to move in with her aunt, but was refused and therefore, forced to the streets. It was obvious that common struggles and tragedies had brought these women together. Misery loved company and these women had made a bed of companionship.

"Bloody hell! I'd like to meet the person who decided to put a heel on women's boots! A fine idea that was!" Liz moaned as she took off her boots and rubbed her feet. The women laughed as the chatter turned to lighter things. Mary's eyes began to get heavy as she got comfortable in her bed with an arm of Kate's draped over her, and a snore from Annie on the floor next to the bed. Still, Abby could not completely relax. She sat there by the fireplace with her knees tucked to her chest and gazed at a shadow that walked by the window several times until finally it stopped directly in front of it. She got up to see what it was, gasping as she glanced out the window. He was standing beneath a lamppost, watching the women.

He held Abby's gaze and slowly, slowly raised the thumb of his right hand and dragged it across his throat from left to right.

"Mary!" she screamed. "Why is Joseph out there staring at us?" By the time the others had moved to the window, he was gone.

"Oh heavens, of all the men I had to get involved with. Are you sure that was him, Julia? You know you've had a really long day and we're all tired." It sounded as if Mary didn't want to believe it, maybe because it frightened her, or maybe she didn't have the energy to deal with it any more.

"I saw him as well," said Liz. "It looked like he was fixing his tie, and then he just turned around and walked off."

Mary was fast to correct. "Joseph doesn't own a tie."

"Oh, right. Well, maybe we're just tired. Julia, let's get some rest."

Abby just wanted Conal back and sleep was the furthest thing from her mind at the moment. She wearily backed up to the corner of the fireplace. She couldn't take her eyes off that window, afraid of what might happen if she were to let her guard down even for some much needed sleep.

"Well if t'were Joseph, he's gone now. Let's all just get some rest," Mary told the girls in a motherly voice.

The five women were crowded but cozy in the little room. It was about ten feet wide and twelve feet long with a fireplace, a bed, a table, a chair, and a wash stand. Abby got as close to the fireplace as she could to stay warm. All she could do was pray that all of this had been nothing more than a bad dream and maybe, just maybe—if she slept, she would wake in the morning to her former life and far away from this one.

Thirteen

The cell rang with the sound of bells, clang clang clang, ringing on an endless loop. The noise filled Conal's head, making it difficult to concentrate. His footsteps fell into rhythm with the bells as he padded down a dark hallway. The floor was damp, cold seeping through the soles of his shoes. But the smell was gone. Unlike every other inch of Whitechapel, there was no overpowering stench of rotting food, whiskey, and sweat.

Clang clang, clang clang.

The bells grew louder. Conal quickened his pace, fear and curiosity driving him toward the noise. Around the corner there was a figure, standing about thirty feet away. Abby. As Conal drew closer, he saw she was in a cell, dragging a tin cup back and forth along the bars. Here were his bells.

"I can hear them, Conal," she called. "I hear them calling to me." She was pointing above.

"Abby? Hear who? What are you talking about? What are you doing here?"

"Conal, where are you? Where did you go? Why did you leave me?"

"I'm sorry, Abby, I had to, but I'm back, I swear. I'm coming!" He began running but he might as well have been stuck in place. The blackness grew until it nearly enveloped Abby, but Conal could make out a shadow. In the dim light, a faceless man appeared, a cape draped around his shoulders. He stood silently behind Abby. His eyes bored into Conal's for no more than a couple of seconds, but it felt like an eternity. Conal opened his mouth to scream, but no sound came out. It felt as though a hand were wrapped around his throat, cutting off his oxygen. He gasped and gagged, trying to cry out, but she couldn't hear him.

Her eyes widened in horror, and her screams were muffled as the man pulled her into the shadows. When she was gone, Conal's voice returned and he became hysterical.

"ABBY!" he screamed. Then he came to, awaking to another nightmare. His joints were stiff from the cot, and the clanging noise was even more real now than it had been in the dream.

"Everyone hop to it," the constable called as he dragged his billy club along each and every bar of the cells.

A breath of air whooshed from Conal's lungs. It was just a dream. Reality was horrible, but it had only been a dream.

Sometime before waking, someone had slid a breakfast tray into the cell. A bowl of lumpy mush, an undercooked egg and a hideous concoction that was meant to pass for a drink. If Conal hadn't been so hungry he might have vomited, but as it was, he would have eaten worse just to get something in his belly.

Tumblety was staring at him, mumbling while he twisted his mustache. Conal ignored him, shoveling spoonfuls of mush into his mouth. The faster it went in, the less he'd have to taste.

"So then, who's the girl? I heard you screaming for her in your sleep."

105

"Don't you have your own women to think on, Tumblety?"

"I've exhausted those memories a long time ago now. Jail will do that to you. Give a man something to live for, eh?"

Conal shook his head. He held his breath and guzzled the orange liquid in his tin cup. Tumblety sat across from Conal breathing heavily, his mouth partially opened with a slight grin and a wide-eyed stare. "What's the matter, Tumblety, your meds wearing off?" Conal laughed. What had seemed to be friendliness the night before had revealed itself to be something more sinister and Conal wanted no part of it.

Tumblety stood, his eyes boring a hole through Conal, searching for something. Conal was grateful they were in cages; at least the bars would keep Tumblety away from him.

The cell block door creaked open and Smith came barging through.

"Get up, Twelve. You've got another visitor."

Conal looked up eagerly. He didn't dare hope that it was Abby, but he didn't care if it was the Ripper himself, so long as he got away from Tumblety's prying eyes.

"Don't get too excited, I'm sending her in here. You've got ten minutes."

Conal's heart thudded as he watched a woman walk through the door. She wore a long lavender dress with a lace shawl draped across her shoulders, and her hair piled elegantly on top of her head.

"Brother," she cried in a loud voice when she reached his cell. "I was so worried about you!" She gave Conal an urgent look, pleading him to play along.

Brother? Well, this should be interesting, Conal thought to himself.

Abby looked at him quizzically, but he reached through the bars to take her hands.

"Thank God you're all right," he whispered.

"Brother?" Tumblety chuckled from across the aisle. "You're a sick one, ain't ya?"

"Friend of yours?" Abby was smirking.

Conal dropped his voice to a whisper. He cringed as he said the words. "He thinks we're lovers."

He could see Abby's face color, even in the dim light.

"I see. Well, that's ridiculous," Abby objected.

"Well, well, ha! There she is, you liar, there she is! Cattle! They're all cattle!" Tumblety barked as he struggled to fight for a look at Abby before he was forced down the hall. "You know what they do to cattle?" he said to the Smith.

"Move your arse," Smith ordered as he grabbed Tumblety's arm and directed him down the hall.

"Forget about him, looks like you've done all right. Where'd you get the dress? Did you make it back to Maybrick's? Where did you stay last night? I saw you walk off with some woman...but I was worried one of those jerks had caught up with you again."

"No, I'm okay. Are you hurt? How are you holding up in here?"

"I've been better, but I'm surviving. Look, Abby—"

"Right, we'll catch up later. What have you found out?"

Conal took a deep breath. He needed to talk quietly and quickly, they didn't have much time and Conal had to let Abby know the danger that was out there.

"Well, I know when and where we are."

"1888, right?"

"Yes. We're in Whitechapel, in the East End of London. Ring any bells?"

Abby bit her lip. "No, should it?"

"How about the name Jack the Ripper? He's the serial killer who—"

Abby's face twisted in fear. "I know who he is, Conal. In this town?"

"Well, we just landed right smack in the middle of it."

"When? Are you sure about this, Conal? How do you know?"

"Positive. I did a report on it when I was in the ninth grade."

"A report in the ninth grade, Conal? Are you kidding me?"

"Laugh it up, but I'm not kidding, Abby. Look, history is history. When I researched this, I never forgot it. Well, at least most of it."

"Conal, the ninth grade was a long time ago but...okay. If anyone would remember it, you would. So the murders, have they started yet? How long do we have? There's a lot of people in this town. Is it really something we need to be concerned with?"

"Don't do that, Abby. Don't be one of those people that thinks 'it'll never happen to me.'"

"All right, all right, we did just time travel, so I guess you have a point. So when, Conal? When does this all start to go down?"

"Any day now. You have to be careful, Abby."

"Can we actually die here?"

Conal didn't answer. Her mind was already three steps ahead, sharing his worst fears. "I don't know," he whispered. If either of them had to worry about that, it was Abby.

"Who was the woman you left with last night?"

"Her name is Mary. She works in a confectionery shop and...and she's a part-time prostitute." She turned her head, but Conal could see the tears glistening in her eyes. Fear knotted in his stomach.

"She took me home, introduced me to her friends," Abby went on in a trembling voice. "The girls, she called them. Most of them...they also work on the street."

Conal raised his eyes upward, not wanting Abby to see his worry. This couldn't possibly get any worse. He was locked up for who knows how long, and Abby was palling around with prostitutes just as England's most notorious serial killer was about to begin his reign of terror.

"What are we going to do?" The tears were gone; Abby's face showed nothing but resolve.

"I'm working on that. I remember that the lead detective on the Ripper case was named Frederick Abberline. The first thing I did when I got booked was ask to see him."

"And? Did you get to talk to him?"

"Yes. I left out certain parts of the story like—the whole visiting from the future by way of a time machine—but I think I managed to convince him I know something about this case. I gave him a few leads to chase, and he agreed that if I turned out to be right, he would release me."

"And in the meantime?"

"In the meantime, you need to stay safe."

Abby nodded. "Mary won't let me leave her side."

"Abby, you said Mary is a prostitute. The Ripper is going to target prostitutes."

"What choice do I have, Conal? You saw for yourself last night that the proper women in this town haven't exactly taken a liking to me. Mary has, and she's been kind. So have the girls. I don't feel right leaving them right now, especially when you're stuck in here. Besides, Mary is tough, and there's strength in numbers. It's rare that at least a few of them aren't together. Believe me, I'll be safe with her until you're out. But I'm not just going to stand around and wait for something to happen. There must be something I can do to move things along."

"Do you remember the victims' names?" Abby went on.

"You aren't going to try and stop one of these murders, are you?"

"Conal, if a woman I know is about to be brutally murdered, then yes, I'm going to try and stop it. I can at least warn her, or tell Mary she needs to keep the other girls close."

"Abby, we don't know exactly how these murders played out. You can't go messing with history."

"The names, Conal. I know you're worried about me, and I appreciate it, sincerely. But please, give me the names."

Somehow he knew. In his gut, Conal knew even before he saw the horror register on Abby's face.

"Mary Kelly, Annie Chapman, Liz Stride, Polly Nichols, Catherine Eddowes, Annie Crook. The last one, Annie Crook, she doesn't end up one of the Ripper's victims, but from what I remember, there's going to be some kind of raid at her apartment, I can't really go into detail right now, but this will mark the beginning of the murders. "

Abby's knuckles were white as she gripped the cell bars for support.

"Abby?"

Abby remained silent.

Conal felt a chill shoot up his spine. He lowered his forehead on the bars of his steel cage. "Abby... What are the names of your friends?" His eyes remained closed. *This cannot be happening.* "It's them, isn't it?"

As Conal lifted his head to look at Abby, she very subtly nodded her head and very softly replied, "It's them."

Conal took a deep breath. "The last victim," Conal said quietly. "Mary Kelly. There's speculation about that, though. There are some who believe Mary Kelly escaped from the Ripper with a baby, Annie Crook's little girl. A body thought to be Mary's was found, but it was so badly mutilated the evidence was never conclusive. Some theorists say it was actually another girl, one who had just begun running with their circle of friends. Julia, her name was, if it's true."

Abby's head snapped up.

"What did you say?"

"Julia. The last victim's name might have been Julia, not Mary Kelly, but no one actually knows."

Conal watched as Abby's hand flew to her mouth, fingers shaking.

"Oh God, Conal. Oh God." She doubled over, gasping for air.

"Abby, are you all right?"

"I'm Julia, Conal. I'm Julia."

The door swung open.

"Time's up, Twelve. Say goodbye to your wench.'

Abby spoke quickly. "The girls call me Julia because I didn't give Mary my real name. I'm Julia. Conal, we've got to find a way out of here. I don't want to die."

"Let's go, Miss!" Smith was stomping down the corridor.

"13 Miller's Court. That's where I'm staying. Get out of here, Conal, and come find me."

And then she was gone.

Fourteen

A dull throbbing in his shoulder woke Conal the next night.

"Get up, you sod," a voice hissed. Conal's eyes cracked open in the darkness. A shiny black boot was pressed against the rough cloth of his prison jumper.

"Did you hear me, boy? Get up. It's half past three in the morning. I'm not waking you for a chat and a cup of tea."

Abberline kept his voice low, and he was impatient. He ushered Conal out of the cell, and back to his private office. Conal noticed he did it without the shackles this time. His heart fluttered; a flicker of optimism.

"How did you know?" Abberline was sitting across from him, and Conal noticed deep bags under the other man's eyes.

"Know?"

"Don't play coy. You told me that there was going to be a raid on Annie Crook's place, and that's exactly what happened yesterday. I want to know how you knew."

Conal ignored him. "What happened?"

Abberline sighed deeply, looking past Conal. "By the time I got there, it had already begun. The door was smashed in so badly it looked like whoever did it had used a battering ram to bust into the place.

"It was supposed to be a quiet day in the Crook household. Annie was doing the dishes; her husband was relaxing nearby. She heard the thud of heavy footsteps, then pounding at the door. Annie wanted to hide her husband, but it was too late. Too much in that little home of theirs gave away that this was no ordinary working man who lived here. A black hand-stitched leather shoe, laces untied, sat at the foot of the stool. A brogan, an undeniable luxury item.

"It didn't take long for the intruders to bust down the door, maybe five strikes. Annie gave them the fight of her life, screaming for her husband to save himself. Neither of them were any match for the small mob. The men subdued Annie and dragged her away from her husband and her baby girl. Her husband was immediately taken into the men's custody.

"That's what I managed to wheedle out of some of the folks who had been around for the raid, though most of them were too scared of the mob returning for them to say much. The child was gone, but there was no sign of struggle in her room, so it's hard to say what might have happened to her."

Conal shook his head. "That's awful. The poor kid."

"Yes, it's a most unfortunate situation for the girl."

"I appreciate the debriefing, Inspector, but why did you drag me in here in the middle of the night? Are you going to let me go or is this just some cruel game?"

"Three people are missing. I can assure you, this is no game. Further, I can't let you go. Not quite yet."

Conal's temper flared. "What more do you want from me? Want to wait and let a few murders happen, sit back and see how that plays out before you decide to listen to me?"

"Watch your tongue. I don't want any murders on my watch anymore than you want your prediction to come true. But I need answers from you, and I'm not letting you skip off into the sunset before I have them."

Conal's head dropped. He rubbed a hand over his eyes, feeling a headache beginning. "What do you want to know?"

"First of all, in a city as overpopulated as this one, the strangest thing has happened. There was a raid on a civilian's home in the middle of broad daylight, and yet no one seems to have seen or heard a thing. I wonder if you might know why that is, being that you are the soothsayer here."

Conal's head jerked up, but Abberline silenced his protest with a warning look.

"Second, why would a well-to-do man who could afford to stay in one of the posher neighborhoods in the city be living in a middle-class flat with his wife and baby? And speaking of the child, where is she? Can you tell me those things? Or do your premonitions run out here?"

"They're not premonitions," Conal snapped. He worked his hands, needing to keep himself busy before he punched one of these ugly white-washed walls. "I do have some answers for you, Inspector, but I'm hesitant to give them to you."

"Oh? Not in such a hurry to get back to your loved one?"

"My resolve is sound, Inspector, I'm just not in a hurry to end up in some psych ward because you decide I'm a lunatic."

Abberline grinned, and the flicker of light from the oil lamp highlighted the stains on his tobacco-ravaged teeth.

"Seems that's a chance we're both going to have to take, eh? You were right about this raid. Crazy or not, I need to know what you know, so I can save the lives of some presumably innocent people."

Conal eyed him suspiciously. "Does that mean you're not planning to send me to a crazy house?"

"Fair is fair. You prove to me that not only can you help prevent these murders, but also that you're not the one committing them, and I have no reason not to let you go free. A bit off in the head, you might be, but you don't appear to be a threat to society, from what I can tell."

Understanding dawned on Conal's face. "You think I might be the killer. You don't want to let me out, because you need to prove first that I'm not behind these murders."

Abberline shrugged. "I don't see any other way. Now, let's get back to this raid. What else do you know about it?"

"Annie Crook is married to a wealthy man, a very important one. They live somewhat covertly to avoid drawing attention to themselves, but obviously they were on borrowed time. You say that the neighbors are skittish, they don't want to give up anything they might know about what happened. Ask yourself, why might that be? You represent Scotland Yard, I can't imagine this is a problem you typically run into. Who would the people fear more than the police?"

Abberline waved his hand impatiently. "Obviously it was someone of power who ordered the raid. I've already gathered that. But why? Why would they order the raid, and why take a husband and wife? If it was just him who was in some kind of trouble, one would imagine they would have left her behind, caused less of a scene. But someone wanted Annie, too.

Conal glared at Abberline. "Now you're getting it. Remember, he's a wealthy gentleman. And she's a Catholic girl. It's a bit of an odd pairing around these parts, wouldn't you say"

"What are you getting at?"

"Well, Inspector, would it be odd or not for someone quite powerful to be married to a common Catholic girl?"

"Odd? I'd say preposterous would be more like it. Even someone with the humblest political aspirations would know that was career suicide."

Conal hung his head, staring at the ground while he waited for Abberline to figure it out, then he looked off to the side and casually suggested, "What about someone who thought they could get away with it?"

"I'd like to see some lovely lord attempt to pull that off," Abberline scoffed.

Conal said nothing, letting the idea sink in. After a moment, he said quietly, "Or?"

"Or?" Abberline held up a hand to Conal in a halting motion. "Someone from the Royal Family? You'd better watch what you're suggesting. That's treason, you know. The Queen and the Royal Family are all staunch defenders of the Church of England, everyone knows that. To marry a Catholic would bring utter shame to the family. That would be treason as well."

"All the more reason to keep it quiet, don't you think?"

"If you have a point, let's be getting to it."

Time to roll the dice. "Annie Crook is married to Prince Albert. He's the husband who was dragged from his home, separated from his wife and daughter. Among the common folk, and to Annie, he went as Eddy.

He risked his entire life and fortune to be with the woman he loved. Now he'll never see her again."

Abberline's eyes were narrowed. "You better not be speaking nonsense. What will happen to them?"

"Happened, you mean. There's a good chance it's already been done. Prince Albert has received a severe reprimand from the Crown, but the whole ordeal will be kept quiet, so as not to cause a national scandal. Annie Crook was seized, and is probably being used as a lab rat, her body brutalized and defiled, her memory erased through some kind of lobotomy. No doubt she has already been taken to a mental institution, where she has been declared insane. Her torturers will claim they were trying to help her, though what they have done to her is utterly inhumane."

"Where was she taken?"

"Oh, no. That's for you to figure out. You'll not get anything more out of me, not until I get something in return."

"I already told you I can't let you out yet."

Conal nodded. "I heard you. But not another helpful hint until I'm free. On second thought, there is one. The first murder will take place tomorrow, just before 4 a.m. The victim will be a middle-aged woman named Polly, a divorcee, and a mother. She's a prostitute who took to the streets to feed her children. When you see her body, you'll know I'm not the murderer. Perhaps then you'll let me go free."

Abberline escorted Conal back to his cell.

"One more thing," he whispered as he turned the lock. "Where's the little girl?"

"I don't know, unlike the murders, this Annie Crook scenario I have only learned of in theory. I'm learning of its validity as it happens, the same as you," Conal answered sadly.

117

Once Abberline and the guard left Conal having confirmation that the theory was now an actual possibility pulled out his tablet he made some additions to his suspects.

Suspects:

Kosminski - lunatic, thinks all women are whores and must be dealt with.

Tumblety - fixates on uteruses and thinks women should be dealt with like cattle.

A Royal Conspiracy (Sir William Gull, Walter Sickert, Charles Netley) want to keep Prince Eddy's secret from getting out. Gull, Sickert, and Gull's driver Netley were all together at The Ten Bells.

Fifteen

There was a man, and a flash of gold, just for a moment. Conal watched him as the gold shape became clear. A pocket watch. The man seemed to be repairing it. He pressed so hard on it his hands begin to shake. He leaned down, close to the watch, blowing so hard a plume of dust rose from the small object. He snapped it shut and laughed as he slipped it into his pocket.

Conal struggled to make out the man's half-reflection in the shine of his freshly polished shoes. The man worked his shoes with a cloth, faster and faster, at a feverish pace.

The polishing stopped abruptly and the man turned, looking directly at Conal. His eyes were boring through him, but Conal couldn't make out his face, it was a blur around his eyes and he couldn't be sure if the man could see him. *Does he know me?* Conal thought.

The man chuckled, a low, evil sound. Conal's heart was pounding, there was a deafening ringing in his ears.

The man folded the white cloth neatly, laying it down carefully on the dresser. He moved to the sink and began to wash his hands. These were most certainly not a working man's hands. They were smooth, with no callouses or scars. His hands were trembling as he dried them.

He reached for a small jar, pouring some powder on the opposite hand, then he licked a thin line of white. Within moments, his breathing became more even, his body more relaxed.

He moved to an open carrying case, where several blades gleamed in the dim light. Insanity danced in his eyes as he smiled at the case.

"Foolish bitch." His voice was throaty, ominous. "I know for certain she's arranged a rendezvous with him in Whitechapel. So be it, my mind is firmly made. London it shall be and why not? Is it not an ideal location for my work? Whitechapel, Liverpool; Whitechapel, London. No one could possibly place them together."

Whatever goodness had existed in him once was gone. His victim didn't even stand a chance. He slipped pure white gloves over his hands and closed the case.

"Yes, yes. It is time."

Conal caught only glimpses of his face as he moved through the shadows. The figure slipped on a cape and a top hat.

"They will pay for what they have done," he threatened. "And you, stranger, will get to sit back and watch it all happen. There's nothing you can do to stop me, and should you try to intervene, you will indeed change history by being the only man as my victim. Oh yes, you weren't so arrogant as to think I didn't know of your presence here, were you? You are a testament to my triumph, proof that I have given birth to the twentieth century."

He's talking to me. He knows I'm here. He sees me. How? Fear created a knot in Conal's throat.

"Rest easy. You won't be alone long, she will die, too." The man cackled manically as Conal yelled.

He hit the cold ground hard, with nothing to break his fall. He awakened to his arms glowing red again up to his elbows and a small pair of eyes stared at him. A rat. It was only a rat.

"What the hell is going on in there?" Smith's gruff voice rumbled through the cell block.

Conal shook his arms free of the red orange glow. "Nothing. Just talking to a rat," Conal replied.

"Who do you think you are, mocking me?"

"Goodnight, Constable."

Conal laid back down on the mat, a hand over his heart to calm his racing pulse. Was it all really just a dream? It had been so real, that sick bastard had looked him right in the eyes and threatened Abby.

Conal didn't sleep again that night. Whatever that was, a vision or nightmare, after that, he'd rather stay awake thinking about all of the books on time travel and relativity he had ever read, trying to recall the report he did in the ninth grade, and replaying everything that had happened from the moment he got on that stage. *Come on, Benjamin, what did we do before that time machine took off? There were so many dammed distractions, Tristan, Colleen, and Abby. Abby, yeah, maybe she'll remember some of the things I did. God, I wish she was here.*

Sixteen

"Come on, let's hurry," Polly said to Abby, ushering her through the City. "It's getting late. We'll need to get going if you're hoping to see your brother."

Abby nodded, but paused to take a second look inside a store window as she was passing. She recognized a kindly looking man, the one she recognized from her first nightmarish day back in history. She glanced at the paint on the window, MAYBRICK COTTON. "Polly, I need to stop in here for just a minute." Five tiny bells tied to some red fabric attached to the door handle bounced against the glass of the door, jingling as Abby and Polly made their way inside.

"Mr. Maybrick, is that right?" she asked. He was diligently counting bills. He paused and stared at her blankly for a moment, then recognition dawned on his face.

"Ah yes, you're the girl I saw the other day. I hardly recognized you. You were a bit more scantily dressed then. You polished up quite nicely. I must admit I'm not so sure how happy I am to see ya quite so covered up."

Abby squirmed a little with such an awkward remark.

He smiled. "I'm sorry, I didn't mean to make you uncomfortable. I simply meant that now it seems you won't be needing to purchase one of my Bunny's favorite items." He chuckled.

Abby sighed in relief as the awkwardness of his comment faded. "I know. I'm sorry, I found a few friends who have helped me a great deal. But I saw you in here as my friend Polly and I were passing by and I—"

Maybrick waved to a customer exiting the store. "Thank you, Sam, always appreciate the business," he called.

The man replied, "Say hello to Flory and the children for me." He looked back at Abby. "You'll not find a straighter, more upright businessman than James Maybrick. A true gentleman."

"Go on, Sam, you're far too kind and you're embarrassing me. I'll see you next month." The redness in Maybrick's cheeks faded back into his normal bland rosy beige color as the bells on the door jingled. Sam tipped his hat to the girls and walked out. "I'm sorry, now, where were we?"

Abby smiled. "Well, I just wanted to say thank you for your offer to help my brother and me. Not everyone has been as kind as you, and your kindness was encouraging."

She glanced toward Polly, who was standing in front of a mirror trying on a bonnet. She hoped Polly wouldn't overhear and start asking questions.

There was no reason to worry. Fortunately, Polly was oblivious to anything except the hat she was wearing. "What do you think?" she asked.

Abby opened her mouth to reply, but Maybrick cut her off. "You look absolutely smashing, like an entirely new woman!" he declared with a broad grin.

Polly blushed. "Yes, it is quite jolly, I must say." She paused for a moment to adjust it.

"Indeed," Maybrick replied. "It's of my wife's favorites."

Abby noticed a photograph on the counter. "Is that your family?"

"It certainly is. My wife Flory and our children. That was taken outside Battlecrease, our family home."

Polly peered over Abby's shoulder at the picture. "That's a good-looking family you have," Polly said.

"Thank you, ma'am," Maybrick said with a proud smile.

"Yes, your wife looks lovely and your children seem sweet," Abby chorused.

"Well, as much as I appreciate your kind words, ladies, I'm afraid it's time for me to close for the evening. Is there anything else I can do for you?"

"Ring up the bonnet," Polly said. "I'll take it."

Maybrick refused to charge full price, offering Polly a fifty percent discount. He was being generous. The hat was finely made and worth far more than he was getting from Polly. Abby wondered if he had taken pity on the older woman. The hat was beautiful but Polly was not, and Abby couldn't help feeling sad as she watched Polly admire herself in the mirror. She turned to Abby, showing off a couple of fancy poses, her smile revealing five gaps where teeth had been a long time ago.

Polly walked with an extra bounce in her step as they made their way toward Scotland Yard.

"You're worried about your brother, aren't you, love?"

If only you knew, Abby thought with a shiver. *I'm not sure if I should be more concerned about him or you.* "I'll feel a lot safer when he's free," was all she said.

"Safer? Oh, don't you worry, Julia. Whitechapel may seem an unfriendly place, but between us girls, we always look out for one another and we survive just fine. We'll look out for you, too."

"That's kind of you, Polly. I suppose it's just reassuring to have a man around."

Polly nodded, frowning. "I understand. I always slept easier at night when William, my ex-husband, was home. When it was just the children and me, I could never quite feel at ease. I was always frightened by the drunks and the scum crawling around the neighborhood." She laughed. "But look at me now, I've become that which I so judged and feared. But we're not speaking of my woes now, are we? Speaking of your brother, it sounds like you two are close. A little too close for a brother and a sister," Polly scoffed, nudging Abby in the arm.

Abby knew she didn't mean any harm, and obviously she didn't know what she was saying. But her words still made Abby's heart pound fast in fear. She couldn't risk anyone finding out the truth about her and Conal.

"We come from a close family," Abby said, more tersely than she had intended.

"Ah, well, I'm looking forward to meeting him anyway. What did you say his name was again?"

"I didn't." Abby's hand flew to her mouth, unconsciously chewing at her thumbnail as she thought. It was bad enough she was lying about Conal, but worst of all, she hadn't told the girls they were marked for murder.

"Julia, look, there's Mary over there. Mary! There you are! Where have you been hiding? We've been worried sick!"

Mary hurried over, but the dark circles beneath her bloodshot eyes gave away her distress. She grabbed both of them and pulled them into an alley.

"Crooksie's gone," she whispered, tears filling her eyes. Abby noticed Mary's hands were shaking, and that she kept pressing them together to control her fear.

"What do you mean, 'gone'?" Polly was wide-eyed.

"The other day, I was out with little Alice. I took her to the park so Crooksie and Eddy could spend some time together, and when I came back, the front door was busted open, the house was torn apart and there was no sign of either of them. The whole place had been ransacked in broad daylight, but no one will say a word. Alice and I hid around the corner when I realized something was wrong, and I watched a man go into the house. He was well-dressed and official-looking, maybe a detective, but I'm not sure. He appeared to be looking for something, but he came out empty-handed."

"Have you gone to the police?" Abby asked. She felt sick at the news.

"No, and you would do well to keep this to yourselves, both of you. We'll only make matters worse if we call attention to it; for now, I took Alice to the convent I stayed at a couple years back, so she's safe for the time being. That's the best we can hope for at the moment."

Abby nodded miserably.

"I'd better be going," Mary said. "From the looks of it, you should, too, or you'll miss your chance to see your brother tonight. I'll see you girls back at the flat."

Abby reached out to hug Mary goodbye, feeling clumsy and helpless.

Neither she nor Polly said anything as they walked toward the jail once again, that extra bounce in Polly's step had turned to dragging feet and heavy shoulders. She scanned the area as she walked, looking for potential customers or any opportunity to get a drink. Abby was so distracted by the thought of what happened she nearly ran over a kid handing out the paper. Polly tugged Abby out of the way as they walked

126

by. Abby just stared at the child, wondering, "Where were ya with that paper yesterday, kid?"

Before Polly could ask Abby what she meant by that, a man across the street called out to Polly and she paused, giving him a smile.

"Just a moment there, handsome," she called.

"Julia, love, it appears my new bonnet is turning my fortunes already. I don't want to let this one go, after hearing that news about Crooksie, this old girl needs a drink. You'll be okay the rest of the way, won't ya, love?"

"Wait, Polly, aren't you going to come with me? I know you need the money, but I really think—"

"You'll be fine," she interrupted. She squeezed Abby's hand. "The jail is just up the road, and you look like a respectable woman now. No one will bother you, and you'll be with your brother shortly."

She didn't wait for Abby's response as she crossed the road. Abby could hear her giggling to the man, saying something about him needing to buy her a swig of gin before he got to take her home. Abby watched until they disappeared around a corner and she could no longer hear Polly's laugh.

Seventeen

I met a gin soaked, bar-room queen in Memphis,
  She tried to take me upstairs for a ride.
She had to heave me right across her shoulder
Cause I just can't seem to drink you off my mind.
It's the honky tonk women
Gimme, gimme, gimme the honky tonk blues."

Conal's voice grew louder with each round of the song, echoing down the cell block. It was as if he was drunk on frustration and boredom. He paid no attention to the shouts demanding quiet, the threats to his life. A few of the inmates even joined in his singing.

How fitting. A song from a group of Englishmen banging on about a gin-drinking prostitute. Conal grinned in spite of himself. It was almost too good.

Smith's voice broke through his solitary serenade.

"Twelve, let's go! Your sister's here again."

Conal bolted upright, his brow wrinkling with concern. Abby. *What was she doing here?* He stood up and paced anxiously. *It's gotta be after sundown, she should be inside for the night.* He walked over to the bars of his cell in angst to see if it was really her.

Fortunately, Smith was kind enough to allow Conal the interrogation room for the visit. Maybe Abberline had put in a good word for him.

"What are you doing here?" he exclaimed as soon as the door closed.

"Checking on you and our little situation, of course."

"Yeah, but why the hell did you come so late? You shouldn't be here. You have to be careful. It's dark outside. Did someone come with you?"

"Polly walked most of the way. We got about halfway here before a customer summoned her." She shook her head, in sadness or disgust, Conal couldn't tell. "I'm starting to realize that's just the way things go here. One minute they're here, the next minute they're trotting off at the glance of some john. I hate it, Conal. They're too good for this. They're—"

"Abby. I know you've become fond of these women, but please tell me you haven't said anything."

Abby's eyes flashed. "Anything about what? How they're all living their sorry lives on borrowed time? That they're only days away from being murdered by the world's first serial killer?"

Conal waited a beat. Abby sighed, throwing up her hands.

"I'm sorry, Conal. You didn't deserve that. It's not your fault this is happening. It's just...you're in here, these girls have targets on their backs, and I can't do anything to help anyone."

"Abby, listen to me. I know you're frustrated, but you need to be smart about this. You're running around all over London with a bunch of women who are marked for murder, and now traipsing around a jail after dark with no one to protect you or see you home. You're not going to be much help to anyone if you end up dead."

Abby's eyes filled with hot tears that threatened to spill over, and her voice shook when she spoke. "What do you know about it, Conal?

129

You sit in this jail every day, just waiting to be released. I'm the one who has to survive out there every day. The girls are kind, but they're asking questions, ones you know I can't answer. How long until their generosity—or their time—runs out? Then what? Are you going to make some room for me in that cell of yours? I don't need any lectures about staying safe."

Conal rubbed a hand over his eyes. Stress knotted in his shoulders; fear in his belly. He had to make her understand.

"I know it hasn't been easy for you to keep hiding the truth and to survive out there. I hate that you're the one in danger walking around this god-forsaken place instead of me. But you need to get back to the apartment as soon as possible. You shouldn't have come here. Tonight is the night. The Ripper will begin his murders tonight, and you need to be off the streets. You're scarcely safer around Mary, but I have to believe that he'll only attack when they're alone, so you should be safe."

"And what, their lives mean nothing?" Abby swiped at a tear streaming down her cheek.

"Of course they mean something, but yours means more to me, and yours is the one we have a chance of saving. Abby, I have no idea if we can change what's going to happen to these women, or if there's time. Why do you have to be so damn stubborn? Please listen to me. You need to go home and stay there."

"You don't understand, Conal. You have no idea what this is like."

"Abby, have you forgotten why I'm in jail in the first place?"

Her eyes snapped up, narrowing.

"I was defending you." His words came out with barely a whisper, and he regretted them as soon as they were said.

"I see."

Abby shoved back her chair and stalked to the door. She banged on it with the flat of her palm. "Constable! Our visit is over. Please open the door."

"Abby—Julia—dammit." *I didn't mean that, I'm sorry.*

"Goodbye, brother," she said. She didn't even look at him as she stalked out.

Conal glimpsed Abby as she slipped out the door. The sky outside was blood red, and the smell of smoke came in on the wind.

"Fires in the city tonight," Smith said. "Worthless lower class, always causing trouble."

He led a remorseful Conal back to his cell.

✳✳✳

Outside, Abby's footsteps fell hard on the pavement. She lifted the shawl to shield her mouth from the smoke, but it still stung her eyes. She refused to turn back to look at the prison, anger and grief roiling in her heart.

With each step, her anger grew. She thought back on her arrival in this horrible excuse of a city in this barbaric time. She hadn't asked for any of this. "Why is this happening to me?" she wanted to scream. She would have traded any night arguing with Tristan, or suffering the insults and coldness of her parents to be out of this detestable mess.

She retraced her steps up the damp cobblestone street from the jail, and approached an unfamiliar corner. Looking all around, she searched for anything recognizable. It did no good to talk to passersby. The women shot dirty looks at her and the men only tried to grope her and proposition her. Rushing from corner to corner getting completely turned around, she was flustered, and finding anything that looked familiar was becoming more and more unlikely.

"Was it Hanbury I turned at? Or Brady Street? Dammit, Abby, remember!" She breathed heavily, refusing to cry again. "Come on. You can do this. Don't fall apart now."

A movement across the street caught her eye. *Okay, I just need to stay calm and maybe this guy can help.* For a split second, Abby lifted her hand to wave down the man for some help. The man was watching her...and he looked familiar. Abby knew that face. "Oh my God, that's the pervert from the cell across from Conal. How had he been released and not Conal?" As he stepped a foot off the curb, Abby did an about face, avoiding eye contact.

The man tossed his cigarette to the ground and started toward her. Abby whipped around a corner, quickening her pace. From the corner of her eye she could see Tumblety was moving faster and getting closer; she could hear his footsteps. "Fuck it," she blurted and broke into a run, barely breathing as Tumblety began to chase her through a narrow street shaded by old oak trees. The moonlight barely cut through the thick canopy of leaves, except for a single sliver stream of light hitting on a tall wrought iron gate partially hidden by bushes. As she came to a desperate halt, she could see the gate was too tall and speared at the tips. She was going to have to squeeze through the bars.

Tumblety drew closer as Abby began squeezing herself through the bars. *Come on, get through! Get through.* With one final push her tiny body popped through the gate, her heels sunk into the damp muddy ground, her long dress catching on branches. She yanked them free as her rage propelled her forward.

She looked back and could see Tumblety at the gate, but his girth wouldn't permit him through the bars; a small reprieve.

He grabbed the bars in a sadistic fit, pressing his face against them. "I see you," he mocked.

Abby's foot caught in her dress and she lurched forward, breaking her fall with her hands. Fresh soil had flown in her eyes and her mouth. She looked down as she was crawling forward, and when she raised her head, a large gray block of stone stood in front of her. with a large 'R.I.P.' engraved on it. "The cemetery. Oh my God, I'm almost home."

For a brief moment, Abby thought she might make it. She ran hard, envisioning the door to Mary's warm apartment. Jews Cemetery wasn't far from there. A few more minutes...

Tumblety kept pace with her, running the perimeter of the wrought iron gate. Abby refused to look at him, afraid the sight of his manic face would make her lose her courage. Every second counted.

What the hell does he want with me?

The idea had barely formed in her mind when she saw Tumblety heading straight for a break in the fence. Within seconds, Tumblety was again closing on her, clambering over gravestones in his pursuit. Abby could feel him getting closer, then with a guttural wail that echoed through the desolate cemetery, Abby felt a jolting pull on her hair and her tired footsteps came to a halt. The last thing Abby was conscious of was being thrown to the hard ground, struggling for air against a gloved hand clamped across her mouth. Silence settled across Jews Cemetery and the world went black.

✳✳✳

PRESENT DAY:

Edie's warm hand, tattered with age spots, lightly shook as it closed over his, bringing him back.

"Conal, dear..."

He shook himself. "Sorry, Edie. The story's just bringing back a lot of memories I hadn't thought about in a long time."

She nodded knowingly.

Sadness and recognition flickered in her eyes. "I'm so sorry, dear. I didn't realize."

Conal pinched the bridge of his nose.

"You remind me so much of my Daniel."

"The man you lost?"

"Oh, I wouldn't call him lost. I believe he's somewhere out there, watching out for me until I join him, wherever he may be. You remind me of him, and I guess I'm hoping you get your happy ending sooner than he and I will have ours."

Conal smiled and cleared his throat.

"Well, go on, then. I believe it was just about time for you to be getting back to what happened to Abby."

Eighteen

WHITECHAPEL: 1888:

His mouth was dry as cotton, and his tongue felt swollen, as though he had been on a bender all night. If only.

The all-too-familiar creaking permeated the silence as the cell block door lurched open; still Conal refused to open his eyes. He could hear footsteps approaching his cell. *Keep moving, don't stop for me.* Maybe if he kept sleeping, this all would be a bad dream.

"Get up. There's been a murder."

Ugh! No reprieve from my nightmare today. "What? What time is it? Someone was murdered? Who?" Conal sat up on the bed with reservation.

"I don't know who was murdered just yet, so save your questions. Put these on and pull yourself together." Abberline tossed a lump of clothing next to Conal.

Conal strained to see the clothing in the light of Abberline's lamp. "Where did these come from?"

"Nevermind where they came from. All that matters is that people don't see a constable of Scotland Yard roaming the streets with a prisoner. You'll act as my partner."

"Your partner?"

"Yes—a silent partner, for the most part. I'm calling you the new Chief Inspector of the City of London Police Department, if anyone asks. It's a mouthful, I'll grant you, but that's to our advantage. People will lose interest before the full title is even out of your mouth. The less you're noticed, the better."

Conal stared at him, waiting for the next twist.

"I represent Scotland Yard; as such, I retain my rank of Chief Inspector of the Metropolitan Police. Consequently, you shall be acting in a cross-jurisdictional liaison manner to which you shall better be enabled with anonymity. The City Police shall issue their reports to you on my behest, believing you to be of my office, as my department shall be briefed upon your presence, keeping tensions mum regarding said jurisdictional boundaries. As there are no City Police personnel attached to my office, no one will know who you are but what I allow them to know. Now, I have not spoken to anyone of our previous conversations, so perhaps it's best to keep this between us, yes?"

"Spare me the bureaucratic bullshit, Abberline. I'm your silent partner. I got it."

Abberline frowned, his jowls swaying slightly. "Are all Yanks so easily lost when deception is involved? I dare say, how America achieved independence simply confounds me. To put it simply, I have orchestrated the necessary events and protocols to facilitate all that is required and that is all you need know. I fear I was not forthright with you. It was necessary not to inform you of my 'plot,' as I was unsure, because of your manner, if you could stay quiet about my plan until I had your identity in place."

"But I didn't give anyone my identification. No one here knows who the hell I am. No one is going to believe I'm your partner. Last time I checked, they don't let Yanks in Scotland Yard."

"Thus the silent partner."

Conal laughed, a short bark of sound. "Great. I'll mime my way around the crime scene."

Inspector Abberline leaned forward and looked Conal straight in the eye, a death stare. "Listen very carefully. For our purposes, this ruse is necessary. No one is more aware than I am of your ineptitude and unworthiness of a badge. But what choice do we have? I need you at the crime scene, and I need the beggars who will be watching at every turn to believe you're a figure to be respected. Otherwise, all will be lost. Now pay attention. You have withheld being a detective from all, save myself, for purposes of your own work. As such, you shall claim the need to remain mum regarding your endeavors and therefore silence all further professional inquiries. That is your story. Don't forget yourself. And don't mistake yourself for my equal."

Conal's neck was sore; the pressure building there was making him feel his head would explode. He rubbed at the base of it, then reached for his clothes.

"How do you intend to explain my sudden elevated status to the happy guards?"

"The report against you has been 'lost'; as any identification was missing, the ability to follow through accordingly was lost with the complaint. With your release, there is no prisoner. If there is no prisoner, there is nothing to investigate. Unless you'd rather stay here and continue getting acquainted with your new friends?"

A smirk crossed Conal's face. "Let's go, Abberline. Women are dying while we're busy jerking around in here."

"Good chap. Here's your badge; keep it on you at all times."

Conal glanced at the badge: James McWilliam.

How many times in his life had he wished to be someone else, begged the man upstairs for a new identity? Now he had the chance and would have given anything to have the humdrum life of Conal Benjamin back.

"Who's James McWilliam?"

"He's a real detective, unlike yourself. The true James McWilliam is currently assisting Pinkerton's men in America on a manhunt and his work requires him to take an alias. His work is...of a private nature. Throwing his name around as though he's still in London will keep people off the scent; keep them from finding out he's gone."

"What if he comes back? You aren't at all worried he might get a little peeved that I've stolen his name?"

"I saved James' life once. He owes me."

"You—you saved his life?"

"When James began with the Constabulary, he was proud, but foolish. He became familiar with a woman of the streets, totally unbecoming of a man in his position. Unfortunately, the prostitute didn't share James' amorous affections and soon she tired of his attention. The little bitch was about to take a blade to him, but I caught her in the act."

"You knew it was going to happen."

"I didn't, as a matter of fact. He had mentioned the girl to me, and I paid it little enough mind until I realized she was a street walker. I couldn't have James embarrassing us all, tarnishing the name of Scotland Yard. I began following him, seeing to it that he kept his foolishness behind closed doors. James is the type who moons about like a puppy

138

when he catches the scent of a bitch he likes. One night, James told me he was going out for a walk, and what do you know? A few minutes later, I realized I was itching for a stretch myself and took out after him. Of course I knew where he was going. This time, the girl wasn't the simpering tart he liked her to be. She was demanding his money, and holding her arm behind her in a queer way. Turned out she was concealing the blade she intended to use to slit his throat and steal his money. Fortunately for our Mr. McWilliam, I intervened before she had the opportunity to indulge herself."

"You're a regular hero, Inspector," Conal said with a smirk.

Abberline gave him a sharp look. "Whatever you do, stay away from the City Police jurisdiction. Some of them will recognize our charade, and I don't need them crawling up my arse if they start getting suspicious. Think you can handle that?"

"I can try."

Conal slipped the brown pin-striped jacket Abberline had given him across his shoulders. Had he not been concerned that the next words out of Abberline's mouth were going to be a proclamation of Abby's death, he would have been impressed with himself. Between the blazer and the white button down dress shirt, tweed pants, and smart brown derby, he almost looked his part in this nightmarish world.

"Of course, by the time James returns, you'll need to disappear. Once he's here, I'll need to declare you a fraud and a con man, and I won't be able to offer you my protection anymore."

"Good to know. All right, Abberline, if you're finished with all your chit chat, I suggest we get moving. I'm done with this place."

"Won't be missing your friend Tumblety at all?"

The thought of the man made Conal uneasy. "If I never see that lunatic again, it will be too soon."

"Let's go." Abberline ushered Conal out of the prison block and onto the street, then hurried him into a carriage. When they were safely settled inside with no one around to eavesdrop, Abberline gave Conal a hard look. "Now, are you going to tell me what in the hell is going on?"

"Me? What about you, Inspector? A woman has been murdered and you refuse to tell me what happened, or even who it was."

The darkness within the carriage made it difficult, but Conal could see Abberline's lips set in a grim line. "You won't get any information from me until you tell me the truth about who you are."

Conal sighed an exhausted breath. *Think of Abby, you need to save Abby. It's the least you can do. It's probably all you'll ever get to do.* "Inspector, listen. I'll tell you the truth. You let me out of jail; you're taking me along for the ride. I owe you this much. But I give you fair warning. You're not going to want to believe me. Hell, I wouldn't believe me if I were you. But you have to know, I am telling the truth."

"Enough with the qualifications." Abberline reached into an inner pocket in his blazer and produced a flask. The scent of whiskey flooded the cab as he unscrewed the cap. Abberline tilted the flask to his lips, but his eyes never left Conal.

"The truth is, I don't how I got here, Inspector. I don't understand. I'm not from here; this is not my world."

"We've already established that, son. You don't need to remind me you're a Yank."

"No, it's not about being a Yank. I don't belong here, to this place or to this time. I'm from America, yes, but I'm also...I'm also from the future." Conal paused, waiting for Abberline.

"You don't take me very seriously, do you?"

"No, Inspector, I do, in fact—"

"No one who took me seriously would possibly speak such rubbish with a straight face when I have just released him from jail; put my trust in him. Is your aim to make a fool out of me?"

"Inspector, just listen. I am telling you the truth. I don't understand it any more than you do. But why would I make this up? Why would I risk my neck and—Ab—er my sister?"

"How would I know your motivations? All I know is, you've been carrying on to me for days about these murders and how you can help me prevent innocent people losing their lives to a madman, but when I give you the chance, you begin rambling like a charlatan or a halfwit."

Conal's anger flared. "Why would I lie about this? Haven't we been over this already?"

Abberline swigged his whiskey again, then waved a hand at Conal to continue.

"I'm from the future, Inspector. I understand it almost as little as you do. One minute, I was there, playing around with a time machine trying to impress a girl, the next thing I know I was sprawled next to some stables over a hundred years before I was even born. What in the hell else do you want me to tell you?

Inspector Abberline remained silent, looking at Conal, then outside of the carriage, almost as if in disgust.

"It's funny; some people dream of traveling through time their whole lives. They romanticize this idea of going back through history, or forward into the future, glimpsing what might be. Well, I can tell you, time travel isn't all it's cracked up to be. No offense, Inspector, but this is the last place in history I would ever have sent myself. No idea if I'm going to make it out of this alive, with the world's first serial killer beginning one of the worst sprees in history."

Before he even realized what he was doing, Conal found himself telling Abberline the whole story. The exhibit, Abby, seeing her with Tristan. His frustration of seeing them together; what a jackass Tristan had been. The time machine, the wrenching through time, waking up in this hellhole of history.

When he had finished, Abberline sat quiet for a long time.

"Are you going to lock me up?" The silence was almost worse than the contempt.

"We're here." Abberline ground the tips of his fingers back and forth along his forehead with a look of astonishment on his face. How could it have come to this? A career built on discretion, intelligence, the highest standards in Scotland Yard decorum and ethics. Now he had a murderer on his hands and his best lead was some crass lunatic American who believed he had dropped out of the sky from over a hundred years in the future.

"Inspector, if my memory is correct, then the first victim will have wounds to the throat and the lower abdomen. I've been locked up this whole time. I'd have no way of knowing that from the scene. If that's true, you'll know I'm not lying."

Abberline didn't answer. The carriage had jolted to a stop. He replaced the flask within his jacket and swung the carriage door open.

"Where are we?"

"We're going to see whether you're a liar or an accomplice to murder."

Things had seemed a bit surreal for Conal up to this point, but now the reality of the situation was finally hitting him. They stepped directly into a throng of reporters clamoring for information. Conal didn't need Abberline's warning to keep him quiet. Terror sat cold in his gut. If he

142

was right, it wouldn't be Abby. But what if he was wrong? 1
been here the first time around. 't

Abberline shoved the reporters aside and they approach
poorly covered body. The thin white sheet was soaked through
blood. A pair of boots poked sickeningly from beneath the sheet, and
hem of a lavender floral print dress was partially exposed. That was th
color Abby was wearing... Some sort of medical examiner knelt on the
ground, a black bag opened next to him. A figure rushed by them, mouth
covered, gagging.

Conal's hands began to turn red again with that burning hot
sensation, and unlike his usual episodes of glowing red arms, everything
around his fingertips became blurred. He quickly stuffed them in his
pockets, beads of sweat began to run down the side of his head. He began
to feel wobbly so he grabbed on to the Inspector's shoulder.

"It can't be." Conal gasped aloud. "No."

Inspector Abberline grabbed Conal as hard as he could to pull him
away as he tried to race forward to grab the sheet off of the body.

"Remember yourself, Mr. McWilliam."

Conal looked past Abberline and felt bile rise in his own throat, a
shaky breath came out. His hands cooled, he moved to wipe at his eyes,
but Abberline batted away his hand.

"I said remember yourself."

Conal could hear the constables whispering to each other. "Strange
behavior for the head of City detectives."

"Everything all right, Inspector?" asked a constable.

Inspector Abberline snapped back, "Might I remind you there is a
cadaver a couple feet away? A woman has been murdered. Does this
picture look all right to you? Now I suggest you go out front and help
keep anyone from coming in here without authorization and give us

143

...e constable was surprisingly disobedient, looking at some ...estioning, almost suspicious eyes for a moment. "Now, Con...ordered Inspector Abberline.

Co...with suspicion written on his face he replied, "Right, sir! Right

"Move aside," Abberline barked. He motioned for Conal to kneel ...ith him beside the body. He wasted no time and drew the sheet back.

It wasn't Abby. The pale face, the lifeless eyes. They were not hers. Yet Conal was overcome with grief. The woman's plump cheeks; yesterday they had held life. Now they sagged on her corpse. The sweet, sickening smell of death drifted from her body. But her eyes were full of shock and pain. Conal would never forget those eyes.

"Her name was Mary Ann Nichols, Inspector," one of the constables said. "Her street name was Polly."

The fact it wasn't Abby set Conal at ease; yet he felt nearly as sorrowful as if she had been the victim. This woman had deserved to die no more than Abby had. Prostitute or not, she was a human being, an innocent woman who had loved and been loved, had meant something to someone. Now she lay here cold on the pavement, mutilated, dead.

Inspector Abberline began examining the body. Using a thin metal rod the size of a pen he pulled from his vest pocket, he gently opened Polly's mouth.

"Four or five teeth missing... a circular bruise to the face... The victim has a deep laceration from left to right, approximately eight inches in length along the throat. It appears as though her windpipe has been completely severed all the way down to her spinal cord."

"Weapon?" Conal asked for no other reason than to hear Inspector Abberline validate aloud what he already knew.

"These wounds were not made with a pocketknife; they were made with a much longer, sharper blade. No apparent injuries or blood to the chest, but deep lacerations have been made to the lower abdomen. Two or three inches from her left side is a somewhat jagged wound, it's extremely deep. The culprit stabbed the victim several times across the abdomen in an extraordinarily vicious fashion." Abberline's face was solemn. "What rage could drive a man to do such a thing?" He steadied the slight tremble in his hand, then continued his examination.

"The work of a mad man, aye, Inspector?" A man peeking out from behind a constable chimed in. The speaker was in street clothes and he walked out from behind P.C. Thain, who was standing by with his arms crossed rather smugly, a hint of a grin on his face. He pushed his glasses up the bridge of his nose to examine Conal's presence. *Where did this guy come from?*

"That'll be enough," Conal snapped, looking back at the man. "Show some respect for the dead."

"Slain," he replied. "So much worse than just dead. People die all the time of natural causes, safe in their beds. The slain have life wrenched from them, brutally, forcefully, violently."

"I'm sorry, but who are you?" Conal challenged.

Abberline's head snapped around. "James," he said tersely, "we've more important things to be concerning ourselves with." Inspector Abberline gathered bits of evidence from the scene, drawing a white handkerchief from the pocket of Polly's dress, a piece of broken mirror, and a comb.

"Do I need to ask again?" Conal stared at the man, waiting for an answer.

"Detective McWilliam, I am Dr. Ralph Rees. Detective P.C. Thain was one of the first to find the body and took it upon himself to come wake me immediately."

"And? What have you found?"

Rees peered at him through beady, narrowed eyes. The man's face was drawn and gaunt, untrustworthy. Conal disliked him immediately.

"Are all the detectives in your division so defensive, Detective Abberline?" Rhees asked.

"Indeed. I hope you can understand why?"

"This woman is—was—a prostitute, gentlemen. If I am not mistaken, prostitution is not entirely uncommon for Whitechapel. I'm sure there will be another ready to take her place on the street and in the back alleys of the city within the day. Now, as I have told Constable Thain, I can't be of any help, You'll have to discuss the cause of death with the Coroner. If that's all, I should like to return home and go back to my bed."

Inspector Abberline dismissed him with a flick of the wrist and a curt goodbye.

"Detached S.O.B., isn't he?"

"Try to focus on the task at hand, Mr. McWilliam."

Conal tried his best to keep the disdain from showing on his face. Didn't he care at all? A woman lay butchered at his feet, yet his face registered almost no emotion at all. Conal could not allow himself to forget that this woman had been alive a mere few hours before, or that she could have been Abby.

"What happens now?" Conal asked. The crowd of reporters and gawkers remained, but hung back now.

"We send the body off to the medical examiner, wait for the autopsy report. And you find a place to rest that head of yours or grab yourself a pint. Whatever you must to settle your mood. You're a detective, not a madman, at least, that's what you're supposed to be." Abberline flagged a driver and insisted Conal get into the coach.

"13 Miller's Court," Conal muttered to the driver. He wondered if Abby even knew yet about Polly.

Nineteen

"Open up! Scotland Yard!" When there was no answer, Conal pounded harder, his fists raw and red. "What? Why are you looking at me like that, Inspector?"

"Why bother knocking? You might as well break down the bloody door." Inspector Abberline darted a glance around the common area in front of the flat and shook his head. "Try to have a little self-control or you're going to look like the damn foot patrol. Are you sure this is the place? It's 13 Miller's Court?"

"Open—"

"Quit your whining, ya sod!" The door swung open to a suspicious-looking woman. "What in the hell is bloody wrong wit' ya coming around here this time o' night?"

"I'm here to see Julia," Conal demanded.

"There ain't no Julia here!" Her eyes darted to Abberline, then lit with recognition. "You! You're the one who was snooping around Crooksie's place. Where is she?"

"Madame, I cannot discuss an ongoing investigation."

"No, of course you couldn't. Useless lot."

"Are you Mary?" Conal didn't care about this showdown between the angry woman and Abberline. He was there for one reason and one reason only, Abby; he needed assurance that she was alive, that she was okay.

"What's it to you if I am?"

"Mary, Mary, let them in!" Abby rushed forward, breathless, pushing past Mary and hurtling herself into Conal's arms.

"I take it this is your long-lost brother, then."

"Mary, I'm Detective James McWilliam and this is Chief Inspector Frederick Abberline from Scotland Yard." Conal darted a quick look at Abby, then plunged ahead with the story, hoping he had read the situation correctly. "Yes, I am Julia's brother. I've been very worried about you." Abby still clung to his arms, tears in her eyes.

"You can't imagine what I've been through!" Abby's hands trembled. She had sworn to herself that she would keep her cool, but the relief of seeing Conal, the mere fact they had both survived another day, left her weak with relief.

"Yes, Mary, this is my brother, James, the one I've been telling you about."

Conal adjusted his posture with Abby to one more brotherly and reached forward to shake Mary's hand.

"You are Mary, then, I take it?"

"So I am. Well, Julia's beloved brother is a welcome guest in this house. Come in." She said nothing to Abberline, but didn't stop him as he crossed the threshold.

Abby stood nervously beside Conal. The tension hung thick between them. They needed a few moments alone, away from Abberline's watchful eyes, where they could speak freely, without this ridiculous guise of being siblings. But that was out of the question.

"So James, how did you end up in jail if you're a detective?"

"Please, James, allow me," Abberline interjected. Conal had no objections. He knew it wouldn't do any good to be tripping over his own emotions again. It would only be more puzzling to display his fondness for this sister.

"By all means, Inspector. Take it away."

Abberline frowned, turning to Mary. "You see—Miss Kelly, is it? Mr. McWilliam's arrest was an unfortunate misunderstanding. The constabularies on duty were unaware James is a Chief Detective. He's from City Police and acts as a liaison between our two departments. When I discovered what had transpired at The Ten Bells, I requested that James stay a couple of days to determine if he might gather any information from his fellow cell mates on further crimes. I'm sure we can all appreciate wanting a safer London. We both believed it could well prove profitable, and after all, it was only temporary. Of course Julia was told; James didn't want her worrying herself sick while this ruse was being carried out. But as I'm sure you understand, it was also essential that she not tell anyone, lest she compromise the operation."

"And?" Mary's skepticism of the story was evident. "Was this...operation a success?"

"Though I'm not at liberty to go into any details, we believe so," Abberline said with confidence.

Abby grabbed Mary's hand to try to reassure her. "Now do you understand why I couldn't tell you anything about myself? I just couldn't take the risk of letting anything slip."

"Of course, love. I always knew you had good intentions." For some reason, Mary had taken to Abby. Where she was suspicious and guarded toward Conal and Abberline, she was warm and reassuring toward Abby. Conal couldn't help feeling a tug of jealousy. He had known Abby for years and he still couldn't shake his feelings for her, sweaty palms and all. Mary had known her a few short days and already theirs was a more intimate relationship than Conal had ever come close to achieving with Abby.

"Julia, when we came in you said something about not knowing what you had been through...what did you mean?" Conal needed to break the uneasy silence that had fallen.

"When I left the jail last night, it was dark. I could see the sky lit up in the direction of the docks, there were several fires. I was upset and I wasn't thinking about where I was going."

"Why didn't you come back? Surely one of the constables could have helped you."

"Oh, Con—James, give me a break. I saw what the men in that place were like. I wouldn't walk through a crowded square with one of them, never mind alone in the dark. Anyway, I saw your friend from the jail, the crazy one in the cell across from you."

"Tumblety." That guy should never have been let loose on the streets. He belonged where he was, in a cage. What did you do?"

"I couldn't quite place him at first, and mistook him for a friendly face," Abby went on. "I waved to him to get his attention, then remembered where I knew him from. I tried to get away, to avoid him, but he followed me. I tried to run. I thought I had lost him by running through Jews Cemetery, but he kept coming. He just wouldn't stop. There were plenty of women about but he wanted me. Why me, James?" Abby looked at Conal with fear in her eyes.

"I don't know. Maybe he picked up some fascination with me." Conal's face reddened with anger. *Dammit, this is my fault! All of it.*

"He kept shouting something about cattle. This man is a fucking lunatic."

"Cattle? Yes, he mentioned on more than one occasion that women should be like cattle to the slaughter. Inspector, we have to find this sick son of a bitch."

"How did you escape this...lunatic?" Inspector Abberline had produced a notebook—the inner pockets of his jacket appeared to be a treasure trove of useful items—and he scrawled across it as Abby spoke.

"A constable keeping watch in the cemetery saw me running and grabbed me. But I hit the pavement and blacked out for a time. When I came to, he lectured me about being in the park after hours, but listened up close enough when I described the man who had been chasing after me. By then, this...Tumblety was gone. The constable saw to it that I was all right and walked me here. I haven't left since."

Conal took a deep breath and sighed. He grabbed Abby by the shoulders, looking her in her tear-filled eyes. "I'm sorry, It won't happen again. I promise." Conal knew there were no guarantees, but she was trembling again and he needed her to relax.

Mary reached out and grabbed Abby's hand. "Certainly, the poor thing had a horrible fright. She was shaking when she showed up at our doorstep." There was an edge to Mary's voice. If this brother of hers hadn't been speaking to her like a child, perhaps Julia wouldn't have rushed off as she did, and would never have seen this mad man in the first place.

"You're a lucky woman," Inspector Abberline said. There was no use putting it off any longer. "It's time we get to our purpose here. You ladies live at this establishment, is that correct?"

"This is my home, and Julia is my guest."

"It's my understanding that several other women live here?"

"What business is that of yours who lives under this roof?"

"No need to get defensive, Miss Kelly. It is, however, in the best interest for all of those close to you, especially any that you may be residing with you, to hear what I have to say."

"Mary, maybe you should just tell him what he wants to know."

"You come clomping in here demanding answers, but where are mine? When am I going to find out what's happened to Crooksie? The life of one woman means nothing to you but she means a great deal to me."

"I assure you, Miss Kelly, I have no information on the whereabouts of your friend, Annie Crook. Even if I had any information on her disappearance, there's no way that I could share that. As it happens, Miss. Kelly, I'm asking because I have some grave news. I believe you and your consorts may be in a good deal of danger."

Abby could see Mary was tightlipped and wasn't going to be any help, even if it was for her own good. She stepped forward, despite the risk of Mary's displeasure. "It's just Mary and I for now. Liz and Annie found lodging elsewhere. Kate is probably staying with Polly at her old place tonight."

Agitated, Mary put her hand on Abby's arm, interrupting. "What's so important that you need to speak to all of us? No authorities have ever given two shits about us. You tend to the people with the money and forget about the rest of us. Women and children constantly being pushed around. Children wander the streets, filthy and starving, and who's there to help them? Your men don't even care, and I doubt they'll care much more about Crooksie."

"Thank you for your keen observation of the otherwise obvious, Miss Kelly. I'll be happy to arrange an appointment with the Queen so you can discuss the endless shortcomings of my force. Now, as much as I would love to sit here and discuss how incredibly difficult it is to get any aid from the Queen, we came here for another reason. I bring news of another of your friends, a woman by the name of Mary Ann Nichols."

"Polly? What's happened to her? Where is she? Is she all right?" Mary's face had gone the color of ash. She clutched desperately at Abby's arm. Abby moved to her side, wrapping an arm about her waist for support. None of them was so naïve as to think this was good news.

"I'm sorry, but Miss Nichols' body was found at approximately 3:45 a.m. on Buck's Row this morning. She's been murdered."

Abby gasped and made eye contact with Conal. "What? How? Polly...I just saw her...we were just with her, just before I came to the jail to see you."

"We have no answers as yet, except that she was murdered." Inspector Abberline wouldn't have been at liberty to give out any information even if he had any.

A wail emanated from Mary as she lunged toward Inspector Abberline, her fists flying at his chest. "This is your fault. You let this happen, you bastard!"

Conal grabbed Mary as Inspector Abberline staggered backward. Mary fought against Conal's arms, sobbing.

"Miss Kelly, I am very sorry for your loss, but I can assure you, I had nothing—"

"You had nothing to do with it? People like you have everything to do with it. You sit on your arses while people starve and women are forced to walk the streets just to feed themselves. And what do you care about the likes of them? We get eaten alive out there, and you turn your blind eye while the johns do despicable things. And now Crooksie is gone and Polly is dead because of you!"

Inspector Abberline straightened his jacket. This one was going to be problematic. It wouldn't do to have her shrieking, calling attention and drawing the neighbors.

"Mary, I know you're upset about Polly, but Inspector Abberline really does want to help."

"Be that as it may," Inspector Abberline said curtly. "The fact remains that your friend is dead. A tragedy, to be sure, but you'd best listen up if you don't want another of your sisters to go missing."

Mary shook Conal off, and glared at Inspector Abberline. She stood still, but tense, as though ready to pounce again.

"I cannot go into detail as yet, but we have reason to believe that whoever killed Polly may also target the rest of you. I don't think it's a stretch to see that two women from the same line of work who occasionally bed down together and have been assaulted recently is not a matter of coincidence."

"Why would someone want to kill us?" The rage in Mary's eyes had receded to utter sorrow, tinged with terror.

"That's what James and I are trying to determine."

Abby pulled Mary closer to her, and the two embraced. The grief was plain on both their faces. "What are we supposed to do in the meantime?"

Conal shifted uncomfortably. He knew Abby had to play the part if they were going to get by without too many questions being asked about their tenuous story. But she was getting a little too familiar.

"You'll need to stay off the streets as much as possible," Inspector Abberline said matter-of-factly. "Particularly at night, though I presume that goes without saying. Right now we have to operate under the assumption that we're dealing with the same person who happens to have a special hatred for women in your line of work, given the murder, the disappearance of Miss Crook, and Julia's chase into the cemetery."

"Thank you for your advice, Inspector," Mary said with ice in her tone. The woman was a whirlwind; Conal was beginning to wonder how stable she actually was. "You can go now." Mary reached for her coat, and indicated for Julia to do the same. Her new "sister" was a step ahead of her, already reaching for her own.

"What are you doing? Did you hear what I just said?" The inspector was baffled.

"I heard you, Inspector. But if you think I'm going to stay at home while my friends continue wandering the streets, not knowing there could be a murderer after them, you're out of your head. Besides, Polly was with all of us. We at least deserve to mourn together."

"No, Julia, Mary, you can't do that. It's still a couple hours before daylight." Panic made Conal's voice shrill. "You heard what the Inspector said."

Abby fired back, "Mary's right, the other girls need to know. If there is a murderer out there, they're in danger, too."

"Putting yourselves at risk isn't going to save their lives. The Inspector is handling it."

Abby pulled Conal to the side, whispering, "Look, he's only supposed to kill once tonight, so I should be safe. At least we'll have tried. Anyway, we'll be fine. Mary and I will be together."

"You're right, so there's no reason to leave this apartment. Stay put for awhile, okay? Trust me," Conal whispered.

Inspector Abberline had had enough. These women were irrational and impossible. "I have to insist that you stay where you are. If you tell me where the other women are, I'll speak with them as soon as possible and let them know of Polly's death. But you can't go traipsing about the streets."

Mary said nothing, but removed her coat. Her eyes never left Inspector Abberline's.

Conal spoke rapidly and insistently. "Please promise me that you're not going to go out there. Abby, things are dangerous enough for us, please don't put yourself in even more danger."

"I'll be fine. It's not fair for them to be out there without any warning of what could be waiting for them."

"I know, it's horrible, but you can't risk yourself just to tell them. Go to the other girls in the morning if you have to, but not tonight. Look, I need to go with Inspector Abberline right now. I'm going to check on the time machine, see if I can't get it to work again. With any luck at all, we'll be able get ourselves the hell out of this mess and go home."

Abby nodded, looking away with tears in her eyes.

"I'll come back as soon as I see to the machine. I'm going to stay here tonight with you and Mary."

"Fine." Abby struggled to keep the tears at bay. She needed to think right now and she couldn't do that if she were in hysterics.

Conal promised again that he'd be back, and left with a warning to not answer the door for anyone except himself or the inspector.

Twenty

Hay fluttered frantically, filling the stables with a choking, earthy scent. Conal's trembling hands tore at bales of hay, at tarps, at the piles of aged dung hiding just beneath the straw. All of it flew through the air, to no avail. "Where is it? Where the hell is it?" *This can't be happening! Why isn't it here?*

Conal's heart raced as panic and nausea set in. He had been through each stall three times before Inspector Abberline could say a word. Conal's face turned white as he grabbed on to the side of a stall, trying to resist the urge to pass out. "We can't be stuck here!" Inspector Abberline stopped him.

"You've been through every inch of ground, every pile of shit in these stables. If your machine was still here, you would have found it."

"This can't be happening. That machine was our only way home, our only slim chance at making it back to normalcy. Who would take something like this? No one here could possibly even know what that machine is! I don't even fully understand it!"

"Novelty. From your description, this is a machine the likes of which has never been seen in Whitechapel before. Someone probably thought they could make a profit off it."

Conal thought he would cry. Wasn't it enough? Wasn't getting hurtled back through time to this horrific time in history with Abby enough, without losing their way home as well? Conal clenched up his hands. He glanced at them. *Red again.* He chuckled listlessly. *Why can't I just be normal?* He rubbed his hands over his face and sank to his knees. "How am I supposed to do this?" he words breathed through his gritted teeth.

Inspector Abberline sized up Conal. "All right, James, pull yourself together. If the machine is as bizarre as you say it is, no doubt we'll hear about it or it will turn up somewhere. In the meantime, we have a murder to solve. Let's go over again who your suspects are."

"Inspector, what is it that you aren't understanding? This machine is our only way home. You said yourself that I'm on borrowed time. When the real James McWilliam comes back, you'll declare me a fraud and I'll be a wanted man." Conal accepted that it was likely the Inspector didn't believe a word he was saying about the time machine, and aiding Conal in finding the time machine was most likely a charade in order to get Conal to help him find the Ripper.

"Let's get some perspective here, James. You need to get home and I understand that. But ultimately, you have options. You and that sister of yours can leave Whitechapel, you can survive. Unless this murderer keeps killing her friends. What would any of it matter if your sweet sister met her end here in Whitechapel as well? Do you think she'd care if you devoted yourself to finding your time machine then?"

Conal let the panic and exhaustion wash over him. He knew he was losing his grip but he had to be strong for Abby. Inspector Abberline was right. What would anything matter if he lost Abby?

He gazed up at Inspector Abberline. This guy wasn't exactly a beacon of stalwart courage and great intellect, but he was all Conal had. "Fine. You win. Where do we go from here?"

"Start by getting off your arse and cleaning yourself off. Let's get the names of those suspects."

As he swept hay from his tweed jacket, Conal thought hard. "Given what happened with Julia in the cemetery, I'd say Tumblety is the number one suspect. He chases one woman down, is thwarted by a patrolling constable who happens to be in the cemetery, then another woman ends up dead a few hours later? A bit too coincidental, if you ask me."

"Indeed. And then? You said there were a number of potential murderers."

They left the stable and Conal shivered. "After Tumblety, there's Sir William Gull, Gull's driver, Charles Netley, and Walter Sickert."

Inspector Abberline narrowed his eyes. "This is the conspiracy you spoke of? In which you believe they are working for the Royal Family to keep the secret?"

"Yes, exactly. Judging by what happened to Annie Crook, there's a strong possibility that I'm right about that. She's not coming back, is she?"

"James, I don't know what's happened to Annie Crook. But I admit, your conspiracy theory isn't entirely lunatic. If what you suggested about the Prince marrying Annie Crook is true, then her mistake was becoming involved with a member of the Royal Family, even a seemingly kind one.

Foolish and naïve. Why anyone would want to get mixed up with that lot is beyond me."

"You think they're behind her disappearance and Polly's murder then?"

"It's not totally out of the realm of possibility. But this news about your sister and Tumblety. It's highly suspicious. We already know the man isn't in his right mind."

"He would scream from his cell about women, terrible things. The man is a lunatic, and he has some weird vendetta against the opposite gender. Could it be that there are two separate plots at work here?"

"Difficult to say at the moment. I won't rule either of them out. But it's high time we paid Gull a visit. Whether or not he had anything to do with the whore Polly's death last night, I have a strong sense he knows what happened to Annie Crook."

"But what about Tumblety? If nothing else, we know the man is dangerous. Gull and his cronies will be easy to find. Tumblety likely knows all the dark corners where he can hide."

"Your information is useful, James, but leave the strategizing to me. Francis Tumblety has been something of a regular in Scotland Yard. I'll have my men out looking for him. It won't take long to pick him up. Now, go back to the flat and get some rest. Next I see you, we'll be paying Gull a visit."

Conal didn't have it in him to argue. "You're the boss, Inspector."

They continued back to the road. Conal felt he had aged fifty years since he and Abby had landed here.

"Is there anything else that bears discussing before we move forward?"

"There are a number of other suspects, or at least history has named them so," Conal said. He tried to focus his mind, fighting the frustration and fatigue clouding his thoughts. "Behind Tumblety and Gull, the next suspect would have to be Kosminski, the guy who was in the cell next to mine when I first arrived. He's as crazy as Tumblety is, perhaps even more unstable."

"Indeed. Anyone else?"

A burning spread behind Conal's eyes. "That's all I have for you at the moment, Inspector. I promise I'll give you whatever information I know as they come up. I'm dead on my feet. You know I want to help, but I need to sleep, even for a few hours. There are more than a hundred suspects in the Ripper case, I couldn't possibly name them all for you right now, anyway."

"Yes, of course, I'll escort you back to Miller's Court."

"What will you do after that?"

"While you rest, I'll visit the coroner, see if he has any new information that may prove useful."

They didn't speak again during the coach ride back to Miller's Court. Conal fell asleep on the ride, his head lolling against his chest. Inspector Abberline woke him with a gentle shove when they arrived.

As Conal climbed down from the carriage, they both heard a clamor from within the house.

"What in the bloody hell...?" Inspector Abberline sprang from the coach. He and Conal bolted toward the open door.

There was a man looming over Abby. "Get the bloody hell out of here! You don't belong in this place! We've got no room for the likes of you," shouted the man. He whirled on Mary. "Don't let them poison your mind, you're better than they are."

"Is there a problem here?" Conal's voice was growing shrill again. His nerves were frayed to the point of breaking. One more thing and he might well snap.

162

The man glared at Conal. "I want this whore out of here! I pay for this place for Mary. Her whore friends are no good, low-rent women. All they'll do is drag Mary into the sewers with them. I refuse to allow it. She's far too good a woman for that."

"Keep your bloody flat, then!" Mary yelled. "You don't own me. If I can't entertain who I like, then I'll be done with this place, and with you."

"Mary, how can you say such things? I work so hard to take care of you, to provide you with shelter so you don't have to sell yourself, and yet you still insist on letting the whores tramp through our home. You should remember your place as a woman, Mary."

"Remember my place as a woman? You'd best watch your tongue, Joseph. You may have paid for this place, but this is not your home. It was your choice to pay, I never asked for your help. This is my home, and you don't belong here."

Joseph tried to grab Mary's arm, only to have her quickly shrug it away. His face reddened with fury. "Women cannot survive without men, and you would do well to remember that before I turn you out with nothing but your life as a wench."

Inspector Abberline pulled his badge from his breast pocket and held it up for Joseph to see. "That's enough of this. It's time you moved along and leave these good women alone, unless you'd like to spend a night in the jails of Scotland Yard."

"This is my place!" Joseph protested. Spittle flew from his lips.

"So you say, but it was my understanding that this is the home of Miss Kelly. I'll inquire with your landlord as to who has paid the rent on this lovely home, and we'll settle the dispute then. In the meantime, I suggest you act like a gentleman and leave these women alone."

"Bollocks!"

"Now!"

The man brushed past Conal, shoving his forearm into Conal's chest, checking his body into the wall as he stormed out.

Abby looked shaken, but unsurprised.

"Are you all right?" Even in his state of exhaustion, Conal couldn't shake the overwhelming desire to protect her.

"I'm fine. But Mary, you need to stay away from him." She turned to Inspector Abberline. "Isn't there anything you can do to keep him away from here?"

"I can't lock him up if he hasn't committed a crime," Inspector Abberline said. "But your friend here is right. It's best to stay away from that one."

Conal had reached his limit. "Is anyone in this town not a psychopath?" I swear the next guy that so much as touches me, it's no more Mr. Nice Guy."

Abby's head snapped to Conal, startled.

"I'm sorry," he said quickly. "It's just there doesn't seem to be too many quality guys in this city, no offense, Inspector."

"None taken."

"Ah, Joseph's not such a bad man," Mary said, her tone softening. "His name is Joseph Barnett, might not seem like it now, but somewhere inside, he's still got a decent soul. The sour lout's just feeling sorry for himself because he's had a rough go lately. Joseph's no real threat, though," Mary professed. "He used to leave work early because he would get wind of some rumor that someone had seen me working the streets. That drove him mad, so he would leave in the middle of work to check on me and make sure I wasn't, as he liked to put it, 'whoring myself out.' His boss finally had enough and told him there were plenty other men out there that could clean a fish. I, of course, had enough of his antics long before that. I needed the place, though. I admit there was a possibility of

us being something more. There was a time he could be quite charming...
But all that is gone now, and..."

"And so now he has no place to stay so he wants to stay here with
you," Inspector Abberline finished her thought

"Precisely. So he sees my girlfriends as responsible for me doing
what I have to do, and the idea of any of them staying here angers him
even more. He wants the two of us to stay here like a happy couple.

"From the looks of it, Mary, any decency in him is buried rather
deep. He's made it pretty clear that I'm not welcome." Abby's words
carried a bite.

"No doubt the decency's been gone from that one a long while,"
Inspector Abberline said brusquely. "Don't be forgetting this is the East
End of Whitechapel. You won't find many unsullied souls here."

"He just doesn't take kindly to rejection," Mary muttered, more for
her own benefit than anyone else's. "He only wants to be loved."

"Well, James is here now, so he can ward off any other intruders, if
you're able to rouse him from his sleep. It's time for me to be off."
Inspector Abberline made for the door, eager to be out of this cathouse.
"James, I'll be back for you. Get your rest. I'm going to need you with a
clear head straight away."

Twenty-One

The corpse of Polly Nichols was lying on the ground, vacant eyes staring into the sky. Conal could see a man kneeling over her. He was wearing a cape; and a top hat with the brim shadowing his face.

There was an open surgical bag resting next to him. The man withdrew a clean white cloth, then dragged it along the length of a bloodied blade. Slowly and methodically, he wiped the red stains from the dagger. The metal shined clean, he discarded the bloody rag on the street.

The man pulled a pocket watch from inside his vest, opened it, checked the time, then snapped it shut. The watch dangled on its chain over the dead woman's body before the man replaced it in his vest pocket.

"I'll take the next soon after this one's gone cold," he said. "I can't delay my pleasure too long." He gathered his bag and began walking down the street. "Julia," he sang lightly. "Julia..." The man disappeared into the fog.

Conal tried to run after him but something was holding him back. He looked down at his legs, they were mired in cold, dead fish, and in his hand he carried the bloodied blade. He struggled against the dead animals, but began to sink.

✱✱✱

Dripping with sweat, Conal woke to his reddened hands and arms. He lay there for a moment, fascinated. Seeing them glow like this in the dark brought him back to a childhood memory. It was like when he used to play with flashlights in the dark, holding them to his hands so he could see what was inside of him like an x-ray. It wasn't the skin that was turning red, it was something inside him that was giving him some kind of translucent effect. He vigorously shook them and wiped the sweat from his brow. "This is all I need, some messed up birth defect to get worse while I'm more than a hundred years from home."

Abby woke in a panic. She clutched at her blanket as she sat up in the darkness. Taking short shallow breaths, she wiped her eyes, forcing herself to focus.

"Conal?" Barely a whisper.

"I'm sorry," he murmured hoarsely. "Bad dream, I guess." Conal stretched his hands in the darkness, grateful Abby didn't see. They ached, as though they had been cut raw. Beads of sweat ran in rivulets down the back of his neck.

"Must have been. You all right?"

"Yeah, sometimes they're just so real, it's hard to shake myself free of them." He stared into the darkness.

"Sometimes talking helps."

"That's all right. I don't want to keep you up."

Abby sighed. "Conal, we don't know each other very well, and we're not exactly getting acquainted under the best circumstances. But we're all we have right now. And I can't have you breaking down on me."

Conal bristled. "Don't worry, Abby, I'm not breaking down on you anytime soon."

"When this is all over, maybe we'll go our separate ways and never speak to each other again. But we need each other right now, and I'm worried about you. The exhaustion, the bad dreams. Everyone has their breaking point."

A weight settled across Conal's chest. How the idea of Abby disappearing from his life again felt like a worse fate than spending the rest of his life in Whitechapel mystified him. *I'm pathetic.*

"I'm not helpless, you know," Abby said suddenly. "You don't need to treat me like some fragile doll who's going to shatter if you give her some bad news."

"Yeah, I...I'm sorry. I don't mean to treat you that way. That's probably the guilt talking."

"The guilt?"

"I don't exactly relish the fact that I got you transported back through time to the seediest part of London during one of the most dangerous periods in the city's history. Or that, thanks to me, you ended up falling in with a crowd of prostitutes who are being targeted by the world's first serial killer."

"Conal, stop. If you want to tell me about your dream, fine. But I'm not interested in hearing you wallow in self-pity about the terrible situation we're in. I was there that day, too. I was angry at Tristan, and glad you showed him up. I didn't have to get on that machine. This is just as much my responsibility as it is yours. And I want you to talk to me about what's going on. Like it or not, we're in this together."

A beat passed before Conal spoke. "I keep having these dreams about him."

"The Ripper?"

"It's as if he can see me, and he knows we're here. He's mocking me. I hear him, I see him. He's inside my mind, taunting me."

Abby moved closer to where Conal lay. "When I was a little girl, probably six or seven, I used to have this recurring dream that I was being chased by my parents. They were furious about something and they would chase me down this block. I remember I would get so scared that I couldn't even scream for help. Anyway, I would always reach this tall gate blocking me, and I could never get it open. It was locked every time. Finally right before they got to me, I would belt out a scream. I'd wake up in tears every time. I couldn't even run and jump in my parents' bed after to feel safe."

"My God, that's horrible, Abby. Didn't they come in and check out what was wrong?"

"No, I had to cover my cries with the pillow. If they had to get up for me, that would have been bad news.

Conal's heart sunk, thinking of what Abby must've felt.

"Okay, let me finish." Abby smiled moving on. "I knew I had to get through this, so one night, I had the same dream again, but while I was in the dream being chased, I told myself over and over, the gate is unlocked, the gate is unlocked. When I got to the gate, it swung open and my parents disappeared. I never had the dream again." I think they call it lucid dreaming. It's worth a try."

It wasn't lost on Conal that this was the first night he and Abby had ever spent together. When he had imagined it before, somehow he hadn't expected talking about childhood nightmares to be their primary activity.

"So you're saying that one night I'll dream that I catch the Ripper and the nightmares will end?"

"All I'm saying is don't let it overpower you. Remind yourself that you're in control of your dream. You're stronger than he is. He uses fear to control people. Don't let him do that to you."

"Easier said than done."

Abby laughed. "That's probably the first honest thing you've said."

"How's that?"

"This is the first time you haven't tried to put on your brave face and be Conal the Hero."

"What are you talking about? I've got it under control. There's no brave face."

Abby groaned, shifting back to her sleeping position. "Goodnight, Conal."

The rest of his sleep was without nightmares, but restless nonetheless. It was as though his subconscious was trying to tell him something, and refused to let his guard down.

✳✳✳

Conal woke to the sounds of Inspector Abberline's carriage outside. He peered through the dirty window panes to see him lumbering up the walk.

Conal shoved open the filthy window.

"Just give me a sec! I need to wash up and throw on my shirt."

"Good to see you're up and about. Hurry along, there's much work to be done."

Before Conal headed out, he pulled out his tablet and pencil, updating his list of suspects.

Suspects:

Kosminski – lunatic, thinks all women are whores and must be dealt with.

Tumblety – fixates on uteruses and thinks women should be dealt with like cattle.

A Royal Conspiracy (Sir William Gull, Walter Sickert, Charles Netley) want to keep Prince Eddy's secret from getting out. Gull, Sickert, and Gull's driver, Netley were all together at The Ten Bells.

Joseph Barnett – jealous boyfriend, resentful toward the girls, has access to Mary's flat.

Conal tucked the tablet and pencil in his pocket and glanced at the women. Mary was in a surprisingly deep sleep, given Polly's death and Joseph's intrusion the night before. *I hope she's getting better sleep than I did.* Abby turned restlessly, but didn't wake.

Gathering his coat, Conal paused, contemplating waking Abby. *I think I did enough of that last night.* He took one last glance at Abby and closed the door behind him. "So what's the plan today, Inspector?"

"Today is a very important briefing for the investigation. I'll need you to pay attention to everything I tell the men on hand, and step in if you see I'm leaving anything out or you remember anything that may be useful for them to know. And try to keep your emotions in check. It's enough that I have to worry about a murderer running about town. I don't need to worry about an unstable partner as well."

"Switch places with me for a day and we'll see how stable you are, old man."

Inspector Abberline rolled his eyes. Another gulp of the whiskey seemed to sustain him. The carriage bumped along the cobblestone streets.

171

"Inspector, any chance we could pop off for a bite to eat before this pow wow?"

"Perhaps I'll answer you when you begin speaking like an intelligent life form."

Conal shook his head. "You Brits, always thinking you're superior." Conal's stomach churned, making a loud grumbling noise. "How's that for a life form? Did you catch that?"

"Are you telling me you're hungry?"

"Bingo!"

"There's no time before the briefing. Your appetite will have to wait a little longer."

Conal shrugged. "You're the boss. Besides, you're buying."

When they arrived at the station. Inspector Abberline and Conal stepped out of the carriage and walked up the steps to Scotland Yard. He noticed the place on the ground that had been stained by his own blood the night he was booked. This made Conal cringe and his nerves tighten. This place was a sight he would never welcome.

Inspector Abberline led him to a small room packed with other officers. A hum of chatter rose when Conal and Inspector Abberline entered.

"These are London's finest, huh?" he muttered.

Inspector Abberline ignored him.

"All right, quiet down, men. We have much to discuss and time is of the essence. You all know why we're here. Now, let's review the suspects.

"First, some of you may remember Michael Ostrog. We've had some complaints about him in the past. Ostrog is five feet eleven inches, has dark brown hair, and gray eyes. Being of Russian and Polish decent, he has an accent, along with a peculiar past associated with doctoring, and is usually seen cavorting around with surgical knives. As he is reported as being seen commonly here in the East End, I daresay he shan't be difficult to find.

Inspector Abberline's voice droned as he reviewed the profiles. Conal struggled to stay alert. He made no mention of the royal conspiracy theory, but that was just as well. You didn't go messing with the British monarchy without hard evidence, and even then, you were probably better off keeping your mouth shut.

"I want these men found yesterday," Inspector Abberline went on. "If there are any holes in their alibis as to their whereabouts at the time of last night's murder, they are to be brought back to headquarters immediately. Furthermore, I expect everyone to keep their eyes and ears open. Use the citizenry as lookouts for these men to keep informed of our suspects' comings and goings. Any questions?"

"Sir, there have been rumors and whispers concerning a man named John Pizer, known as 'leather apron,'" one of the officers piped up.

"Fair point, same goes for Pizer. If he has a weak alibi, I want him brought in as well."

"We need to keep our names clean, and the people happy. There's nothing worse than a shoddy public uproar. I want foot patrols doubled along Bucks Row, Brady Street, Commercial Road, Cannon Street, Leman, and all the way down to Wentworth. I also want us working all the way up to our Middlesex jurisdiction lines. Keep your wits about, gentlemen, because there's no telling if he's only after prostitutes. It may be any woman; your sister, your mother, or even your own wife. Let's see if we can't keep another murder from happening on our watch, shall we?"

The other officer raised his voice again.

"Sir, are we not over-extending ourselves for this murder? We've had murders before, what's so special about this one? After all, Mary Ann Nichols... I mean, she was only—"

"Yes, Charles, she was only what?"

"Forgive me for saying, but she was only a prostitute, sir. We're treating this as if the bloody Queen herself was the victim."

"Only a prostitute. We have thousands of prostitutes in Whitechapel, most of these women aren't doing this because they enjoy it. These are mothers, sisters, and daughters selling themselves just to have some money for food and shelter. Most of them do it to survive. Now if we let this murderer go, we might as well let them all die."

No one spoke.

"Right. Before we adjourn, there's one other matter that bears discussing. Chief Detective James McWilliam of City Police has had an item stolen from him, a scientific instrument being used in the service of the Royal Family. Here is a sketch of the missing item."

Inspector Abberline made up a fictitious purpose of the machine in order to protect the legitimacy of its importance and handed out copies of a sketch drawn up by the Scotland Yard sketch artist based off of Conal's description. "This chair is in development for sale to the Colonies as a means of execution in a more dignified, albeit untraditional, manner. As this project is of international importance and scientific discovery, any facts or information will be treated with the highest importance. It was last seen by the stables on Commercial and Church Street."

"This instrument is truly of the utmost importance. Your discretion in this instance is vital to national security." It was the first time Conal had spoken. "The Queen herself will be most grateful for your assistance."

Inspector Abberline stiffened beside him, but Conal didn't miss a beat. A little incentive was good for morale.

Twenty-Two

Winds whipped around the Colony Hatch Lunatic Asylum. Dry dying bushes wrapped around the ominous structure that looked more like a castle. It was three stories high, the rust covered walls decorated in old ivy. The courtyard was like a small deserted park. The lawn had all but completely dried up and had already sprouted weeds.

Pigeons flew away as Conal stepped out of the carriage behind Inspector Abberline. His boots crushed the brittle grass as he pushed his wavy brown hair from his eyes to get a better look of the structure. *I already hate this place.* Conal put on his hat and readied himself for what lay ahead.

"James, I'll go on inside and pay our friend, Sir William Gull, a surprise visit as we planned. I suspect if they have anything to hide, they'll be preoccupied plenty with me and they won't suspect you on the premises. Why don't you have a look around the property, see if you can find something, or someone, out of place."

"Right! Huh! That's the first time I can remember us actually agreeing on something." Conal made his way to the back of the building, where he found windows casting light into rooms below. He tapped at them using his foot, but none shook loose. Patients occupied some; most stood empty. He moved toward a six foot high wall nearly entirely concealed by bushes and ivy. Within the yard, an orderly herded patients back inside. *Only one orderly.* Conal pulled himself over the wall and shimmied along the outskirts of the yard, attempting to stay inconspicuous among the patients. When the last of them had entered, he grabbed the doorknob and slipped in.

As Conal made his way down a short hallway, he peeked around a corner, where he could see an orderly speaking to someone through a small barred window of a steel door As others were being placed in rooms. Some of the resident patients spoke gibberish but the haunting cries and moans of one of the poor souls locked up really haunted Conal..

Stay focused, Conal, you came here for a reason. Just see if you can find anything and get out. Conal stayed hidden near the door until the orderly had finished his business. The moans of the insane echoed off the cold walls of the sanatorium. *A little more detail to Inspector Abberline on where I came from and I could have been right here with these people.*

As Conal worked his way through the halls, he approached a small cluster of doctors and orderlies turning a corner. One of the orderlies with the group banged at the doors to quiet the screaming patients. Conal backtracked, running his hand along the wall, heart now hammering against his chest. His hand found the cold handle of a door, he shoved it open and disappeared. He could smell the strong odor of bleach and other cleaning supplies. He felt around until his hand closed around something wet. Lifting it, he could sense it was a mop. It was a maintenance room. He felt around in the room until he felt a pull chain light switch dangling just overhead. He pulled it, turning on the dim light. It was on no more than three seconds before the bulb became unbearably bright and burst over Conal's head, sending shards of glass and porcelain flying through the room. *Great!* A small trickle of blood marked the place where a shard of glass nicked his hand.

Conal cracked the door slightly, allowing a sliver of light to filter in. There was a long white janitor's coat hanging on the door that was a dead ringer for a medical coat. He took off his hat to shake off some glass and set it on the shelf. He brushed off more glass from his lapel and shrugged on the white coat. *Not bad, not bad at all, it just might buy some time.*

He watched the group of men, about ten or twelve of them, walking rapidly down the hall. Sir William Gull, the older, well-to-do man from The Ten Bells led the group. "What the hell are you up to, Gull?" Conal whispered to himself.

A man heading toward the group from the opposite direction paused at a room and let himself in. Two orderlies followed. Conal heard someone else approach, but couldn't make out what he said.

Conal slipped out of the room, keeping his head down. He walked down the hall, trying to keep his pace even but slow enough to catch the conversation. Someone mentioned Inspector Abberline's name; this was a much-needed distraction.

As he reached the door, the orderlies burst from the room, dragging a woman with them. She appeared exhausted, though not deranged. Her hair was matted and deep circles made rings around her eyes. "Where's my daughter? Let me go! I want to go home to my daughter!" The commotion provoked a fresh chorus of wails from the other cells. "Where is Alice? Please let me go home to my baby!"

Crooksie! It had to be.

The man who interrupted Gull continued whispering to him fervently, something about an inspector. Gull nodded and said something to the orderly. Then he turned to the group.

"Gentlemen, it seems a rather important matter has come up that I must attend to," he said in a bored voice. "Please do forgive me, we will have to continue this tomorrow evening." *Nicely done, Inspector.*

Gull looked at the orderlies and nodded. They dragged the woman back to her room, shoving her inside. She fought, her legs thrashing around, screams echoing down the hallway. "Let's quiet it down, sweetheart. You wouldn't want to bring any unwanted attention to yourself now, would ya?" One of the orderlies tried to cover her mouth with his hands and was met with a full, firm bite.

"Bloody hell! Let go! Let go!" He threw her to the ground.

"Bugger! You bloody whore!" He clasped his bleeding hand and scrambled out of the room as the second orderly slammed the door to her room. It was labeled 101 on the front. The orderly looked at Gull for permission to leave. "Excuse me, sir."

"Of course, go on, get that taken care of."

When the woman who must have been Crooksie had been locked away, the orderlies and the rest of the group casually strolled toward the double doors as if nothing was wrong. Conal joined in on their subtle small talk conversations, blindly agreeing with whatever the hell they were droning on about. *The bastards.*

When they reached the end of the hall, Conal doubled back to her room. He opened a small five by five steel framed window to her cell and looked in. She wasn't curled up in some fetal position in the corner of the room like he expected. Instead she was pacing angrily. "Annie Crook?"

The second Annie made eye contact with Conal, she went at the window as if she was going to reach through and pull Conal in with her. "Where's my daughter? Let me out of here!" Annie screamed when Conal looked through the window.

"Ma'am, you don't understand. That's what I am trying to do. I'm here to help."

Crooksie's voice was tired and weak. " What do you want from me? Please, just let me go." She fought back angry tears.

"Ma'am, please, I'm not going to hurt you. I'm a friend of Mary's."

She raised her head. "A friend of Mary's? The hell you are. No doubt you've got her locked in here as well, and this is just another one of your tricks, one of your God-forsaken games to convince me I'm insane."

"No, Annie, I swear to you. You are Annie Crook, aren't you? Your friends call you Crooksie, right?"

"Who are you?"

"My name is James, and today, I'm your new best friend, okay, Crooksie?" Conal smiled. "I'm a friend of Julia's, her brother, actually. You remember Julia, right? Mary introduced you two, you and Mary helped her with a couple of dresses just before you—"

"Before I was kidnapped," Crooksie finished for him. "Where's my daughter?"

"I'm not entirely sure, but I have a pretty good idea. I need to focus on getting you out right now, okay? I'm working with Scotland Yard. We're trying to figure out who did this to you."

"You're working with Scotland Yard? What interest would Scotland Yard have with helping the likes of me? Every one of you is in the pocket of the Crown."

Can't blame her for being suspicious, Conal thought. *But why does everything have to be so damn difficult?*

"Crooksie, I know you have no reason to believe me and I can't guarantee everything will go back to the way things were before all of this happened, but I can promise you this. I can stand here explaining everything to you until those guys come back, and you can stay here with them, or you can come with me and I can get you the hell out of here."

Crooksie was silent for a moment.

"Crooksie, this may be your one chance to find your daughter."

Crooksie's eyes filled with tears. She pressed her lips together, nodding. "Get me the hell out of here," she whispered.

"Good choice." Conal quickly scanned the frame work of the door. Wood! "A steel door with a wood frame!" One of the good things about this era was the engineering and the security wasn't very good, so it was easy see these doors weren't going to be all that difficult to get open.

"Hang on, Crooksie, I need to find something to pry the door with. I'll be right back, don't worry."

Conal ran back to the closet. "There has to be something here I can use." As soon as Conal opened the closet door, the ward doors opened. "Dammit! He's back." Conal slipped inside to stay out of sight of the returning orderly. The orderly methodically jingled a large ring of keys and his footsteps moved at a speedy pace, pausing and speeding up again — going door to door looking for something or someone in particular.

"Hold tight, Crooksie," Conal whispered.

As they drew nearer to the closet door, Conal held his breath and grabbed hold of the handle tightly with both hands. He could feel the orderly grab the handle, trying to twist it back and forth. "The bloody key's not working!" The orderly paused for a moment. Conal pressed his ear to the door, waiting for what felt like an eternity. Whatever this orderly was contemplating, Conal considered knocking him out and pulling him into the closet if he took any longer.

Finally he could hear the orderly's footsteps walk briskly away.

As Conal opened the door, his eyes immediately focused on a flat piece of metal, examining it briefly. It resembled some kind of a tile scraper or crowbar with a smooth flat end. It was perfect. Conal clenched it and ran back to the locked cell. Conal motioned for Crooksie to not make any noise as he worked the flat end in between the door and the frame. He worked at prying and tearing away at the wood frame. "Come on, you damn door, open up!" The halls filled with screams and howls from the surrounding patients. Conal struggled "Have to... get it... open!" He worked a gap between the wooden frame and the door. He leveraged all his body weight on the tool, finally popping the door open. Conal quickly threw the bar onto Crooksie's bed.

Tears rolled down Crooksie's bruised and sunken in cheeks. Her lips were dry and cracked and she had dried blood smudged on her face from the orderly's hand. Her hair was ratty and knotted.

"Let's get the hell out of here, shall we?"

"Why are you doing this?"

"I'll catch you up on that later. Come on, we've got to move right now. That orderly will be back any second."

She limped slightly and her frail body shivered as she walked.

Conal reached for her elbow. "See, no need to worry, I look more like a doctor helping a patient. Just forget I'm a fraudulent detective smuggling a captive out of the insane asylum." Conal led her out the back door. Crooksie turned to him when they reached the wall.

"I can't make it over this."

"Think of your daughter— you can do this, okay? Now hold on."

A vague fierceness returned to her eyes.

"I'm going to lift you up. You pull yourself over. It's not a far drop if you can't hang on, there should be some bushes on the other side, they'll break your fall if you slip."

He cradled her like a child, then pushed as high as his arms allowed. Crooksie was naturally a light woman; and no doubt she had lost weight

181

during her stay in the asylum. But she was stronger than she looked and grabbed on to some of the ivy, pulling herself over.

Crooksie held on to the wall covered in dying ivy, scraping a gash in the side of her upper right arm as she lowered herself. She felt the sting, but she was okay. " I made it, I'm all right."

As soon as Conal heard her land with a soft thud on the other side, he quickly followed.

Crooksie's arm stung. He wrapped the jacket he found in the closet around her shoulders, a poor attempt at concealing the white standard-issue asylum gown, but perhaps it would buy them a few seconds.

Conal wrapped his arm around Crooksie and walked her straight to the carriage, then helped her in.

"We have to wait for Inspector Abberline. He'll be along soon, just keep your head down and we'll be all right."

Crooksie slunk lower in her seat.

"I'd just as soon let the Inspector find his own way home."

"Crooksie, can you tell me what happened when you were abducted?"

Crooksie looked away. She knotted her hands together to stay the trembling. "It was horrible. They burst in on us, without any warning at all. We weren't hurting anyone, just having a night together at home. It was a happy night, too, one of those that feels special in no extraordinary way. I was washing the dishes when they came. Eddy and I had just had the loveliest supper, venison with stewed potatoes." Crooksie brushed a tear from her cheek, sniffing back another. "Alice was off at the park, thank God above. They didn't even knock. They went for Eddy first." Her voice broke off.

"We didn't even get to say goodbye. Once they had him, they went for me. Those bastards dragged us off, no word about where we were going...Alice must have been so scared when she got home. I don't even know what's happened to her." Annie's shoulders shook with silent sobs. She looked past Conal and suddenly shot straight up.

"Eddy!" She leaned across Conal to peer through the carriage window; her overwhelming fear from a second ago forgotten.

"Oh, thank God he's all right. I knew he'd come for me once he was free. He is royalty after all, they couldn't keep him from me forever."

Conal watched the hope brighten Crooksie's eyes, then fade just as quickly. "What the hell's he doing with him? They're the ones that took him, too."

Eddy stood at the front of the building, laughing and clapping Gull on the back as though they were old friends. As though the man had nothing to do with Eddy's own abduction or his wife's imprisonment in an insane asylum, or his helpless daughter being abandoned. Conal knew the theory and it included Eddy.

Inspector Abberline and Sickert stood with them as well; the only one that seemed to be getting any attention was Inspector Abberline.

"Eddy, no, it can't be. What's going on?" A wild look of panic had come into her eyes, and Conal worried she was about to blow their cover.

"Crooksie, stop. I don't know what's happening, but you can't go out there."

"I have to go to him. He doesn't know I'm here, I have to tell him. We have to find Alice together. How can he believe these are good men after everything they've done to me? You don't know what they've done, James. I won't let them have Eddy."

Conal grabbed Crooksie's shoulders, forcing her to hear his words. "Crooksie, look, I'm not going to sugarcoat this for you. You've been through hell and back, and if anyone deserves the right to confront their spouse, it's you, but now is not the time to go picking a fight with your Prince. Do you trust Eddy?"

"I...I don't know what I believe now. I want to."

"Then trust that he knows what he's doing. If you go out there right now, you'll be locked up again and you'll be in for a hell of a welcome back party. I don't know what they did to you last time, but you can bet that whatever treatment they have for escapees is worse."

Crooksie eyed him warily. "But what if they hurt him?"

"Focus, Crooksie. Your daughter, remember? Eddy looks fine. In the meantime, you need to find your daughter and disappear."

If the records were accurate, the Ripper's final victim was never conclusively identified. She was murdered in the dark, in her sleep, and though people speculated, no one ever knew who it truly was.

That had given rise to the theory it was Julia who was the last woman to be murdered by Jack. But if Annie Crook actually escaped from the asylum, it would be her and not Mary Kelly who took Alice into hiding, a lifesaving reprieve for Abby and Crooksie, but an unfortunate turn for Mary. If she hadn't been the one in hiding, she was most likely to be the final victim.

Conal felt embattled inside. Abby would be safe now and history would likely play out as it's supposed to. *So why the hell do I feel like I'm writing Mary's death sentence, like I'm the one responsible for her death?*

Crooksie stared hard at Conal. She sat across from him nervously, her hospital gown filthy beneath his tweed jacket. "I need to be with my daughter."

"It's too risky for you to wait here any longer. Can you ride a horse?"

Confused, Crooksie nodded.

"Good. Wait for me to get inside, so I can distract Gull and the rest of them. Once we're gone, unhitch the horse and ride for the convent. When you reach the convent, ask for the Mother Superior. Everything you will need is there. And wear this."

He handed her the Inspector's coat. She quickly shrugged out of Conal's tweed jacket and pulled on the inspector's coat. It looked less foolish than Conal's, the inspector's smaller frame was a far better fit.

"It'll have to do." Conal righted his own coat on his body and reached for the door.

"Remember, not until we're all inside and none of us are watching."

"James...thank you." She gave Conal a hug.

Even in this moment of urgency, her hug made Conal blush. He awkwardly hugged her in return. "You're a strong woman, good luck, and don't stop for anyone." He gave her a friendly squeeze, jumped down from the carriage and headed toward the entrance of the asylum.

Constable Charles Richins, who had driven the carriage, stood at the entrance. He was about six foot six, skinny with a bit of a belly, tobacco stains on his teeth, and in need of a shave. He wasn't what Conal pictured as the image of protection, but despite his appearance, he took his job as serious as anyone on the force and he was looking bored.

"Richins, come with me. Let's see if we can't hurry Inspector Abberline along."

Twenty-Three

It didn't take long for Conal and P.C. Richins to figure out they weren't welcome at Colony Hatch Asylum.

"Don't look now, Richins, but here comes the welcoming committee."

Two orderlies approached as soon as they walked through the door. Though Conal could no longer hear the screaming patients, the smell of the hospital was sickening. How many families had been duped into believing this would be a safe place for their troubled loved ones, only to find them more insane than they'd been the day they arrived?

"Is there something we can help you with, officers? We're past visiting hours tonight." *Wouldn't want to frighten away potential customers*, Conal thought.

"Thank you, but we won't be needing your help. We're here with Inspector Abberline, and I see he's right over there." Conal flashed his badge at the guard and headed in Inspector Abberline's direction. He motioned for Richins to follow.

"All right, gentlemen, I suggest you get back to whatever it was you were doing. Go on now, you heard the detective," Richins said, pushing them back with a firm nudge of his billy club. "You wouldn't want to give me a reason to bring the both of you in for obstruction."

"It's all right, gentlemen. Let them through," Sir William Gull sounded off. He motioned to let Conal and P.C. Richins through.

The two approached Inspector Abberline, where he was accompanied by Gull, Sickert, and Eddy, fully decked out in his red and gold royal uniform.

"James, I believe you've already met Sir William Gull and Mr. Sickert." Inspector Abberline raised his eyebrows at Conal from behind the small group.

"Long time no see." Conal gritted his teeth. It would do him no good to knock these two out right here and now, but that didn't quell the urge.

Gull spoke up. "Yes, Inspector, we've met. But let's put our unfortunate first meeting behind us, shall we? Tell me, how is that fiancée of yours?" Gull smirked as he recognized the subtle strange look Inspector Abberline had let slip.

Conal was certain he'd have to explain to Inspector Abberline why Gull referred to Abby as his fiancée and not his sister. He ignored Gull and turned to Sickert. "How's that eye of yours, Walter?"

"It's fine, thank you." Sickert smiled smugly.

"If I'm ever in need a sparring partner, I'll give you a call." He winked and gave Sickert a pat on the shoulder.

Sickert yanked his shoulder and slightly raised his hand in a defensive manner, giving Conal a very sour smile.

"James, please meet His Highness Prince Albert."

Conal beamed an overly friendly smile at the Prince. He extended a hand.

"Pleasure to meet you. It's Eddy, right? You weren't at The Ten Bells like your two constituents here." That comment aroused an uncomfortable silence and a wave of panic washed over Eddy's face. Only Crooksie called him by his nickname. Conal continued. "No, of course not. I wouldn't think it would be normal for someone of your standing to be in a place like that."

Eddy stammered a hello with his brief handshake, then let Conal's hand drop.

Inspector Abberline interjected. "Yes, well, James, I'm quite through here, so we can be on our way."

Conal semi-circled Gull and Sickert, drawing their attention away from the window, where they would have easily seen Crooksie struggling with the horse. "Inspector, have you asked His Highness about his relationship with Annie Crook?"

Inspector Abberline gave Conal a curt nod. "Yes, I think we covered just about all we needed for the time being. Was there something in particular you wanted to ask?"

"Indeed. I do have a few pressing questions for you gentlemen. Specifically for you, Your Highness. Have you any information on the current whereabouts of your wife, Annie Crook?"

"His wife? That's mad! I think you've been greatly misinformed, sir. To even suggest such a thing is absurd and an outrage. If the Prince was married, I assure you the entire nation would know about it. And it would certainly not be to an insane, low-born, Catholic woman." Gull appeared to think he was the ringleader in this operation.

"Oh! Please forgive me, Your Highness," Conal said facetiously. "I thought you went by Eddy? Do accept my apologies if I have overstepped myself, Your Highness. Apparently I'm mistaken. Annie Crook is not your wife? I guess our work here is done." Conal was reluctant to interact with Gull and Sickert if he could help it. "I'm glad that has been cleared up...I'm also glad to hear Annie Crook is considered to be an insane, low-born, Catholic woman. Thank you for that insight, Sir William. I wasn't aware of that. Were you, Inspector?"

"Watch your mouth, sir. This is the Prince to whom you speak." A sheen of sweat had broken out across Eddy's face. Gull frowned, but wouldn't let Eddy respond to the question.

"Inspector Abberline, who is this impudent officer? Has he forgotten he is in the Queen's service, and is addressing a member of the Royal Family as though the Prince was some common man on the streets?"

Silence wouldn't work with this one, after all. "Perhaps I shall address you, then," Conal said to Gull. "If you don't want me speaking with the Prince, I have a few questions you might answer yourself. For one, what were three men of the Palace doing in a seedy bar in Whitechapel? Doesn't exactly seem like your kind of establishment, carousing with the commoners. But then, maybe it's exactly your kind of crowd. If memory serves, and I believe it does, you were soliciting the services of a woman you believed to be a prostitute the night I was beaten and dragged off to jail." He grabbed Sickert's arm, squeezing tightly, and leaned into his ear. It was at that moment he could see Crooksie escaping, riding off on the horse from the carriage.

"And let's not forget, assaulting an officer is an offense against the Crown," he whispered against Sickert's ear.

Sickert threw him off. "Let go of me, you oaf, before I have you imprisoned again. Do you really think the Queen cares about the affairs of peons like you?" Inspector Abberline moved to step between them. "Always something with this kid."

An orderly approached them timidly, a look of terror on his face. "Forgive me, Doctor, but one of the patients has gone missing." The boy looked as though he expected to be slapped.

To his credit, Gull maintained his composure. "Which one?"

"The patient in 101."

Conal prayed recognition did not show on his face.

"That was Mr. Andrews' room," Gull said evenly. A cool customer, this one. He knew perfectly well Eddy's face betrayed nothing. What was his game?

The orderly's eyes widened when he saw Conal. "You! You were in the hallway lingering about the room. You let her out!"

"Her? I thought you said it was a Mr. Andrews who had escaped." Conal gave Gull a curious look.

"Now, orderly, calm down," Gull said, ignoring Conal's probing stare. "The detective is a member of Scotland Yard. We can't go around accusing esteemed officers of freeing dangerous patients."

"What do you mean by her?" Conal insisted. "Was it a woman in room 101? After all, that's an important detail when searching for this poor soul."

Sickert and Eddy were both sweating now. They knew it was no Mr. Andrews who had gone missing from his cell. "101 contained Mr. Andrews; he was released earlier this morning. You must pay closer attention to who is admitted and released to and from the hospital, boy."

The orderly's eyes had widened and he lowered his head in obedience. "Yes, Dr. Gull. Right, my mistake, Doctor." It was obvious Gull was covering. It was obviously a lie. Even the orderly couldn't help but look puzzled.

"You will now have to excuse me, Inspector, if you're finished? I'm sure you understand."

"Yes, of course."

"One last thing, Your Royal Highness, sir," Conal began. Inspector Abberline stiffened.

"James, you just can't seem to leave well enough alone," Inspector Abberline grumbled.

"I'm sure that if you did have a daughter named Alice and a wife named Annie, who loved and trusted you to protect them above all else, you would stop at nothing to keep them safe. Surely, they would come first, even before your loyalty to the throne? After all, a man's first loyalty is to his family, right?"

The Prince walked over and gripped Conal by the elbow, dragging him away from the others. "You do overstep your bounds now. Do not presume to speak to me about my love for my wife and child."

"My humblest apologies, Your Royal Highness, the idea of letting your wife be locked in a cell and your daughter raised by strangers to avoid political suicide is, of course, preposterous. I'm afraid Yanks like myself lack patience for such actions. Please excuse my lack of manners." Conal hated showing any kind of humility to these men, however, he also wanted to keep his own head.

Conal wrenched out of the prince's grip, not waiting to hear his answer. "Inspector, Richins. Shall we leave these men to their business?" They swept out of the building and down the front steps toward the now horseless carriage.

For all his swagger as a Scotland Yard Inspector, Abberline made his apologies on Conal's behalf as well, then ushered Richins out the door.

"What were you trying to do back there, James? Are you insane? You must be more careful. I hope you understand the magnitude of what you just did." The inspector sighed.

Abberline had plenty to talk about and could have kept going on about Conal's reckless behavior until his thought process was halted. "What in the bloody hell happened to our carriage? Where is our horse?"

He looked all around and then eyed Conal suspiciously. Richins began to whistle, a signal for constables nearby to come to their assistance.

"Richins, Richins! That won't be necessary." Conal waved him off. "Inspector Abberline and I will be walking from this point."

"What do you mean we will be walking?" Conal walked ahead and buttoned his tweed jacket against the breeze.

Abberline had popped his head into the carriage and came out just as quickly. "And my bloody jacket, too?" Abberline stared hard at James as he walked down the drive. "James, are you familiar with the word inconsiderate? It means without using any thought!" To his further ire, Conal laughed.

"What's the matter, Inspector? Been awhile since you were on foot patrol? Come on, it'll be good for you. Besides, I'm pretty sure someone needed that horse and your jacket more than you or I."

"Considering that we have enough on our plate already, I'm going to turn a blind eye to this, James. However, I'm going to assume if there were a Miss Annie Crook committed to Colony Hatch, that she quite possibly has indeed escaped from room 101?"

"I would say that would be a safe assumption, Inspector, if there were a Miss Crook, of course. Yep! She would be long gone, and with any luck, she might just find her daughter as well. So, what about you, Inspector? What exactly did you find out?"

Neither spoke for several moments.

"Something's amiss with Gull and Sickert, that's for certain. But I'm inclined to disagree with the notion of their guilt as far as the murder of Polly Nichols is concerned. Gull was helpful, almost too helpful, when I asked for the records on Miss Crook. No doubt they're up to no good where that one is concerned, and I still haven't sorted out her husband's involvement in the whole thing. But that doesn't give them motive for slaughtering her prostitute friends."

Conal nodded thoughtfully. "I'm thinking along the same lines. Gull and Sickert are palace men and will do anything to keep the reputation of the monarchs untarnished. They have every motive for abducting Annie and keeping her and Eddy apart. But that doesn't explain why they'd murder the other women."

"Well, if they thought Annie had shared that information with her friends—"

"Fair enough, But they have solid alibis." Abberline reached for his flask of whiskey, but found himself patting at thin air. "Where is—" He threw his hands up. James wasn't like to answer even if he knew.

"Gull and Sickert were at Buckingham Palace attending a ball for the Queen the evening Polly Nichols died," he went on. "Sickert and Prince Albert retired to their separate quarters at the Palace at the end of the night. Gull had taken ill and was seen by a colleague several times throughout the evening. Gull is not a very threatening man to begin with, let alone when he's bed-ridden. You saw him today; the man is but a slip of a thing and not like to get his hands dirty with the business of killing."

"I have to agree with you, Inspector," Conal said. "I don't think he would be able to stomach murdering anyone. If I were to give my best guess, they abducted Annie and interrogated her, just as we suspected. Then, when they were confident there was no one else who knew about her marriage; they were going to use her as a test subject for their brain experimentation. Maybe they'd let her go once they had addled her mind beyond the point of coherent speech or memory."

"Poor lass," Abberline murmured. It was a rare moment of empathy for another soul. "Weak in body though Gull might be, he is a clever and manipulative man, and without much feeling for the troubled patients."

193

"You agree, then, that she's better off being out of that institution and away from them?"

Abberline shrugged. "Perhaps. She'll have to live her life looking over her shoulder, always watching for what's coming up behind. But if she can make it and find a bit of happiness along the way, Godspeed to her."

Somehow Eddy's involvement created more discomfort for Conal than anyone else. Gull and Sickert were twisted, for sure, but Eddy was her husband. He had risked everything to be with her, had shared her home and her bed. They had a child together. Conal wanted to believe that Eddy's camaraderie with Gull and Sickert was all part of a master plan to free his wife and find their daughter. If it wasn't, it could be that Eddy was the most evil of them all.

"You did good work today," Abberline said grudgingly. "But you've got to keep that temper in check. I don't know what things are like where you're from, but you put all three of us at risk today."

Conal turned his face into the wind. "That might not be so bad," he said. "I'm beginning to realize there are some fates worse than death."

Conal turned his face into the wind, pulled out his tablet and erased the Royal Conspiracy as a suspect.

Suspects:

Kosminski - lunatic, thinks all women are whores and must be dealt with.

Tumblety - fixates on uteruses and thinks women should be dealt with like cattle.

Joseph Barnett - Jealous boyfriend, resentful towards the girls, has access to Mary's flat.

194

"Conal, you look like you have seen a ghost. Your hands are freezing."

"Until now, I've only relived this in my mind. So many times, so many moments, so many regrets.

"That chill that was in the air. That was in the air, Conal, you mustn't let your despair ice over your heart."

"That was the first day when I had thought death might not be a worse fate than going in that horrible place. Had it not been for my guilt over Abby, I might have given in. After all, I was no hero. Those women would have meant nothing to me if Abby hadn't been among them.

Twenty-Four

"You sure you don't want me to wait with you, Julia?" Abby turned toward Dark Annie, who seemed to Abby to deserve her nickname less and less. The air had turned cold but Abby didn't mind. She had been gazing out at the Thames river, taking a rare moment to drink in her surroundings for no other reason than the sheer pleasure of it.

My first time in London and all I've done is hide out from a madman who might murder me if he mistakes me for a prostitute. "No Annie, I'll be fine. I'll wait for James at the first tower. There'll be plenty of people around if someone gives me trouble."

Annie looked unconvinced. No one would accuse Annie of wearing her heart on her sleeve, but she had taken Polly's death quite hard. Julia might be a new recruit, or whatever it was Mary claimed her to be—a new pet project perhaps—but Annie didn't want to see another woman dead. And this one was scared as a kitten, refusing to leave the flat without escort. Well, who could blame her? Whitechapel wasn't a kind place for newcomers.

"If you're sure, then. I suppose I'll see you at Mary's this evening, or perhaps tomorrow."

Abby smiled. "Goodbye, Annie, and thank you for a lovely day. It was a treat to get out of the house."

Annie waved and hurried off into the darkness.

Abby's smile fell as she walked toward the first tower. Playing the part of the sheltered innocent was exhausting. *I should be used to this by now. I've been playing it my entire life.*

The secrets were necessary, of course, but acting like a simpleton was getting old, fast. "If I manage to make it home or escape the jaws of death by the Ripper, I swear I'm starting over," Abby vowed, not for the first time since she had arrived in Whitechapel.

Abby hadn't known Conal well in high school, but had been right to assume he was a nice guy. Perhaps a little too nice.

She thought back as she looked out across the river. He had been a bit of a loner, if memory served. Shy, kept to himself, never went to dances or football games, never dated anyone, at least as far as Abby could remember. She frowned. But she had tried to talk to him, hadn't she? Yes, that one time at the locker. Conal had been the only person who had even been mildly supportive on her first day as the new girl in their class. She had hoped that they'd become friends but when she tried to talk to him, he had mumbled something she couldn't make out and walked away. The next time they had seen each other, he had caught her crying in the parking lot. It almost looked like he wanted to say something but Tristan pulled up.

Abby blushed at the memory. *I should be ashamed of myself.* She wanted to question why she had ever dated Tristan, but wondered if the better question wasn't why did she still even have contact with him?

No. *I'm not going down that road.* Abby could hear the first thrums of self-pity beginning and the new her, the one who would materialize when one or the other of the nightmares she was currently living ended, didn't go in for that. Nevermind that her parents had never encouraged her, had called her a nuisance, ugly, and incompetent, had refused to nurture any dreams other than taking over the store when her father retired. Amazing how long they had kept that one going. Their stubbornness was surpassed only by hers. She was amazed she had held out this long, persisting even when they ignored her declaration that she wouldn't be taking over the business and that if her father was planning an imminent retirement, he'd better start looking for more help.

Abby had always wanted to be a scientist, but that dream had been dashed with her first failing grade in freshman biology. Despite vows to get a tutor, study harder, beg her teacher to let her take the exam again, her parents wouldn't hear of it. "We always told you that you weren't cut out for science. Stick to the business courses. Those will serve you once you're done with school."

What would Conal think of that? Somehow Abby suspected that even if he didn't believe she had what it takes, he might not tell her that to her face. She felt a little guilty for being so harsh with him sometimes. Why should he give me credit? I don't give myself any, and I act like a brat whenever he comes home after spending the day searching for a man who might try to kill me.

Abby straightened her shoulders. She would make it up to him tonight. Perhaps they could go to dinner, walk around the city, spend some time outside the grottiness of Whitechapel. She looked about her, realizing suddenly that she had been waiting for a long time. Quarter past seven. Not so bad. Maybe he just got caught up with Inspector Abberline, or got lost.

Thirty minutes later, Abby wrangled with alternating bouts of fear and anger. Conal wouldn't just leave me hanging. He's supposed to be with the inspector, so I'm sure nothing bad has happened to him, and if something did, then I'm sure the inspector would've let me know. No, we made plans, and if he's not here, I'm sure he has a very good reason.

A breeze picked up, whipping her hair about her face as she tried and failed to still her temper. An internal battle began within her between reason and her own insecurities, which threatened to overwhelm her. Wow, I think I'm being stood up. It's okay, it's not like this was a date. Damn right it's not a date. If it was, it would most certainly be our last.

The crowd on the bridge was thinning. Abby angrily swiped at a tear on her cheek. I'm not going to cry over this.

It was somewhere around eight-thirty and she was going it alone. She had no choice but to walk now before it became any later and riskier than it already was.

Unlike any other night in this foul city, it was as if she didn't exist. The town paid so little attention to her, she was bumped into without notice, no apologies, no angry people calling her a whore, and no dirty looks. She felt incredibly unimportant and homesick. She might as well have been a ghost. Even Tristan would have paid her more attention. Her heart was full of disappointment and fear as the rain came down and she headed back alone.

✳✳✳

The clock boomed. Conal shook himself awake. Stay alert, man. This is no time for sleeping. He slumped in a chair in Abberline's office. How are we still here?

This shouldn't have taken more than a few hours. When the breathless officer had run up to him and Abberline, shouting for their attention, Conal had thought for a moment they might actually have a break in the case.

"Inspector!" the man had screamed. "We've found something!"

"Something or someone? You were supposed to be sniffing out that dog Tumblety."

"We haven't found him yet, sir, but I have news on the...well, the Queen's special project."

Conal instantly stood from his chair. Could it be that they had found his and Abby's way home? Being hopeful was my first mistake. I should have known it was too good to be true.

"Did you find it?" he gasped, over eager. Most likely he was giving himself away, but if it was true they had found the machine and it worked, it didn't matter who knew, or who thought he was a lunatic.

"Yes, sir, we found it. Sullivan was over by Britannia and overheard a couple of men talking about some kind of odd machine, said it looked like some kind of throne or one of those electrocution chairs you hear about being built in America. They found it lying in some stables. So Sully figured that had to be it."

"Where is it now?" What do I care about what some losers in Brittania think of the chair? So long as I'm able to get home, I'll send the damned thing back to them once I'm there.

"I questioned the men, but all they could tell me was that they sold it to some fellow on the street from Middlesex for four pence. The bloke bought it to sell for parts."

"I thought you said you found the chair."

Abberline laid a hand on Conal's arm to stay his rage.

"Forgive Detective McWilliam. He's so eager to please the Queen, you see." Abberline's grip tightened as he continued. "This man thought to sell it for parts, is that right? I suspected as much might happen. Did the man you spoke to have a name?"

"No, sir, no name. If he had given his name, it would still be difficult to find him, what with him being out of our jurisdiction. Less, of course, if Chief Detective McWilliam could help us out."

"Help? You mean do your job for you." Conal yanked his arm out of Abberline's grip. "Did they at least say if it's still in one piece, or if it's been butchered to cheap parts yet?"

"I don't know, Detective McWilliam." The officer was beginning to cower. "We're lucky we got this much information. They weren't too helpful in the first place, what with not being partial to the uniform."

"Keep looking."

The officer nodded and hurried back into the night.

"You didn't have to be so harsh with the lad. I thought you'd be thrilled by his news."

"The machine is still somewhere in London. There's no time for celebration yet. We don't know where exactly it is and some genius who wants to make a quick buck is trying to bust it up and sell it for parts. Seems to me we're not much further than when we started."

Conal pulled up a chair as his thoughts tugged at him. Faint glimmers of optimism were tamped down by his anger and frustration. Still, perhaps it was worth mentioning to Abby. A bit of good news would be a nice change for once. Abby! "Shit!" He bolted to his feet. "Abberline, I've got to go. I was supposed to meet Julia hours ago."

"Your sister? She knows you're working on this case. I'm sure she understands."

How could I have been so goddamn stupid? "No, this is different. I have to go."

"James, we still have leads to discuss. We could find this machine of yours. Any moment, we could get the man's name who has it and have it in your hands by tomorrow morning."

"Then I'll be back in the morning. Julia doesn't know the city well yet, she could be lost or hurt. I'll see ya, Inspector."

"Wait, have you lost your mind? It's my carriage you're using."

Conal grabbed his tweed jacket and sprinted out of the building. Abberline struggled to keep pace.

What he hadn't mentioned to Abberline, of course, was that he had just passed up his chance at wooing the girl of his dreams, the one who got away. Finally he had a chance to spend time with Abby, reintroduce himself to her as something other than the shy awkward loner he had been in high school. Now she probably hated him or worse.

He ordered the driver, an officer named Longley who was taking Richins' post for the evening, to drive to Miller's Court as quickly as possible. Mary was about to enter the flat when Conal arrived.

"Mary, is Julia home?" he demanded.

She looked taken aback.

"No, James, she's not. She said she wanted to see if any stands were still up at Spitalfields. Truth be told, she seemed upset and I think she wanted to be alone but was too polite to say so. But a hankering for fruit as an excuse for needing a good cry will not get by Mary Kelly."

Panic seared through Conal.

"So you let her go out alone?"

"I had some business to take care of at the convent and asked her to stay until I got back, but she still left. I've never seen that sweet thing in such a mood."

"What's the date today?"

"I don't know, why?" Mary looked puzzled.

"WHAT'S THE DAMN DATE?" He closed his eyes, as if that would help him remember.

"It's the eighth, Mr. McWilliam," Abberline shouted from the carriage. "Is the date of particular relevance?"

"Hold on! I have to think." Conal clutched at fistfuls of his own hair, pacing in front of the building.

Mary rolled her eyes.

"The eighteenth or the eighth, the eighteenth or the eighth?" he muttered over and over. He struggled to recall an article he had read years earlier. Suddenly he began to feel the tingling, the heat, and menacing laugh boomed somewhere in his brain.

"Oh shit! Inspector, I think I'm wrong. It doesn't happen on the eighteenth! It was the eighth! My God man, it's tonight! We have to go now!" He dashed frantically back into the carriage and screamed at Longley to move. The horse startled at the sound of his shouts.

Mary would likely put him out tonight, but he couldn't be concerned with that now.

"Are you certain, James? Are you sure you're not just..."

"Inspector, we need to move fast." Conal's look of desperation was all the convincing the inspector needed.

"I'll take the carriage and go after Miss Chapman. You take P.C. Longley and go after Julia on foot. Now calm yourself and tell me, is there anything else you remember? What time, where? Some detail that might save Miss Chapman's life?"

"No, that's all. I just know that it's tonight and it's supposed to be Annie Chapman. But if you run into Kate or Liz, get someone to escort them home immediately. Longley and I will try the Ten Bells. You start at the Alma Pub. Inspector, we have to find her."

Conal's hands shook violently. Abberline was right. He needed to calm himself.

The Alma pub was very popular among the prostitutes because of its central locale and plenty of back alleys nearby. Abberline rode off in a hurry.

The fog had rolled in heavily, making the foot search for Julia all the more difficult.

Conal ran down alleys and streets with Longley on his heels. Their footsteps fell heavy and panicked on the damp roadways.

"Longley, we need to split up. You take Dorset Street and go around the back way. I'll head up Commercial. Alert any constables you come across."

Longley looked uncertain but was given no time to protest. Conal sprinted down a block, running until a shrill whistle nearby stopped him in his tracks.

Conal followed the sound, which was being made by a constable attempting to control a growing crowd. Heart banging against the walls of his chest, Conal shoved through the gathering, elbowing people aside and declaring himself a detective, more than grateful that at least to these people, his title placed him above reproach.

He knew even before he reached the front that the spectators were ogling a body. Though it was not an uncommon sight in Whitechapel, it still piqued the citizenry's morbid interest.

The body was not the one he'd both feared and expected to see.

It was that of a man who had hung himself, and had been decomposing for a week before anyone found him. The discovery had been made by the landlord when he made his rounds handing out eviction notices.

Conal swallowed the bile rising in his throat.

Whitechapel wasn't a place people came to live. This was where people came to die.

"Constable, maintain this crowd until back-up arrives. And see that no one desecrates the body."

Again without waiting for response, Conal whirled on his heel and sprinted back the way he'd come.

A bright half moon glowed down on the city, but struggled to cut through the fog. The eerie effect and the scent of death had turned Conal's stomach to jelly but he dared not think of that now. Every second could be Julia's last.

A familiar woman was standing on a corner, her cinched up dress and make-up marking her as a sister of the night. A drunk lurched toward her, and as her position required, she urged him on, stink and all.

"Liz!"

"Sod off, you bugger! I saw her first." The drunk made to strike Conal but stumbled and came up short.

Conal ignored him.

"Liz, get off the street and go home immediately."

"James, have you lost your mind? I'm working tonight and you're interrupting. I thought you were a friend to the working girl."

"Liz, please, what you do most nights is your business and I wouldn't interfere, but I swear to you, tonight you need to go home. Don't ask questions, just get off the street and don't come out again until morning."

"You want to give her a go yourself, don't you?" The drunk made for Conal again.

Conal shoved him, hard, and the man sprawled across the street.

"Liz, have you seen Julia or Annie? I have to find them right away."

She raised a brow. Conal noticed she swayed a little herself.

"Oh yeah!" She giggled, burped, then giggled again. "Julia was heading home when I saw her last, should be up that way now. Haven't seen Annie much today, perhaps the darkness is on her again. Ain't been

205

the same since Polly was done for, you know." Liz grew misty-eyed. "Annie was looking for somewhere to sleep tonight, as I recall. Check her usual places. She'll pop up somewhere."

"Thanks, Liz. Now get off the streets, and if you see Kate, take her with you. It's not safe tonight. You know what I am talking about." Conal knew his warning fell on deaf ears, but he had to try.

He spotted Abby when he reached the next corner. She walked in his direction, rubbing her shoulders against the chill.

"Abby! Thank God you're okay. Where have you been? Mary said you went alone, upset, and that you wanted to get some fruit from the market. The market closed hours ago."

"What are you doing here, Conal?"

"Looking for you. Abby, something's wrong."

"Where were you tonight?" Abby looked him square in the eyes.

"We got a lead on the time machine. Abby, listen, I'm really sorry for leaving you hanging and I know you're probably angry, but we have a more immediate problem. The Ripper is supposed to murder another woman tonight."

The defiance drained from Abby's face.

"What? I thought you said he wouldn't kill again until the eighteenth."

Conal ran his hand ran across his forehead and down the side of his cheek "I was wrong. He's going to strike tonight, or at least try to. I spoke to Mary and Liz. Abberline is out looking for Annie right now. But you need to get home."

A set of footsteps rang behind them. Longley.

"Sir, you found her." Longley was panting when he reached them.

"Yes, I did. I will escort my sister home. You go back and check the Ten Bells for Annie Chapman, or if you see Kate Eddowes, see to it she has an escort home."

"They're not there, James. We were earlier, but Kate turned in early and Annie left with someone. I tried to convince her to just come home with me, but you know how she gets. She's had a bad day, things didn't go well with her husband's estate, and she started drinking heavily as soon as we got to The Ten Bells. She said the other girls were taking all of her business and she didn't how was she going to survive, and then when she marked a potential john in the bar, she went after him. I begged her not to, but she refused to listen to me."

"Longley, I need you to find Inspector Abberline and check every other pub and lodging house you can find. Annie Chapman must be found tonight."

Twenty-Five

Abby walked close to Conal, the warmth from his body reassuring her that she was not alone. She never wanted to be alone again in this damned city.

It had been bad enough when Conal had warned her about the reign of terror into which they had been dropped. It had been worse when poor Polly had been savaged by this madman. Now she was racing against time to save her new friend from the same cruel fate.

Abby wanted to prove her fearlessness, but she had always found something reassuring in the idea that bravery means admitting you're scared and facing your fears anyway. She would not be a coward, that much she could promise herself. But she also did not want to do this alone.

They still hadn't spoken about what had happened earlier in the night. Somehow being stood up for a walk along London Bridge seemed less important now, less of a slight. Abby reddened, recalling her anger. I should be ashamed of myself, projecting all of my romantic problems on to Conal.

It was true that aside from Tristan, Abby hadn't had much of a love life in the past few years. Even after she had ended things with him, he would still call her, beg her for another chance, take her to a romantic dinner, and then the cycle would start all over again. Often as not, Abby would end up sleeping with him, just for the sake of having a warm body next to her. Sometimes in the mornings, before Tristan woke to start pawing her again, before the self-loathing set in, Abby would pretend the arms around her belonged to someone else. Someone who actually gave a shit about her.

Conal might be that, she had told herself. He was a handsome guy, and seemed to listen when she spoke, at least to some extent. He had a lot to learn about her, but he seemed to have at least a passing interest in her as more than arm candy and getting laid.

She was bitter. She knew that. She didn't like it, but she accepted it. Shame on me for being so desperate that I would look to Conal to get me out of a bad situation, just like I always do.

If Abby was honest with herself, she had seen the way Conal looked at her sometimes. The panic in his eyes when she became upset, the admiration when they were getting along. Even his protective nature towards her like on their first night in London, at The Ten Bells, when the nightmare really began.

Oh well. No harm done. She hadn't taken advantage of Conal yet. And she wouldn't, either.

"Abby, I'm sorry for not meeting you on the bridge earlier tonight."

Her gaze snapped to him. Had she spoken her thoughts aloud?

"One of the constables came in just as I was getting ready to head out earlier and said they had a lead on the time machine. Someone found it and was bragging to his friends that he was going to break it up and sell it for parts."

209

"You're an asshole!"

Conal stopped abruptly. Then he burst out laughing.

"Is something funny?"

"I'm sorry, I just...I didn't take you for a swearing kind of girl."

Abby rolled her eyes, but allowed herself a laugh as well.

"You probably don't take me for a lot of things. Most people don't."

The tension broke between them.

"So what does this mean, we're stuck with Jack and company for the rest of our lives, however long those might last?"

They resumed walking. The fog was thicker now and a light rain began to drizzle down. They kept even closer to one another now.

"I don't know what it means. I was at the station with Abberline, waiting for the constable to return with more information. He was out searching for the man who has it, to bring him in." He glanced at Abby with a sly grin. "We've told them the machine is part of a special project commissioned by the Queen, to give them some incentive."

Abby's eyes widened in amusement.

"If only they knew the truth."

They fell into silence then, a surprisingly companionable one.

Hours passed and still there was no sign of Annie. A drunk here and there, an anxious citizen rushing home for shelter from the mean streets of Whitechapel, but no Annie Chapman.

A bell tolled. Abby was first to respond.

"It's past four in the morning. Should we have found her by now? We've had no news from Abberline, no word from the police at all... Could you have made a mistake?"

"At this point I don't know what to think. At first I was pretty sure it was the eighteenth, but then everything was taking shape. Then something just wasn't right. It dawned on me that I was distracted, you were alone, and the girls were all out. It was as if fate was setting the scene for something bad to happen. Maybe I'm wrong, but I don't think I am, and it wasn't a risk worth taking. I'm just surprised we haven't heard anything yet."

"Do you think we should go home?"

Silence.

"I don't know that there's anything more we can do. Maybe we should head home." Conal was reluctant but couldn't help but consider there was nothing they could do.

Abby scanned their surroundings nervously.

"I would feel horrible if something happened to Annie and we could have stopped it. But it's been hours and I'm dead on my feet. Looks like you are, too."

"Abby, I don't know that there is anything else we can do. We don't even know if we're going to be able to prevent these murders and we're not exactly doing much good wandering around Whitechapel in the rain.
"

They crept into the flat, taking pains to avoid waking Mary up. Conal took off his soaked shirt and jacket and hung it over the fireplace. He threw some wood on the fire and looked towards Abby to invite her to come get warm but could see she was soaked. He nervously jumbled his next words. "Uh, yeah. Why don't you, uh... I'll just turn around so you can...um..." He moved his fingers in a confused motion so she could get out of her wet clothes.

Abby couldn't wait to be warm again. "Oh, that would be great." She smiled.

"Sure, no problem. My mother would say you're gonna catch pneumonia." Conal laughed.

Abby politely laughed in return, waiting patiently for Conal to recognize the growing awkwardness.

Conal paused a moment, a little flustered before he realized he hadn't turned around yet and Abby was waiting.

"Right! Of course." Conal smiled. "I'll turn around now so you can do your thing. Don't worry, I won't look." Conal turned and shielded his eyes, more in embarrassment of his behavior than to prevent a peek. Do your thing? I won't look? For crying out loud, shut up man!

Abby undressed and covered herself with a blanket. Her trembling hands shook less and less as she absorbed the heat from the fire. They retreated to their separate sleep spaces on the floor, offering each other equally troubled smiles, then each turned to their own disquieting thoughts.

Abby fell asleep, replaying the day she had spent with Annie as the sad woman desperately sought the money her husband had left behind. But prostitutes don't hold much sway in society and her failure had served to further her ongoing depression.

Despair entered Conal's chest with a whoosh, the way it did every night lately. Annie's murder seemed all but guaranteed. Like so many in her trade, her lack of consistent accommodations made her vulnerable and made the option of going home with a man all the more appealing.

A loud banging thudded in Conal's unconscious until it woke him with a throbbing head. "You've got to be shitting me!"

A panicked voice boomed through the wooden door.

"Detective!" The wooden door shook with the impatient banging. "Detective McWilliam!"

He rushed to the door and opened it a crack, signaling for the rookie constable to quiet down.

"I apologize for the disturbance, Chief Detective McWilliam. Inspector Abberline needs you immediately."

"No doubt he has abysmal news for me. Wait here."

Conal crept back into the apartment and slipped into his shirt and jacket.

He leaned over Abby and shook her gently.

He didn't wait for her to be coherent. Open eyes were enough. He had no time to waste.

"Did you have another nightmare?"

"What? No, no. Abberline needs me. I have to go. Stay here and sleep. I'll be back as soon as I can."

"Is it Annie?"

"I don't know. I hope not."

✷✷✷

Annie Chapman's body was found nearby, only three short blocks away from where Abby and Mary were sleeping.

The young constable had led Conal to Hanbury Street, not far from where he and Abby had landed and abandoned the time machine.

Conal repeatedly scanned the surrounding alleys. A man sick enough to murder a helpless woman in such a brutal way was likely sick enough to stick around and admire his work. Perhaps that wouldn't have been a terrible thing. Conal wasn't one for murder, but this was one life he wouldn't mind ending. At least it would mean Abby lived.

The street in front of 29 Hanbury Street was already crowded with gawkers. Some struggled toward the staircase, strangely eager for a glimpse of the dead body.

One particularly twisted individual barred off the staircase and charged a penny for a look.

"Come see for yourself! One penny be all it takes! One penny and you gets a look at the worst murder in London's East End."

"What the hell is wrong with you, man?" Conal dragged the shameless merchant away from the staircase, frightening the others at least a few inches into the street. "A woman has died here and you're selling tickets for a sight of her corpse?"

The man showed no remorse at all, though he didn't protest. He spit at Conal's feet as he walked away. How much had he made off his morbid venture? Conal wondered.

The crowd began to protest.

"It'll be the Tower for all of you if you don't remove yourselves this moment," Conal bellowed.

The young constable led Conal toward the backyard. Inside, they walked down a hall, where a white towel lay bunched on the floor.

A man stood over it, staring down. As Conal approached, he turned to Conal with a solemn gaze. The towel, it turned out, was actually a sheet and it covered the body of the woman who had been Annie Chapman.

Abberline emerged from a back room.

"Right again, James. This time it was worse." The inspector knelt beside the body and drew back the sheet. Conal immediately gagged.

Annie's throat had been cut from left to right. Her head was turned toward the door with her hands flung over her head, as though she had died fighting. She had been torn open from breastbone to vagina and had been thoroughly disemboweled. Her uterus and most of her bladder had been slashed and removed from her body. Her throat was cut so deeply that other than some loose skin, her head was severed from her body.

No amount of reading or studying the Ripper's heinous acts could have prepared Conal for this.

"The Doctor here thinks this is the work of a professional or at the least someone trained in the arts of dissection." Abberline pointed to the man standing over the body.

"Indeed. Whoever did this must have had certain tools to make cuts so precise. And to extract...well, her internal organs. I'm Dr. Baxter Phillips. You must be Chief Detective McWilliam."

Conal shook the man's outstretched hand.

"You seem certain that this was someone with a medical background."

"I have no doubt."

"Forgive me, Doctor, but it seems unwise to presume anything. I could remove organs from a woman's body if I had a mind to. Anyone can. It doesn't take a special kind of butcher to gut another human being, at least not in physical aptitude."

"The kind of cuts this particular butcher made were extremely precise. The man had at least some knowledge of the human body."

Conal looked back at Annie's destroyed body and shuddered.

"In addition to the tools and the know-how, the murderer was likely desensitized toward the body, hardened to blood and death. This also points toward someone in the medical field. Even if it is just a macabre fascination with the human body, he most likely developed his ability through experience. His cuts look like that of a professional; single cuts with methodically straight and steady precision. Not to forget, this was done at night in the dark with limited light to see."

"The body is mutilated. What kind of professional would do such a thing?"

"A deeply deranged one."

"Inspector Abberline, are you finished with the doctor?"

215

Abberline raised his eyebrows at Conal. "Yes, I believe so, unless you have something further?"

"No. I think we're done here. Thank you for your time."

Abberline waited until the doctor was gone to address Conal again.

"Are you all right, James?"

His red-rimmed eyes were answer enough.

"I'm sorry, James. I know your sister was fond of the woman. But we need to move quickly."

"What do you know?"

"We found a piece of crumbled paper with two pills wrapped in it. A piece of torn envelope with the letter 'M' inscribed on it. In the victim's pockets we found two farthings, two brass rings removed from her fingers, two combs, and off to the side was this leather apron." The inspector gave Conal a hard look. And you, James? What insight might you have on this...tragedy?"

Before Conal could respond, another constable entered the dwelling accompanied by another unfamiliar man.

"Inspector Abberline, sir."

"Yes, Laurel? Who's this?"

"Albert Kodosh." He nudged the man forward. "He's a neighbor, lives just nearby."

"What can you tell us, Mr. Kodosh?"

"Well, sir, I do a bit of drinking from time to time, same as anybody else, and well, you get to be my age and you have to get up every now then to go tend to your needs."

"What kind of needs?"

"Toss a piss, excuse me, sir. I was outside earlier tonight tending to my business and I heard a voice from the other side of the fence. I was still half-asleep, but it sounded like someone screaming the word 'no.' I didn't make much of it at the time. Truth is, sir, and I'm ashamed to say it, I was still a bit in me cups and might have imagined it after all. Then there was a thud against the fence, as though something had been thrown against it."

"And you didn't think to investigate?"

"I thought perhaps whoever it was might want their privacy, without me being about relieving myself. What others do is no business of mine. I didn't know it was a body what was falling against the fence."

Abberline had the grace not to criticize the man openly for his vices. His guilt and shame showed plainly on his face.

"Is that all you remember, Mr. Kodosh?"

"That's all, sir."

Abberline waved him off with a brief thanks.

He exploded after Kodosh had left.

"Of all the neighbors, all these sadists and gawkers straining themselves to catch a glimpse of the poor woman, the only one who sees anything is the one who wants to respect the privacy of a murderer."

Conal rubbed his eyes and didn't respond. What was there to say?

He addressed Conal and the constables as he walked toward his carriage. "The coroner will deal with Miss Chapman's body. Detective McWilliam and I will go back to headquarters. The rest of you, find this man they call Leather Apron and bring him in. Check the suspect list. Anyone whose name starts with the letter M, anyone in the medical field, bring them in. Someone find out what these damn pills are. And bring in Francis Tumblety! We need twice as many men on this. Any more witnesses, bring them in, too. Move your arses, we need this bastard found."

Twenty-Six

The day was the most perfect one could hope for in a London autumn.

Despite the living hell each day brought, Conal was determined to make amends with Abby after standing her up.

A breeze drifted off the Thames, lifting Abby's hair from her neck. She closed her eyes, drinking in the warmth of the sunshine and fresh air on her face.

"Why didn't you talk to me in high school?"

"Excuse me?"

"You were the only person who made me feel like I wasn't an alien when I transferred to school. That meant more to me than you could possibly know. But when I tried to talk to you, you blew me off."

"I wouldn't say I blew you off, exactly..."

"I said hello to you and you pretty much turned and ran the other way."

Conal smiled nervously. Damned if he wasn't feeling like that teenage boy again.

"You weren't exactly easy to talk to in high school, Abby. Loners like me didn't exactly mix with social butterflies like you."

She turned to him, propping herself on one arm against the bridge.

"I was the new girl. Being a social butterfly was the only way to avoid being labeled as the weird girl for the rest of high school."

"You seemed to enjoy it."

"I did, actually. I had always been shy growing up, so pushing myself to be assertive and friendly, that was huge for me. That was the first time I had a lot of friends. But that still doesn't explain why you never talked to me. I really wanted to get to know you."

Her words were like a dagger in Conal's heart, forcing him into the land of what if, thinking of all the opportunities he had missed. The pain might have been unbearable if she had told him everything she had been thinking.

The clock tower began to chime.

"That's Big Ben," he told Abby.

She looked at him expectantly.

A tingling sensation burned through Conal's fingers, making it difficult to move his right hand. He attempted to clench them shut and the effort felt superhuman. He cradled the right in the left, rubbing the skin to restore circulation. He shook it out. "Sorry, hand's fallen asleep."

Conal looked out across the river to the House of Parliament, standing golden in the sunset. He breathed deeply. I'm not a kid anymore. Time to do what needs to be done.

"The truth is, Abby, I didn't really like you much in high school. From the day you arrived, I pegged you for a yuppie kid who thought she was better than everyone else." This was the furthest thing from the truth. Whether it was the need to protect Abby or maybe the need to protect himself, Conal was pushing Abby away.

"Oh really? Then why did you help me the first day of school?"

"I hadn't had a chance to observe you yet. Everyone deserves a chance."

Abby's eyes narrowed. "Go on. Tell me what changed your mind." Her mood darkened against the backdrop of a brilliant sky.

"Well, the company you kept didn't do you any favors. Jocks, cheerleaders, prom queens. Not exactly the intellectual cream of the crop. And not exactly the friendliest bunch to people like me, who lived on the fringes of the social order. Look, I was all right. I knew where I stood. But as far as I could see, anyone who would hang out with those people was probably also a spoiled brat. How could they have stood it otherwise?"

"So you thought I was a spoiled brat?"

Conal shrugged his agreement. "If I'm being polite, snob comes to mind." Inside, his heart was breaking. The last thing he wanted was to hurt Abby, but he knew he had to do it.

"Wow. Well, that certainly clears things up for me. And now? Do you still think that way of me now?"

Conal swallowed hard. "For the most part, but I still don't know you very well. You have your moments, though."

Abby's eyes widened in surprise. "Why are you doing this? Are you trying to hurt me? Has my past desire to have friends and be accepted cut you so much that you're trying to punish me now, even if it means being small and petty?"

"I'm just being honest. Anyway, what does it matter? Hopefully we'll soon find the time machine and we can both get back to our lives, where we never even have to speak to each other again."

"Is that what you want?"

"I think it would be best."

220

Abby said nothing more but the hurt that registered on her face was almost too much for Conal to bear. Conal steeled himself against the desperate urge to apologize, to take it all back, to tell her how much he had admired her in high school, how many of his thoughts had been occupied by his longing for her. But he couldn't, not now. Allowing himself to be entangled romantically with Abby would cloud his focus and judgment. If he really cared about her, he'd get her home and give her back all she had lost when she got into that time machine.

Twenty-Seven

The tobacco shop owner looked nervous to see them, but also a little relieved. He wasn't looking for any trouble, and it might be slower to come his way if the detectives were hanging about.

"How can I be of service, gentlemen?"

The man reminded Conal of his grandfather the way he waddled about.

"How is the investigation going, Inspector? Any leads on what happened to poor Polly? I couldn't help but notice the press gave you a good going over regarding your lack of progress."

"Mr. McWilliam and I are trying to locate your friend Pizer. We need to ask him a few questions."

"Seems the whole city is looking for him these days. Mr. Lusk was here earlier asking of Pizer's whereabouts. His band of tag-alongs looked to have grown considerably. They were quite insistent at first that I was keeping my tongue silent regarding Mr. Pizer. They seem to think he's the one responsible for old Polly and Annie Chapman's death. John Pizer's never done anything wrong to me, but I have no reason to protect the man, and I certainly wouldn't keep quiet for no murderer. I'm an honorable man."

"Did Mr. Lusk say anything else about Mr. Pizer?" Abberline had insisted Conal remain quiet during this interrogation, unless his partner was missing something crucial. His behavior around witnesses had proven less than impressive of late.

"He did, Inspector. Said he had fifty whores who could attest to Leather Apron's crazy ways. Kept insisting that I knew where old Leather Apron was."

"And did you tell him anything?"

The merchant shifted his weight and frowned. "I told him where John's brother lives, as I suspect he might have holed up there if he knows a mob's after him. I fear Mr. Lusk might hang him on the spot if he finds him."

The rest of the interview passed quickly enough.

Lusk had made good use of the tobacco merchant's information. He was already at the other Pizer's home when Conal and Abberline arrived, and indeed had a growing band of cohorts with him. They might as well have been standing outside with pitchforks and torches demanding the blood of Frankenstein's monster. A few of them had gathered loose rocks from the street, while others held tight to makeshift clubs. All called for John Pizer to show himself.

His brother yelled to the crowd from the porch. "You're all wasting your time. John ain't here!"

"We know he's in there! I seen him with my own eyes looking out the upstairs window!"

"Gentlemen, please, if that's what you are. Let's not forget ourselves. Give the man some space."

Abberline and Conal pushed their way through to Lusk and Pizer's older brother, Henry. Abberline looked sharply at Lusk. "Is this your idea of searching for Tumblety?"

"Is it yours, Inspector?"

"We're here to make an arrest, unlike you, who seem bent on adding another murder to the horrors this town has seen of late." Abberline and Lusk stared each other down. Conal was about to intervene when the front door swung upon. John Pizer stood in its frame.

"Get me the bloody hell outta 'ere before this lot sends me to a meeting with the Maker."

That John Pizer would decide he was better off with the police than with his fellow citizens was not something Conal or Abberline had seen coming. It was a welcome twist, however. One less struggle to be fought in this endless battle.

"Murderer!" The crowd screamed as he was led away.

"You're going to 'ang!" Lusk called. A wad of spit flew from his lips in Pizer's direction.

"All right, all right that's enough, gents. Step aside, coming through! We'll handle this. Come on, move it!" Abberline held Pizer's arm and dragged him down the street.

Three hours passed before John Pizer had been interrogated, and for the moment, cleared.

He looked as though he might spit at someone if he hadn't been released.

Lusk had been guarding the station, watching like a hawk to see if and when Pizer would be released.

He stormed in not ten minutes after Pizer had stormed out.

"Pizer!" he screamed into the street. "Mark my words, you will hang, murderer!"

"Calm down, Mr. Lusk! Inspector Abberline and I have this investigation under control. Take one more step toward Mr. Pizer and you'll be spending the night behind bars. I suggest you think twice before calling my bluff."

"We've been here for the last three hours with Mr. Pizer going over his whereabouts and verifying his alibis. They have been confirmed..."

Lusk cut Abberline off. "That ain't good enough. All he speaks are lies. We have women, fifty of em', that say he's the Ripper!"

"Mr. Lusk, he has verifiable alibis of his whereabouts. Several officers, including Sgt. Thick, have already confirmed it. Sorry to disappoint you, but he's free to go about his business."

Pizer had heard Lusk's screaming and returned in a fit of his own rage.

"Sod off, you bloody wanker! You want to know where I was the other night? There was a fire at the London docks. You may have heard of it. Took 'em a while to get the fire under control. It must've been midnight when I started back. Seen a couple constables along the way home, and ended up at Crossman's Lodging house on Holloway. Decided to stay the night. The landlord saw me, even had a chat for a while. Smoked my pipe and slept till he woke me in the morning."

"Is this true?" Lusk remained suspicious.

"Yes, Mr. Lusk. It's all been confirmed." Abberline gave him a warning look.

"That's right, Georgie boy. So if'n any of you come around me, if'n you bother me or my brother...perhaps you'll find out exactly what kind of killer I can be."

John Pizer had reason to be angry. He had been more than suggested as the Ripper, he had been proclaimed such by Lusk and his vigilantes,

225

and even the East London Observer had named him the killer. The paper read:

His was not an altogether pleasant face to look upon by reason of the grizzly black strips of hair about an inch long covering most of his face, his thin lips which had a cruel sardonic kind of look that was increased, if anything, by his dark, drooping mustache and side whiskers. His head was slightly bald on top, and was supported by a thick and heavy-looking neck.

Pizer had said the description bore him no more resemblance than it did the man on the moon, but his protests had fallen on deaf ears. It's a tough thing to shake the label of murderer.

"Mr. Pizer, we are done here, so I would encourage you to get moving now before things escalate further," Abberline said quickly. "Oh, and Mr. Pizer, it would be in your best interest to avoid prostitutes and women within London in the future. I'm afraid any further disruptions will only antagonize the populace and put you in the line of suspects once again."

Lusk simply glared after the man, his hatred palpable. He turned his ire on Abberline.

"You have the disapproval of me and many others, Inspector. You should have your badge stripped. You've let a killer go free."

"Mr. Lusk, if you have nothing of value to offer us, I suggest you see your way out."

Lusk thundered out of the building.

"That won't be the last we've seen of him," Abberline sighed.

"Let's focus on what we know." Conal was irritable today and looked more tired than usual.

"Well, James, we've established that the conspiracy theory with Gull and Sickert is incorrect. And Pizer's off the list now as well. You said the Ripper was never identified or apprehended?"

"Correct."

"So we have no idea if he does or does not have a medical background?"

"No, we don't, aside from the doctor's speculations. This psychopath may very well have one, but I also wouldn't dismiss any suspects simply because they're not a doctor."

"Anyone with a history of working with knives or having access to them will be placed at the top of our list, however unlikely," Abberline said. "We have no word on Tumblety yet. Let's redouble our efforts on his whereabouts. The fact that he's making himself so hard to track down makes him all the more suspicious, as far as I'm concerned." Abberline looked defeated for the first time.

"Look, Inspector, you're going to figure this thing out." Conal lied through his teeth. He believed that less and less every day, but a little false hope every now and then might keep them going.

Abberline exploded. "No, I won't, James, and that is exactly the problem!"

That Conal had not been prepared for. He couldn't afford for the despair to get Abberline, too. Much as he was loathe to admit it, he counted on Abberline to keep him optimistic.

"Look, why don't you put away the notes for tonight? Go home and get some sleep. Everything will still be there in the morning and you'll be able to start again with fresh eyes. There's nothing more we can do here today. In the meantime, I need to get back to Julia."

Abberline raised his eyebrows.

"I suppose you're right. I'm sorry for losing my temper. That was quite unprofessional of me."

"Get some rest, Inspector. Clear heads in the morning will do us some good."

Twenty-Eight

The cold and wet had returned to London, leaving the previously beautiful day a distant memory.

Conal glanced at Abby curled on her pile of old blankets beside the fireplace. He hated that he had hurt her, lied to her. He hated to think of the further pain she would endure, but it was inevitable. Abby and Mary had become especially close since the Irish woman had rescued Abby in front of The Ten Bells. With her other friends dying around her, Mary would be sad to say goodbye to her Julia. Conal suspected Julia would feel the same.

If I don't get it together, they won't have to say goodbye because the Ripper might see to it that they're united in death.

Time seemed to be passing quicker every day. Unless Conal and Abberline could stop him, the Ripper would soon make his way to Miller's Court.

The previous two murders had, if anything, proven to Conal that he was most likely deluded in his aspirations to change history. Perhaps he should simply focus on finding the time machine and getting him and Abby away from here forever.

There was, of course, the possibility of simply taking Abby elsewhere in England. Even if they couldn't go home, he could get her far from London so she at least had a chance to live. How likely do you think it is she'd go anywhere but home with you and leave her friends for dead?

Since that day on the bridge, their relationship had been even cooler than before. Abby was polite, but not friendly, and she spent most of her time with Mary, helping her with errands, tidying the flat, stopping for a drink at one of the city's seedy pubs. Conal hated it, but what could he do? He had pushed Abby away and he had to live with his decision.

He turned his face to the dirty window of Mary's flat, watching rainwater streak the grime on the glass.

Conal sat there for the duration of the early morning, taking inventory of all the clues, suspects, dead ends, and victims of this 'ghost' he and Abberline, and Lusk and all his vigilantes were chasing. As soon as they had a suspect in their sights, they would dismiss them. The clues were all organized and deliberate. The Ripper seemed to know exactly what he was doing. He was methodical, precise. Perhaps he was playing the detectives like a fiddle. Perhaps each clue was orchestrated to lead them further and further from his true identity, keeping them preoccupied as he savagely took the lives of more women.

Tumblety was still the foremost suspect, and also the most elusive. The newspapers worked hard at stirring up angst among the townsfolk. Women lived in fear and men were in a constant state of anger and uproar. The entire East End was one murder shy of a full scale riot.

We just need to find the machine and get out of here. Conal felt a little ashamed at how quickly he was willing to abandon the women he knew were marked for death, but the situation seemed hopeless. Abby might hate him, but if he could save her life, he could live with that.

He began to sweat, thinking of the time machine. What if, rather than breaking it up for parts, the opportunist who had seized it accidentally used the machine and left Conal and Abby stranded here forever?

"I'm going to die, aren't I?"

Conal whirled around, startled by both the break in silence and the harrowing words.

Mary stood beside him, wrapped in a sheet, trying to keep warm. Her smile was sad. "You warned us to stay off the streets but we didn't listen. Duty calls, after all. Now two of us are dead. You and that inspector have given an awful amount of attention to this flat and my girls. Seems to me this monster has it out for us."

"Mary, I don't know the future. All I know, the moment we're born, we begin to die. Are you the next victim, or any victim of the Ripper? I honestly can't say. But I do know that the Inspector and I are doing everything humanly possible to prevent that."

"It's always been a hard life here in Whitechapel. Perhaps death will be a sweet release. Maybe once I've gone from this place, I'll be reborn in Ireland. Maybe I'll even see my family again. Even if I'm only a ghost, I'd love to hear me mam's laughter or me da's singing voice. I always did think I'd make it back there someday before I breathed me last." She laughed. "I had even thought to raise a family there. Silly now, it seems."

"Hold on to those dreams, Mary. They'll give you something to live for. This is a terrible time, but when you have something to live for, your chances of survival are so much better."

The sad smile remained. Mary truly was the pretty one, as she had been called. She had begun to get a worn look about her eyes, premature aging from the past few years, which had been so difficult. But her beauty remained in her thick hair, her lovely smile, her otherwise smooth skin.

She might have married a handsome, prosperous man back in Ireland. Life had not been kind to Mary Kelly of late. What a cruel trick that it should now be taken from her.

"What about you, Detective?" Mary came up beside him and leaned her head on his shoulder, mocking him. "What is it you dream of? A life with Julia?"

Conal looked uneasily at Abby, still asleep on the floor, "What about Julia?"

"Come now, don't play coy. What's the real story with you two? I got me six brothers and know a thing or two about how a brother and sister act, and the two of you certainly aren't it."

"Sibling relationships are different in America."

"Ah yes, you Yanks do have some strange ways. I hadn't realized they included falling in love with your own sister."

"In love with my sister? Absolutely not."

Mary slipped an arm about his waist and leaned in close, whispering into his ear. "James, doing what I do, I know men better than most. A smart working girl keeps things simple and fast, but she also learns to keep her customers happy and coming back. Thing is, sometimes the things you do to make a man happy in bed lead him to believe he's in love with you. That's what happened with Joseph. The man is convinced he's in love with me, though he doesn't know me at all. I've seen the way these men look at me many a time, and I've never seen a one look at me the way you look at Julia. Yours is the worst I've witnessed. So I tell you this. You two make horrible siblings, and even worse play actors. No I'm certain there's a bit more to the story here and it doesn't include her being your sister."

Conal said nothing. He wished Abby were awake. She'd be more likely to throw Mary off this scent, if only because the woman wouldn't dare to embarrass her sweet Julia.

"Things have cooled between you two in the past few days. Anything you want to talk about?"

Mary was a beautiful one, but she was too close. Conal hadn't been with a woman in a long time and if Abby woke to see Mary curled around him, there would truly be no chance of reconciliation. He disentangled himself from her grip.

"I should wake her up. I need to get going and she may want to come with me today."

"Ah, you should let her sleep. She's been exhausted lately, fretful and anxious."

"Maybe." Conal didn't really want Mary prodding Abby about their story, not because Abby couldn't handle it, but because of what she might choose to reveal. Abby was hurt and angry and had no one but Conal to talk to. He couldn't blame her if she decided she was tired of the lies and revealed the true reason she had been angry with her "brother" lately. But he also just wanted her around. Now that he had eliminated the possibility of complicating things with romance, he still wanted her by his side for as long as he could have her, even if it meant dealing with her cool silence.

He headed toward the stable, determined that the day would be devoted solely to finding the time machine. Conal walked the city deliberately and consciously, from the stables to Spitalfields to the docks, the hospital, the prostitutes' church, Big Ben. He questioned the constables, who had nothing of use for him.

Daylight was beginning to fade when he entered Maybrick's shop.

Maybrick was bidding a woman goodbye, kissing her lightly on the cheek. He coughed when he saw Conal, straightening himself. Maybrick was not the type of man who expressed affection in the presence of others.

The woman hurried away.

"Ah, the lovely Bunny, I presume?" Conal motioned toward the woman as she swept out the door.

"Have you met my wife? I thought you were new on Abberline's detail."

Conal smiled. "You don't remember me, do you?"

"Of course I do. You were with Abberline when Lusk and his rabble were rioting in front of the tobacco shop."

"We met before then."

Maybrick studied Conal's face, searching for some kind of clue.

"You mentioned your wife to me the first night we met. It's good to see her in person at last."

"Detective, please. I must confess something." Maybrick's face had gone nearly purple. "That woman...that was not my Florence."

He spread his hands helplessly. "I have no excuse, sir, but please...if you could just forget it this once. I couldn't bear for my children to endure the shame."

Conal frowned. If this guy was so worried about his children, he wouldn't be sleeping with some other woman and lying to their mother.

"Mrs. Maybrick hasn't been herself as of late. It appears that whenever I must take leave of town to retrieve my medicinal needs, she has taken solace in the company of another. Or so I've heard. If she can do it, why can't I? But I beg your discretion. A scandal could bring us to financial ruin. As I said, if the children should suffer..."

"Mr. Maybrick, I didn't come here to morally police your life."

"I'm sorry for bothering you with all of this nonsense and even more sorry that you had to see my infidelity. Reasoned or no, it's not a thing a man's proud of."

"Nothing personal, Mr. Maybrick, but your family issues are none of my business."

"Indeed, sir. Now, you obviously came in here for something. What is it I can help you with?"

Conal described the time machine, sweetening Maybrick to him by confiding in him about the Queen's special project. Maybrick had an ego, like most men, and stroking it could only endear him to Conal's cause. It had been a mistake to try and get Maybrick to recall him the night he and Abby had arrived in London. Dangerous, even. But Conal was desperate for information and Maybrick had been the first person who had talked to them.

Well, no harm done. Maybrick was too busy trying to cover up his dirty deeds to notice anything amiss.

The visit to Maybrick proved useless. He knew nothing and kept injecting thinly veiled pleas for the detective's discretion. Conal was depressed by the time he got back to Miller's Court. The walk back had provided him ample time to muse about his lost chances with Abby. Even if she hadn't felt the same way, at least telling her would free him of the burden of harboring his desire for her all these years.

The hour was late when he got to the flat, but Abby, Mary, and Liz were all on their way out.

"Where are you three headed?"

"Girls' night, big brother. No boys allowed."

Conal made for the door of the flat, but turned when they were a safe distance away. They could defy him, but they couldn't escape him.

How foolish could they be? Two of their friends had been murdered in the night and they were off to flaunt themselves at some sleazy bar.

Conal lurked behind them through the night, watching them drink and dance and laugh.

For a moment, he understood. They had been in mourning, terrified they would be next. They needed release from that, needed something to smile about amongst all of the morbid energy. Still, dammit, why didn't they value their lives more? Why risk death over a few laughs?

By the time she was good and liquored up, Liz had found herself a customer. Men were lining up to inquire about Mary's services as well but she wasn't taking on any customers. She wouldn't leave Julia alone, besides, Liz wouldn't listen to caution and needed the money.

One of the constables on graveyard duty approached Conal where he stood, leaning against a lamp post across the street from The Ten Bells.

Did they have to go there? It was as if Abby was begging for trouble, trying to get a rise out of Conal.

"Good evening, Chief Detective. Everything all right tonight, sir?" The man had a young face. He must have been a new recruit.

This has to be the youngest officer I've ever seen. "Evening, Constable. So far, so good, I believe. Just making sure my sister gets home all right."

"From out here, sir?"

"She doesn't like it when I check up on her. Stubborn one, she is. So, here I am."

"Ah yes, of course. The women don't want you scaring off business, eh?"

"Oh, no, my sister isn't a prostitute."

The young man looked confused. "I thought...but she's spending time with Miss Kelly and Liz..."

"They're friends, not colleagues."

The constable nodded. "Right, then. Well, I'll be just be around the corner on patrol if you need me, sir."

"Thank you, Constable. Good night."

Abby and Mary stayed out until the early morning, and when they walked home, arm in arm, they laughed like college girlfriends. For a night, they got to be young again and happy.

Twenty-Nine

September 27th. Nineteen days had passed since Conal and Abby had arrived.

Inspector Abberline slumped at his desk, collar unbuttoned and hair disheveled.

A stack of letters sat in front of him.

"What's all this?"

"Letters, nearly a thousand of them, and all rubbish." Abberline's eyes were red with exhaustion and purple-black bags sagged beneath them.

The inspector picked one up, glanced at it and tossed it to the center of the table.

"Take a look, if you can stomach it. You'll be amazed at how many of your fellow men are willing to take credit for these ghastly murders.

"Don't put too much stock in these, Inspector. You'll get little help from the letters, if that's what you're seeking. There'll only be mockery there. Even if you have one from the Ripper, it's only part of his game. He's watching us, you, me, the women, the vigilantes, and having a laugh at everyone's expense."

P.C. Smith came into the room with another letter.

"Sir, this just arrived from the Central News Agency."

"Oh good. James, looks like we can add one more to this pile of sadistic jokes."

"Place it with the rest, Smith, we shall take a look soon enough."

"Sir, I think you might be wanting to take a look at it now."

"May I see that, Smith?" Likely another fraud, but it was worth taking a look. Conal had read an actual letter from the Ripper, or at least one the history books figured to be the most authentic, and as soon as he saw that the heading said "Dear Boss," he remembered this one was most likely authentic. It read as follows:

Dear Boss,

I keep on hearing the police have caught me but they wont fix me just yet. I have laughed when they look so clever and talk about being on the right track. That joke about Leather Apron gave me real fits. I am down on whores and I shant quit ripping them till I do get buckled. Grand work the last job was. I gave the lady no time to squeal. How can they catch me now. I love my work and want to start again. You will soon hear of me with my funny little games. I saved some of the proper red stuff in a ginger beer bottle over the last job to write with but it went thick like glue and I cant use it. Red ink is fit enough I hope ha. ha. The next job I do I shall clip the ladys ears off and send to the police officers just for jolly wouldn't you. keep this letter back

239

till I do a bit more work, then give it out straight. My knife's so nice and

sharp I want to get to work straight away if I get a chance. Good luck.

Yours truly,

Jack the Ripper

Don't mind me giving the trade name

P.S. wasn't good enough to post this before I got the red ink off my

hands, curse it No luck yet. They say I'm a doctor now. ha ha

There were plenty of reasons to discard almost every one of the letters received. Most were ridiculously written and their facts absurdly borne from nothing more than mere rumor and conjecture. Even the signatures were blatantly off. However, this one was different. This one bore paying attention to. This one would be remembered for years to come.

✳✳✳

When Conal and Abberline emerged from the inspector's office, two constables were standing at the front desk discussing some sort of security issue.

"Excuse me, Detective McWilliam. You asked us to report anything suspicious. There's been word of some trouble with Mary Kelly's former lover, Joseph Barnett, this evening. None of us saw anything, only heard bits of it after. According to witnesses at the market, Mr. Barnett looked as if he'd gone mad. They say he caused quite a ruckus at the market."

Conal rolled his eyes. According to witness accounts, it wasn't a pretty picture.

The rumors of Joseph Barnett's sacking were ugly ones.

"Charlie, you can't sack me! Come on, mate. You can't do this to me. I'm already a month behind on me rent, and if I miss this month, too, I'll be out on me arse!"

Joseph Barnett was not a reasonable man, nor a practical one. Charlie had known that, but he had liked Joseph. He gave him a chance at a job on several occasions. Joseph was a poor worker and his temper was disruptive. A poor sod, Charlie didn't want to sack him. But the man was bad for business. If he wasn't so busy housing whores and trying to domesticate them, perhaps he wouldn't have trouble making the rent. But Charlie said none of that. He didn't need another outburst.

"Charlie, I promise..."

"Enough, Joseph, enough! You had your chance and you threw it away. Time and again you come crawling back, and time and again, I gave you another chance. This is how you repay me: shoddy work and a bad attitude. Now bugger off, I've already gotten a replacement."

"Charlie, I been loyal to you! More loyal than anyone, and for longer than any of these other blokes, I might add. I can do twice the work of any two of them combined, and ain't no way any of them could ever work as fast or as hard as me."

One of the men responded. "Mind your words, ya sod. I got mouths to feed just like you."

"Mind your place, Michael, and get back to work. A sorrier lot I've never hired!" Charlie shouted. "Look, Joseph, you had your chance. Things went awry when you got wrapped up in that whore of yours. It's a shame, but what can you do? We all have our weaknesses over women. Dry yourself out, get it together, and get yourself a new job."

"Don't you bring Mary into this. Say what you will about me, but you'll be leaving her alone."

Charlie turned away. "I meant nothing by it, Joseph. Time for you to be moving on."

"You're a bloody arsehole, you are, Charlie!" With a swift push of his boot to the cutting table, he knocked it over; taking down the fish display with it.

Charlie jumped to avoid the table and its contents, while Michael grabbed a butcher knife that flew through the air. "I've been more than kind, but now you've done it, Joseph Barnett. You get your arse out now or I'll have you arrested."

Joseph staggered off in a blind rage. First Mary, now the job. The man had nothing left.

✻✻✻

"Tell me, Smith, why isn't Mr. Barnett in our custody? I don't suppose anyone was paying attention to see if there was any type of knife on him?"

"No, sir." Smith felt childish beneath Abberline's glare.

"Well, don't just stand there. Track him down and bring him in. And check for a knife when you find him. Do you need me to write it down this time so you don't forget? Seems to me a constable of Scotland Yard would think to bring in any suspicious and misbehaving characters when we're on the hunt for a mad murderer."

"Sir, the market owner insisted he shan't wish to press the matter..."

"Do you take orders from a fishmonger now?"

"No, sir!"

"Go to Miller's Court," Conal ordered. "He's likely headed there now."

"On the double," Abberline snapped. "Unless his paramour, Miss Kelly, has had a sudden softening toward him, I doubt Barnett will get the welcome he's hoping for and that may go hard for her."

"I'd better go down there as well." Conal wasn't leaving Abby's safety in the hands of this timid constable.

✳✳✳

Joseph did indeed make his way toward Miller's Court, leaving a wake of fear and destruction behind him. He hastily shoved aside everyone in his way, yelling at strange women, swigging from a bottle of cheap booze. He was as pathetic as he looked.

Conal and Smith beat him to Miller's Court.

"No problems here so far, James," Mary told him when they arrived. "Just us girls sitting about having a chat."

"Well, look who it is!" Liz's voice boomed from within the flat. Her slur gave her away. "If it isn't Chief Detective Arsehole!"

"Liz, that's enough." Mary stood between Liz and Conal, but the larger Liz shooed her out of the way.

"Have you girls all met this character?" She poked Conal in the chest. "Allow me to introduce him. Chief. Detective. Arsehole." She laughed, a crude, drunk, mean sound.

Smith muffled a laugh. Conal rolled his eyes. Smith had not been a great fan of Conal's since his arrival. No doubt he was loving this.

Liz looked at Smith. "And you, what are you laughing at? You ain't no good to us neither. Letting our girls be murdered the way they was."

"Liz, that's enough. They're here looking after us now, and we're grateful for that, gentleman."

A crash on the street heralded Joseph's arrival.

243

He stumbled to his feet and slouched toward the door, moaning Mary's name. When he withdrew his hands from his pockets, they were covered in blood.

Conal and Smith rushed to apprehend him.

"Whoa! Easy mates, be easy! I cut myself on a bottle of gin. You'd have been proud of me, Mary. I didn't drink any, course there wasn't much left to begin with."

"All right, Mr. Barnett, let's get going." They each grabbed an arm, dragging Joseph from the women, who had gathered in the doorway.

"Mary, don't let them do this. Please, Mary, tell them you love me. You're all I have left. Please, I know you still love me." Abby slipped a comforting arm about Mary's shoulders. Mary didn't say a word as she watched them leave.

Barnett was fairly cooperative when they arrived at the station. Still, misery settled into his bones, and his failures were exposed by his failed attempt to fight back tears.

Conal sat patiently while the Inspector interrogated Barnett the same way he had all the others. And like all the others, there were no grounds for holding him, no evidence to force him to stay. Conal and Abberline came up empty handed again and it seemed as if this was beginning to sound a bit like a broken record.

Joseph Barnett was taken to London Hospital to have his hands patched up, and to keep him under their watch a bit longer. Barnett simply spun his tale for anyone who would listen, about how his beloved Mary had betrayed him and he had no one else left in this world.

"I gave her everything. She had a place to live, food, and my heart, but this is what I get in return. She didn't want for anything and still she allows those whores to come in between us, feeding off her, and now leaves me out in the cold."

When they left him, he was sitting outside the hospital, weeping.

Thirty

Julia and Liz had never really hit it off, but Abby didn't see why they couldn't be friends. After all, Liz was going through a bad time.

Maybe she just needed a shoulder to lean on.

"So Liz, how did you end up here in Whitechapel?"

"How did I end up in Whitechapel? Or how is it that I became a whore?" Liz lived her life in two modes: drunk or defensive. Tonight she was both.

"That's not what I meant, I'd just like to get to know you better. I was curious how you got here, that's all." Abby smiled, hoping she came across as sincere. Liz's testiness set her on edge, which was likely the point.

"Not sure what's it to you, but fine. I'll share. I was born in Sweden. I've two sisters, Rebecca and Janette, and both are beautiful. My father is a very successful doctor and my mother a school teacher. They are very well to do indeed and always have been. Most people would be lucky to associate themselves with my family. As for me, I have been a whore since I was thirteen. Started with my own family at that, I did, so I suppose I can't say I didn't benefit from their fortune."

246

Abby could only raise her brows and gave Kate a look of disbelief.

"Whoring since thirteen. That's quite a feat. No wonder your tits are so saggy now," Kate replied, giving Liz a good ribbing.

It was a full house at Mary's tonight. Abby hadn't spoken much with Kate until now, and she was shocked by the woman's frankness.

"Bah!" Liz laughed. "Come on, Kate, I'm just pulling your leg. Thirteen is a bit young, even for me." Kate had earned Liz's respect and a right to poke fun. "It wasn't always this bad for me." She sat back in Mary's bed and began to tell her story.

"The truth is, I was an only child. My father was a laborer and my mother took care of me. Occasionally, she made extra money by taking in mending. They were good parents, they showed me as much love as any parents could. Eventually, I had no choice except to go out on my own, as my father didn't make enough money for the three of us. I lived rather modestly for awhile. Circumstances that I'd rather not discuss at the moment got the best of me and when I turned twenty-two, I began working the streets and have been ever since. Dropping my knickers is in much higher demand than mending.

"Ah, but you wouldn't know what the fuck I'm talking about, would you, Julia? You've certainly never had to let a hairy old drunk thrust himself on top of you to make the rent or to put a little food in that flat belly of yours. I bet that handsome brother of yours knows a thing or two about that."

Abby was speechless and the room was silent for a moment.

"Liz," Kate snapped sharply. "Must you always be so foul? This is the girl's brother you're talking about."

"I think it's time we were all off to bed," Mary said, returning to the room. "Liz, if you can keep that filthy tongue of yours in line, you can stay here tonight."

"It's starting to smell a little too flowery in here for me, and I'm sure your darling Julia doesn't want me stinking it up with my whorey scent, do you?"

"I was just trying to make friendly conversation. You're the one who turned it into a crude discussion."

"So that troubled you, eh? There's something not right about the two of you. When I seen yas together I could tell... Well, never mind," Liz rolled her eyes. "I'm off in the hopes of better company. A good man to warm this old body and throw me some coin, perhaps."

"Liz, I really don't think that's wise. After what happened to Polly and Annie..."

"Don't you speak to me, you snotty wench. You don't know anything about those women."

"I know enough that they would warn you not to go out there just the same, but if you want to continue being a bitch? Forget it, just go." Abby wasn't one for spite, but she'd had enough of Liz's insults and cutting remarks.

Liz grabbed her worn shawl and stormed out of the flat.

"I'm sorry, I shouldn't have said that. Liz is your friend, and I know you're all grieving."

"Never mind, Julia. Liz is who she is. She got exactly the response she wanted from you." Kate stood to leave.

"You're not spending the night?" Bad enough that Liz wasn't heeding the warnings, there was no need for Kate to be out there, too.

"Liz can be a mean one, but I don't want her out there alone."

"Then we'll go with you." Mary reached for her own shawl, but Kate stopped her.

"Best if you don't. We'll be all right, love."

She hugged Mary goodbye and hurried after Liz.

248

The two women discussed the evening over gin.

"Don't you dare lecture me, Kate."

"Don't go getting your bloomers in a twist, ya cow. I swear I don't know why you always have to be so bloody tense. I'm with you, remember? Julia has been nothing but trouble ever since she's arrived, her and that brother of hers always lingering around. Remember the murders didn't start until those two showed up."

"There's something queer about those two, there is."

Kate relaxed into her seat. Agreeing with Liz was a sure way to win her favor.

Liz took a long swig of gin.

"I was being a bitch, wasn't I?"

"A bit," Kate admitted.

"It's just too much sometimes. She's not from around here and I'll tell you that's bothersome. I don't like the way Mary fawns over her. She hasn't been the same since Julia arrived. Bloody hell, now I do feel like a right bitch."

"Don't worry about it, Liz. I'm sure you're not the first bitchy woman she's ever encountered. You can always apologize tomorrow."

When they had drunk their money, they each worked a customer, only to return with a little more money jangling in their pouches, eager to be drunk.

Liz was on her third john of the night. That was a record for her these days. She was older than the other girls, and usually too drunk and uncomely to get much work.

Just as a man was about to slip her an advance, a younger woman scooched up beside him.

"You sure you want to spend that on old Liz tonight? She's already had a few this evening, and I'm not just talking about drinks. Why don't you come with me? It's my birthday, after all."

"Sod off, you lying bitch."

"I turn twenty at midnight, you filthy old cow."

The man's eyes lit up. Liz stood no chance next to the unblemished young girl.

"Will you let me see your birthday suit?" the man laughed.

The girl giggled. "Of course. For a price."

The man wrapped his arm around the girl and led her away.

Long Liz Stride lunged at the other woman. She was drunk and livid.

The bartender lifted her from where she fell and led her out into the street, not unkindly.

"You've had enough for tonight, Liz."

"Sod off. There's plenty of other pubs." Liz was never known for being gracious.

She stumbled on alone.

Kate snatched her things and ran into the street after her, but Liz was nowhere to be seen.

✳✳✳

A repeated banging sound coming from nearby shook her momentarily from her pity party. It sounded about fifty feet ahead.

"Hey, who's there? Anyone there?" Liz shouted

A door creaked open, then slammed. The pounding continued.

"Shit me! I'm losing me bloody mind."

A man's voice spoke to her from the shadows.

"It's the gate."

"Who's that? You scared me half to death."

"It's just the gate," the voice repeated. "You can see it swinging loose from here." The man stepped forward and pointed. "You see?" Liz looked up ahead at a loose gate across the way opening and closing with the wind.

"So it is. Well, you can never be too safe nowadays. Never know what it is that makes things go bump in the night."

"Here, have some sweets, it will help you relax a little." The man held out his hand, offering Liz sweets as well as some grapes.

"Well, that's right kind of you, sir. I don't mind if I do." Mouth still full, she turned to him. "All right let's get it over with."

"Get it over with?"

"You want to get your pleasure for the night, I take it? Don't think these sweets will count toward your payment."

"Madame, I offer you my kindness and give you something sweet and you treat yourself as a whore. Very telling." He chuckled. "I guess I shouldn't be so surprised. Yes, by all means, I don't want to keep you here too long. Let's get it over with. I think I shall most certainly have my pleasure for the night."

Then, with a haunting blank face he stared at Liz. "Shall we go through here?" He indicated the alley through which he had come.

"Money up front, sir. This ain't for free."

"So like a whore, looking for your whoremaster. Just like the others. There will be no money for you tonight, whore."

The man's face twisted in a serious sneer. Liz knew this was him. She was staring into the eyes of the man who had murdered her friends, and she was about to join them in death.

She took a step back, her mind sober now. Perhaps if she didn't give off that she knew him, she could get away.

His hands were on her in a death-like grip. Before she could scream, he had wound her scarf about her neck and pulled... tighter... tighter... so tight her neck nearly snapped. Long Liz Stride slipped into unconsciousness without another word.

❊❊❊

Approximately forty-five minutes after Liz had left The Ten Bells, Kate Eddowes had followed suit. It had been raining off and on, and the wind was kicking up. She looked around nervously, wishing she had a shot of gin; just a little something to ease the nerves, something just didn't feel right. She quickened her pace slightly.

"All right, Kate," she told herself. "You're a big girl! Let's just hurry up and get home." No reason to think anything was amiss, not really. Most likely Liz had found herself another customer.

Now she hurried toward Middlesex Street, talking herself through her fear. Why should she be more afraid tonight than any other? She could take care of herself.

Still, she couldn't shake the feeling she was being followed. Though no one was there when she looked, she could swear she heard footsteps behind her.

❊❊❊

The stink of rotting food, soiled clothes, and feces gagged Conal. They had been crouched behind the trash can for hours and Conal was sure the stink would be on him for weeks.

Stakeouts are a hell of a lot less glamorous in reality, Conal thought. They had set up just off Dorset Street, by the Britannia, in perfect viewing distance of one of the most well-trafficked pubs in the area.

Abberline wore a pair of plaid trousers with an old long jacket. Conal garbed himself in a pair of faded pants that looked like they had come from a mill worker, along with an itchy wool sweater. P.C. Richins had the unfortunate job of dressing in full drag, strolling up and down the street looking for customers. He wore a whistle around his neck disguised as a necklace.

"Three girls left, and it's all nothing more than a bloody game," Abberline grumbled.

"Abberline, what the hell are we doing here?" Conal asked, not for the first time. They were getting soaked and this farce of having Richins dress in drag was stupid. "We're not going to catch the Ripper this way."

"What do you suggest we do, James? Have you even remembered any information as of late? We could go off what you think you remember, but that's a risk in itself. If the date or location is off again, then we risk being in the wrong place; if it is the correct place, there's still no guarantee that you have the right time."

"No need to remind me." Conal's unreliable memory had been a cause of frustration for him these last two weeks. He had always been able to recall facts easily. However, this was something he hadn't studied in years. It was no surprise his memory was so muddled.

"You've been a great help, James. I just hope you come up with something before it's too late." Abberline looked around, slowly resigning himself to the futility of the stakeout. "Perhaps you're right. There doesn't appear to be anything happening tonight."

Two constables were speaking, gesturing animatedly across the street. One pointed the other in Abberline and Conal's direction.

"Inspector!" the man screamed. He blew his whistle, running toward them.

"Tell me, James. Where you're from, do you have constables half as intelligent as this imbecile coming towards us?" He rose from behind the trash cans. When he reached the constable, he grabbed him by the scruff of the neck.

"Constable, have you gone mad? Your idiocy is jeopardizing this operation." Abberline took a quick look around and noticed a couple of onlookers. "Point your club at Detective McWilliam and talk fast. Make it look good for the public and for God's sake, stop addressing us as police."

When the onlookers noticed it was just another drunk making a scene, they moved on.

"I'm sorry, sir," the constable whispered when they had moved away. "I didn't mean to call attention, but another victim's been found over at Dutfield's Yard. A merchant reported her."

The tingling was back in Conal's hands again and they grew warm and itchy. He had hoped the tingling came from nerves, as it started whenever he became most anxious.

As he had predicted, this absolute circus of a plan had brought them no closer to the Ripper. While they had been watching Richins parade the streets as a woman, Liz Stride was having her throat slashed.

She had been more fortunate than the others. Her throat was the only thing the Ripper had time to cut.

The Inspector looked around the area. It was fairly open. "Someone must have interrupted his work, forcing him to abandon the body," the Inspector concluded. "This won't be enough for him. He has a thirst when he's killing and it's unlikely he's quenched it tonight. He'll be out for more blood."

Louis Diemshutz had discovered Liz Stride's body. The man was terrified. He was a timid man, simple in his ways, and did his best to avoid trouble. He was a jeweler and had been making this late night trip home for about seven years. He worked late to keep food on the table for his family and a roof over their heads.

His voice cracked with fear as he spoke. "I turned the corner and my pony, well, she is already a little bit skittish, but this time she just about drove me into the wall to avoid something in the road. I didn't know what it was at first. I thought maybe she was avoiding some mud that had built up with the rain. I pulled her aside to get a better look and still, it was much too dark. I didn't know for sure, but I just had a feeling it was something bad, so I ran. As I was running home, I ran into to my neighbor Isaacs first. I called out to him a couple of times, 'Isaacs! Isaacs! Where is Margaret?'

"'How the hell should I know? I got my own wife to mind,' he replied.

"'Isaacs, this is serious my friend,' I told him.

"'She's upstairs! Gone to bed I suppose.'

"'Isaacs, I need you to come with me. I'm afraid I have found something awful, too awful for Margaret to see.'

"Isaacs lit a match as we stepped outside. We could see the blood everywhere. Something was blocking the path. When we held the match closer, we could see it was a body. She was already dead when we found her."

"No doubt she would be, with a cut like that. We just sat there in the alley like fools." Abberline blamed himself. The stakeout had been his idea. He could have been out on the streets, in the pubs, not squatting behind trash cans.

"Was it the Ripper?"

"It was. Thanks for your help, Mr. Diemshutz."

Why frighten the poor old man anymore? Conal thought.

Liz's was the first corpse Conal had openly shed a tear over. The woman who had been mannish and worn in life but looked almost lovely in death. She wore a flower in her bosom and clutched a cluster of grapes to her breast.

✳✳✳

Kate had been right to be frightened. Her instincts told her a truth her intellect did not want to hear. The Ripper was on a mission and he would not be deterred.

He played Kate the same way he had Liz: disarmed her with a bit of charm and the promise of some money in her pocket. Kate's senses were dulled from drink, though it likely would have made no matter.

By the time she realized she was in danger, he was too close and too quick for her to run.

Her body was found in Mitre Square, two hundred yards from Middlesex Street. What he had not been able to accomplish on Liz's corpse, he had more than made up for on Kate's.

Her throat had been cut, like the others. The uterus and kidney had been cut from her body and the tip of her nose had been sliced away. The Ripper had taken special care with her eyes, nicking each eyelid and cutting a careful 'V' beneath each eye.

Abberline listed the items that had been found on Kate's body:

A man's white vest

A pair of men's lace up boots

A tin box containing sugar with a strand of fabric

A tin box containing tea

One small tooth comb

One red leather cigarette case with metal fittings

A piece of old white apron

A mustard-tin containing pawn tickets

One empty tin match box

Abberline looked through the items and back at the victim's face. "He's giving it to us. He's telling us who he is. It's right in front of our faces and we can't see it."

"What do you think it is?'

The Inspector slowly paced. "Those Vs beneath each eye, there's something there. There's no question something is here, James."

Thirty-One

"Look at this." Inspector Abberline was shining his lamp over a trail of blood leading down Goulston Street.

"Halse! Has anybody bothered to look down Goulston?"

Detective Constable Daniel Halse was from the City Police. He was over by St. Boltoph's with two other detectives when he heard about the death of Kate Eddowes.

He shot Abberline an irritated look. "I've already given orders to have the area searched. There's nothing there."

Abberline was Metro Police and D.C. Halse was City. There was no love lost between them and one of the many challenges on the growing list of complications was that these murders were all taking place along the dividing lines of police jurisdictions. Getting cooperation from City was nearly impossible. They didn't want to show any signs of inferiority to the Metropolitan Police, and they didn't care if that meant slowing down the investigation. Showing that they were the more capable force was as important as finding Jack the Ripper himself, and they were desperate to do just that.

Abberline stared at the pool of blood at his feet. He looked back and then toward Halse. He crouched to examine the blood, then took a few steps back in the direction of Mitre Square.

"Well, Inspector, don't keep us in suspense. What is it?" Halse relished putting Abberline on the spot.

"He took Stride at Berner Street, that was his plan. It was a perfect night for it: cold, wet, and raining. Not a lot of people out for witnesses, and she would have wanted to be in from the cold. But then our savage culprit was interrupted and that... well, that's what really angered him. Not being able to finish his work because of a man that was far beneath him. If he didn't see Louis Diemshutz as such an incompetent and therefore insignificant man, perhaps he would have killed him, too."

He went on. "What kind of man would stand for that kind of interruption? Not anyone with a sense of pride, I tell you. In fact, it was because of his pride that he not only had to murder someone, but he had to prove his point and do the job right. So he passes Middlesex, and murders Eddowes in Mitre Square. He wanted to show us he did exactly what he set out to do. We need to follow his direction. That's what he wanted."

Hastily we headed up Goulston Street. Conal spotted some kind of rag ahead on the walkway. Abberline knelt to pick it up. Conal held the lamp overhead. A blood-soaked cloth. It was a piece of Kate Eddowes' apron. He examined the cloth and stared down the dark street. "He came from Mitre Square. After the killings, he ran back toward the East End."

Abberline paused. "But why would he be running back to the East End? It's as though he wants us to find him."

Conal shifted the lamp higher. "The man is a lunatic, but he's not entirely unintelligent. He doesn't seem the type of person to live in the East End."

Abberline stared past Conal.

"He's left us another message, James."

Written on the wall behind Conal, were the words: The Juwes are not the men that will be blamed for nothing.

"He misspelled Jews," Conal said dully. Another twist in this never-ending case.

"I want this whole area blocked off. It should be daylight soon and we're going to need to get a picture of this as soon as possible. Longley, I want you to get a photographer."

"Right away, sir."

"That won't be necessary." A man emerged from the darkness. "I want it removed immediately." He was middle-aged, well-dressed, stocky, and proud. He wore a full mustache.

"What are you talking about? Who are you? Of course it's necessary. We're collecting evidence in a murder case." Abberline had no time for interference from these odd characters.

"This is the Metropolitan Police Commissioner, Sir Charles Warren. Commissioner Warren, this is Chief Detective James McWilliam. Head of the City Police detectives, he's liaison for the City Police. He's here to help things run a bit smoother between us and City." Conal actually had to behave as a liaison between the two forces now, and act like he knew what the hell he was doing.

Abberline quickly pulled the commissioner to the side. "With all due respect, sir, we need to at least take a picture of this. I wouldn't think that I need to tell you that with this we can eliminate hundreds of letters, perhaps match up his writing. There may even be some witnesses that saw him in the act of writing on the wall."

"Inspector, might I remind you that with the tensions mounting in this town toward the Jewish population, this kind of defamation could

260

cause absolute chaos. Instead of looking for a murderer, you'll be fighting off riots. I'm sure you'd agree that your time would be better spent on this investigation."

Conal watched their faces and inferred there wasn't much time before they lost a key piece of evidence. They weren't going to get a photograph.

"P.C. Long, do you have something to write with?"

"Of course. I have a pencil and a tablet right here, sir."

"I want you to write down exactly what you see. Keep it to yourself for now and see if you can get D.C. Halse to do the same. Quickly now, we don't have much time before the commissioner wants it gone."

"Yes sir, right away."

Abberline's voice was rising. "This is insane. There are hundreds of incidents that happen every day that could set off riots. You choose this one to act upon. Why?"

"Inspector, don't try my patience this early in the morning. I want this trash gone. Good people don't need to wake to see this."

Abberline could barely breathe with rage. He sputtered toward a constable, telling him to clean it away.

"Let it go, Inspector. Let it go." Conal lowered his voice. "I had both Halse and Long write it down." Both had neatly folded the papers and slipped them to him wordlessly. Unfortunately, in their haste, both had written it down differently. A problem to be dealt with later, one of the many.

Abberline fumed the rest of the way to the station.

"So which one is correct?" He stared at the papers a long time before speaking.

"I don't know. Long says he may have written it wrong. His version reads 'The Juwes are the men that will not be blamed for nothing.'"

261

"And Halse's?"

"'The Juwes are not the men that will be blamed for nothing.'"

They had spoken little on the ride back to the station, the double murder weighing heavily on them both.

And then, of course, was the grim fact Conal did not want to face but could not avoid. Mary Kelly was next.

They reviewed the evidence, debated the meaning of the racial message. They called in Israel Schwartz, a witness who heard the conversation between Liz and the Ripper, and described a man he had seen with Liz Stride to a sketch artist.

They held up photos they had for comparison's sake, but Schwartz was of no help and would not identify the man with any of them.

"I refuse to do it. Our people have enough trouble from everyone else in this town, we don't need it from one another. We go through enough. I won't do it."

"All right, Schwartz, that'll be all. You can go on home." Conal rolled his eyes as Schwartz puttered through the door, upset by the interaction.

"That's cowardice."

"That, James, is Whitechapel. Let's keep going."

The photo bore no resemblance to Pizer, Barnett, or Kosminski, and he was already locked up in an asylum. There was, however, a small likeness to Francis Tumblety.

Conal pulled out his tablet, removing Pizer and Kosminski. His list was getting smaller. He withheld mentioning Maybrick as a suspect because he really had no other reason to suspect him other than what he considered odd behavior. Then again, it might just be that he was over sensitive because he was on edge and wanted to go home.

Suspects:

Tumblety - fixates on uteruses and thinks women should be dealt with like cattle.

Joseph Barnett - Jealous boyfriend, resentful toward the girls, has access to Mary's flat, Hostile.

James Maybrick - ??? Strange behavior, infidelity, last name starts with an "M"

"We need more information about Tumblety. Smith, I want an update on my request out to the States for information on this Tumblety. I want to know if there is anything about this man that can give us a clue where in the hell he is." Abberline scratched his chin.

"We also need to increase our patrol." Conal continued to study his list.

"Yes, well, trying to get Commissioner Warren to help out...well, you've seen what happens."

"What if we get the girls and some of the other prostitutes to start petitioning for more men? We'll go right past Warren. The Queen has to listen then. Surely she must care about the safety of these women."

"It's unlikely that Her Majesty will give a moment's attention to some dirty prostitutes, but it will keep them busy, anyway. I don't need a riot of prostitutes on top of everything else, and God knows they're frothing at the mouth for someone to blame right now."

"As well they should," Conal snapped. "Just because they sell themselves for a living doesn't mean they deserve to be abandoned to this mad man."

Abberline shrugged. "There's more than that, my friend. Prostitutes have few friends save one another."

The killings were getting worse. The Ripper grew bolder with each one. The mutilations, the letters, the writing on the wall. The man felt himself invincible.

"We do need more men," Abberline agreed finally. "More money for more manpower. The force is stretched thin as it is."

"We'll have to go past Warren on that," Conal said cautiously. He knew there was no love lost between Abberline and Warren, but stirring up trouble wasn't going to make the Inspector's job any easier.

But Abberline wasn't going to shy away from an opportunity for a fight with the surly man. "Nothing would give me more pleasure than to stick it to that son of a bitch."

Thirty-Two

Days had passed since the double murder with no further word from the Ripper. Almost as little conversation passed between Conal and Abby.

She avoided him when possible, and granted him a grudging half-smile when forced to communicate. Their relationship was civil, but barely. Abby was nursing her wounds under the guise of respecting Conal's desire to be rid of her. Conal refused to allow his attraction to Abby to overwhelm him and was grateful enough for an excuse to stay away from her.

It was already past eleven at night, and with Abby and Mary gone, Conal lay awake, huddled near the fireplace, nervously waiting for Abby to come home, reminding himself of who he was and where he came from. He was reassuring himself that everything was going to be okay when Abby and Mary walked in. He kept his eyes closed and listened to Abby console Mary through her panicked spells.

"I know it's pathetic, Julia, but I...I can almost understand how Joseph feels. Broken, defeated, a laughingstock. It's no wonder he's decided to take it out on me."

Conal had learned from their conversation that Joseph had stopped paying Mary's rent and she was nearly two months behind, in danger of eviction.

Mary was in tears. "What have I got to live for? My girls are gone, it's not safe to work, and I'm about to become a beggar on the street."

"Mary, don't talk like that," Abby repeated soothingly, a mantra she murmured often these days during Mary's fits. "You're not lost. You can go back to the convent if need be. It might be better...making a clean break from Joseph could be the best thing for you."

Conal remained silent during their conversations. He couldn't imagine his input would be welcome. Abby hated him, he was certain of it, and Mary's opinion of him seemed to depend entirely on Abby's. A man's perspective was not what either of them sought.

And so he allowed himself to become ever more obsessed with finding the killer, sinking deeper into Abberline's world, jaded and cynical, consumed with the job..

"You're all I have left, Julia." Mary was sobbing again. "And you'll leave me soon enough as well."

Conal cringed. He prayed Abby wouldn't get it into her head to stay here, that she wouldn't forget their only real goal was to make it home alive.

"I can't stay at the convent right now. They've got their hands full, and they only take in the most dire cases as it is. Let one struggling prostitute in, you have to take them all."

"What about your family?" Abby prodded. "Surely they'd be happy to see you. Going back to Ireland might do you some good."

Mary snorted. "Julia, I can't buy my rent, let alone passage back to Ireland. Never mind. I'll find my way. I've got business to attend to here anyway."

266

Through half-opened eyes, Conal watched the women embrace, Mary giving Abby an unconvincing smile.

"Enough about me. How are you doing, love?"

Abby dropped her voice to a whisper. Against his better judgment, Conal strained to hear.

"I'm all right. It's just...this...argument with James is getting to me," she whispered.

"Still?"

"I just don't understand it. Am I wrong to be so upset?"

No. I was an ass. You have every reason to hate me.

"I don't know what I did to provoke his anger. Of course I appreciate all he's doing, trying to find this psychopath and keep us safe, but it doesn't mean that I don't hurt when he treats me so cold."

"I know your hurt, Julia, but don't let him get the better of you. When a man treats you like that, brother or not, he's not worth a second thought, let alone any tears."

Conal lay there enduring the torture of listening without being able to respond until Abby and Mary finally settled in to go to sleep.

Thirty-Three

"How was your little vacation, James?" Abberline quipped as Conal stepped into the carriage.

"Difficult. I need to talk to you about getting back home."

"Later. While you were out relaxing, I have been conducting a murder investigation." Abberline tossed a bag onto Conal's lap.

"What do you mean later? What's this?"

Conal opened the bag and took out a long narrow blade. Flakes of dried blood clung to the steel.

"Is this the murder weapon?"

"Perhaps he didn't have time to retrieve it when fleeing the scene."

"This proves nothing. Is this even capable of making the cuts of the Ripper?" Conal was exhausted by this case.

"The coroner seems to think so, though I know you don't put much stock in his word. He even showed me his own postmortem knife and compared the two. They were quite similar. We also received a postcard yesterday." Abberline handed him a small card smeared with dried blood.

Conal peered at it, trying to make out the words.

I was not codding dear old Boss when I gave you the tip. You'll hear about Saucy Jackys work tomorrow double event this time number one squealed a bit couldnt finish straight off. Had not time to get ears for police thanks for keeping last letter back till I got to work again.

Jack the Ripper

Conal glanced at the date on the card. It had been received by the post office October 1st. "Take a look a the date. This was sent out before the press released any reports of the killings."

"Yes, precisely."

"You know what that means don't you? It means that if this letter isn't a hoax then neither is the "Dear Boss" letter, because he's clearly referencing it, along with the murders. I think it's the real deal."

"I'm surprised he didn't deliver the letter himself."

Conal's insistence on finding the time machine took a backseat once again. He'd have no help from Abberline today.

⁕⁕⁕

Mary's bouts of anxiety and depression were coming closer together now. Mary was certain she'd be the next woman taken by the Ripper, and Julia was the only one who could talk her down from her hysterics. Conal always walked out during those conversations.

Abby couldn't understand why. Maybe he didn't know how to feel anything except anger and hatred. She felt a little guilty thinking those things. Conal hadn't had it easy, and her lack of conversation was likely making him uncomfortable. But he was the one who had said he couldn't wait to be rid of her. Put a bit of a damper on any good-natured conversation.

Mary was dangling a thick red apple before Abby in front of a stand at Spitalfields marketplace.

"Care to bite the apple, Princess Snow White?"

Abby laughed until the merchant came and snatched it from her hands.

"The feck are you two about, touching good produce like that? I don't presume you're going to pay for it."

"Ah, come off it, we were just having a laugh."

It was good to see Mary in high spirits again.

The vendor shooed them off.

"That apple looked so good, Mary. I suppose there's too much shame in begging for me to go back?"

"Are you hungry, then?"

"Starving."

Mary's eyes twinkled.

"Let me ask you, Julia, what's better than one of those shiny apples? Two!"

She revealed two apples hidden beneath her shawl and laughed.

In another life, Abby would never have eaten stolen goods, but today she knew what it meant to be hungry. She devoured the apple greedily, savoring the sweet juice that dribbled down her chin.

The women wound their way through the crowds. Abby couldn't remember the last time she had felt light-hearted. Mary made everything seem bright and easy, and Abby found herself feeling increasingly comfortable around her.

They were laughing like schoolgirls and didn't even see a couple approaching them. Abby knocked into the woman hard, sending her to the ground.

"Oh my God, I'm so sorry," she gasped, reaching to help the clearly disgruntled, but beautiful, woman to her feet. "Are you all right?"

The woman made a sour face. "I'm fine."

"No thanks to the likes of you," her boyfriend or husband, Abby couldn't be sure, sneered. He looked at Abby and Mary like they were dogs to be kicked. The woman dusted herself off and the pretentious pair hurried off.

"Mary, did you recognize that woman at all?"

"That sourpuss cow? No, don't think I've seen her before. Have you?"

"I'm not sure," Abby said with a frown. "She seemed familiar to me, but I can't quite place her."

"Sorry for your troubles if you've encountered that one before." Mary made a show of dusting herself off in a mock of the snobby woman and the two fell into a fit of giggles again.

Still, Abby couldn't shake the feeling that she had seen the woman somewhere before.

Who knows who or what I've seen, she thought wryly. *I could have seen her reincarnated sometime in the future.* She put the thought from her mind.

They walked through the market, approaching women, asking them to sign petitions to the Queen. That was one of the few conversations she and Conal had gotten to in the past few days. He had told Abby and Mary of the shortage of manpower to work the case, and both had agreed to work on rallying the women of the city to fight for their right to protection.

Mary nabbed a copy of a newspaper left lying on a bench. She laughed. "Look at this, Julia." The front page carried a story about the Queen wanting more officers working their patrols, and an accompanying piece about Metropolitan Police Commissioner Sir Charles Warren.

"Commissioner Sir Charles Warren is opposed to any increase in Police and deems it unnecessary, but says he'd like to explore the possibility of using bloodhounds," Mary read through a mouthful of apple.

"Does this man even want to find the murderer?"

"Utter incompetent. It's no wonder the Ripper is still out there. Let's go." They rounded up some other women to help, other girls in Mary's network.

✳✳✳

Conal and Abberline were in his office when fifteen angry women descended upon the Yard.

Mary Kelly was known to have class, but she was not shy about making a scene.

She stormed into Abberline's office with Abby close on her heels. She threw the newspaper and petitions onto the desk.

"Have you read this trash? This Warren doesn't want to put more men on the streets until the Ripper is found? Are we less than human because ours is a less than respectable trade?"

"Miss Kelly—"

"No, don't Miss Kelly me. Our lives are at risk. Every night when we leave our homes, we can't visit a friend for a cup of tea without wondering if we'll make it home, let alone try to make a living. Every dime could mean our lives, and you sit here trying to placate me, trying to placate all of us."

Conal gave Abby a pleading look and she returned it with one of defiance. This wasn't about their personal quarrel. This was about the unfairness of a broken system. Abby had a cause and she wasn't letting go of it.

Abberline collected the petitions. "I assure you, Miss Kelly, Julia, I'm doing everything I can. I'll see that these are delivered to the Palace, and I will demand more men. Please relay this information to your cohorts." Abberline dismissed them, much to Abby and Mary's chagrin.

When they left, he looked hard at Conal and chuckled. "That's just what we need. A pack of angry women on top of everything else."

Thirty-Four

So I'm home with my wife and son about 5 o'clock, to eat supper. The wife made me favorite meat pie and mash, and just as we finish grace, I hear a ring at the door. So I say to myself, oh bloody hell! What is it now? The family's already frightened enough. I open the door and no one is there. I say to myself, what the hell is going on? I grab my rifle and I go to take a few steps out on the porch and look around, you know, to make sure its safe. I keep my rifle by the door when I'm at home, just in case. Anyway, I go to take a few steps out and I feel my feet knock something over. There on the ground is this small cardboard box. It came with this letter."

George Lusk thrust a box across the table toward Abberline and Conal and flung the letter on top.

"Made me so sick I couldn't eat. Go on, Inspector, open it."

Abberline opened the box. Out came this indescribably rancid smell. Inside the box was some kind of organ, a rotting piece of the human anatomy. All three of them covered their mouths. Their eyes watered from the stink as they opened the letter.

From hell

Mr Lusk,

Sor

I send you half the kidne I took from one women, prasarved it for you tother piece I fried and ate it was very nise I may send you the bloody knif that took it out if you only wate a whil longer

Signed

catch me when you can Mishter Lusk

"Now Inspector, I want to know what in bloody hell is going on here? When are you going to get this psychopath off the streets? He's sending me kidneys now! What will it take for you to do something? A severed head delivered to your own doorstep?"

That particular prospect hit a little too close to home for Conal.

"You made the decision to get involved, Mr. Lusk. You've let anyone who would listen know you're after this man's blood. Did you think he wouldn't take note of that? Did you think he mightn't come after you, too? I suggest you spend more time protecting your family and less making noise about this murderer."

Lusk stood, knocking over a chair.

"Maybe when one of your constables gets disemboweled and decapitated, you'll take this more seriously."

He stormed out. Lusk was almost as troubling a figure as the Ripper some days.

✳✳✳

The analysis on the kidney came through. It perfectly fit the hole left in Kate Eddowes' body. The kidney was believed to come from a forty-five year old woman who suffered from Bright's disease. Kate Eddowes was forty-six years old and suffered from Bright's disease.

There was little doubt that the letter left for Lusk was a genuine article.

"The writing, though—the spelling. It was almost childlike," Conal said. "He could have been on drugs or...perhaps he's schizophrenic. I believe it's genuine, but it was too different from the previous writings."

P.C. Richins entered the room. "Inspector, we have just received files from the States on Francis Tumblety." He handed him the file. "Here's one on George Chapman as well."

"George Chapman?" That was a name Conal hadn't heard before.

"His given name is Severin Klosowski, who, for reasons I'm unsure of, changed his name to George Chapman. Even his wife doesn't know the real reason. The missus came into headquarters and confided in Constable Richins. She said the two had a fight, that her loving husband threatened to cut her head off."

"Come now, what do we have on Tumblety? I think he's who we should be focusing on here."

Abberline opened the file. They looked it over together.

Conal let out a low whistle as Abberline read aloud.

"Apparently, he had a troubled relationship with a woman years ago and wrote off women forever. He has since then come out as homosexual. In fact, he despises women. The man is known for keeping a collection of uteruses. He has crates full of anatomical parts. In 1865, he was suspected of being involved in the assassination of your former president, Abraham Lincoln."

"Well, I'll be damned. I never knew Francis Tumblety made it into the history books for that little achievement. Abberline, what's wrong with this place? I've never heard of a place so infested with lunatics and killers."

"Have you forgotten that Tumblety is American?"

"No, but of all the places in the world, he chose to come to Whitechapel. That tells you something, doesn't it?"

Thirty-Five

Conal stood in front of the mirror straightening his tie. Abby's gaunt face appeared behind him. This had become their routine as of late, her waking to ask him a question he couldn't answer and him leaving for another day of fruitless work. This morning in particular was more difficult than others to look Abby in the eye.

Conal had long since stopped imagining an alternate reality in which their little ritual was something sweet and romantic. He and Abby would never share that. Abby might not get to share that with anyone.

"Is today the day?" She referred to the final murder, the last one promised by history.

Conal didn't know. He never was really one hundred percent certain of anything and his not knowing left Abby in a perpetual state of fear and discomfort. Her and Mary's lives were like an endless game of Russian roulette. They knew it would come in November, but they didn't know which day.

Abby's moods had begun to swing as wildly as Mary's, from moments of elation and determination to live her life as though each day was her last—and she would quip, it very well might be!—to bouts of deep depression and irritability as she faced what seemed like certain death.

The rap at the door had become so routine Conal would miss it once it was gone.

"Chief McWilliam! Sir!" It was P.C. Smith. He and Conal still kept each other at a distance, but they worked well enough together.

"I gotta go, I'll see you later."

Leaving today was painful. Conal felt a physical discomfort to leave the house and the nearness of Abby behind. Was it because she was now on borrowed time? Was it for all the missed opportunities, the moments they had spent together and not even gotten to know each other?

Abberline picked up on his melancholy the minute Conal walked through the door.

"Cheer up, James. I've got good news for you. We've had a break in a certain investigation." He smirked.

Conal's eyes widened "Inspector, don't say things like that unless you absolutely mean it. My heart can't take it."

"Oh, I mean it, Mr. McWilliam."

"The Ripper?"

"Not that investigation. It seems as though a certain Queen's project that had gone missing has been found."

"You're kidding me. You have the machine?"

"That will be all, Smith." He smiled at Conal when Smith had left the room. "The same fellow who took the machine turned it in to City Police, if you can believe that."

Conal's heart pounded. He didn't think he could take another false lead. Desperate as he was, he dared not cling too tightly to hope.

"Well, let's go get it. I'm sure you can stomach a moment with the City Police."

"As a matter of fact, it's at St. Boltoph's Church."

"The prostitute's church?"

"The very one. City Police are a bit overwhelmed at the moment, and they figured the good people of St. Boltoph's would see to it that it would be returned safely where it belonged."

Conal's fingers began tingling again and he could feel the burning spread through them.

There were so many decisions to be made and so many calculations. Would the machine be fully charged? Would they be able to get back? Where would they land? Would time have passed at home, too?

"James, I'm sure this is big news for you, but let's remember we have work to do."

"Are you kidding me? Are you crazy? Do you remember how long Julia and I have waited for this? You're asking me to risk losing this machine again?"

"There's still a murderer to catch." Abberline gave him a look that reminded him of his father.

Guilt kicked in. Conal nodded, but his heart was no longer in the investigation. If he could get to the machine, he and Abby could leave and be free of the terror. Of course he would have liked to see the Ripper get his, but not at such a cost. Somehow he didn't think Abberline would take that lightly.

A few hours later, the inspector was occupied with an interrogation and took the opportunity to duck out and head to Miller's Court to tell Abby the news. Try though he might to temper his own hopes, he knew giving her this to hold onto would help her get through whatever came next.

Abby was elated. It was the first good moment they had shared together in a long time.

Conal hadn't even finished speaking when Abby threw her arms around his neck and sobbed. He could feel her relief when she wrapped her arms around him and squeezed him as strong as he has ever been hugged.

"We're going home," he murmured into her hair. "We're really going home."

Together they formulated a plan. Conal would work the rest of this day and most of the next, to give Abberline what he could toward the investigation and throw off his suspicions. Tomorrow they would meet at Big Ben at six in the evening, and then they would go to St. Boltoph's together.

"How will we get back?" Abby asked.

"I've been thinking about that since we got here. I can't be one hundred percent sure, but we can't overshoot time, because we haven't lived out our future. So we can't go to a place that hasn't happened yet."

Abby looked puzzled. "Okay, let me ask again. How do we get back home?"

"There wasn't any kind of dial, so we just have to think of the present time we would have been in. Maybe say it out loud or picture our last memory before we left. Think of arriving at the Science Fair."

"You really think that's going to work?"

"We don't have any connection or memories to anything that happened immediately after we traveled back in time, so our strongest thoughts to visualize have to be the present time of where we were from. Honestly, Abby, it's a shot in the dark but that's all we got. I can say this much. There's nothing to say that it won't work. So think it, shout it, whatever you have to do, just keep thinking about the Fair and don't stop until we're back."

"I guess we don't have much choice. Like you said, anything is better than here. "

Her face darkened. "What about Mary?"

"She can stay at the convent like she has before. She doesn't have to be alone. But we can't tell her until the last minute. It's too risky."

Abby agreed but she still hated to leave her friend behind. Mary was the most genuine friend she'd ever had. Leaving her now felt like a betrayal.

"Are you all right with that?"

"I feel like I'm deceiving her but I don't know what else to do."

That evening they put their past behind them and walked one last time through Whitechapel. They had agreed not to speak of the bad blood between them and celebrate the fact they had a chance to make it home.

They walked past Spitalfields and The Ten Bells, though Conal refused to go in for a drink.

"Bad memories."

Abby laughed. "We were off to a good start, though, before...well, before people started trying to buy me as a prostitute."

They even stopped in at Maybrick's, where Conal told him his detail in Whitechapel would be ending soon and he and his sister would be heading home.

Maybrick was sweating and sickly. "You okay, Mr. Maybrick? You don't look so good."

"I'm sorry. I've been a bit under the weather. I'll be fine. It'll be a pity not seeing you two around here anymore. Here, I want you to have something." He pulled a pocketwatch out of a drawer and handed it to Conal. "This way you have something to remember me by."

"Oh, sir, I couldn't possibly..."

Conal noticed Abby staring at the picture of Mr. Maybrick and his wife. As he watched her, she shook off whatever she was thinking.

"Nonsense," Maybrick wheezed. "I insist. Bon voyage and all that."

Conal and Abby left Maybrick's Cotton. "Abby, why were you staring at that picture? You couldn't take your eyes off it."

"His wife looks so familiar. I swear I have seen her before."

The last place they visited was the prostitute's church, to scope the landscape for the next evening. St. Boltoph's was a sanctuary for working girls trying to avoid being picked up by constables on the streets. They could avoid being arrested there. The church was on an island centered in the middle of the busiest corners for business. It was illegal for women to stand on the street corners, so they would avoid being arrested by circling the church. If they were caught not moving at anytime, they would be arrested.

✳✳✳

When they entered the church, Abby walked straight to the front and knelt in a pew. Her strict Catholic upbringing came back to her now, and if ever there was a moment she needed to call upon God, it was now.

She closed her eyes and murmured the words of the Our Father. "Forgive us our trespasses as we forgive those who trespass against us."

But I don't forgive. I don't forgive the Ripper, who has murdered my friends and made my life a living hell. I don't forgive Tristan for being an asshole to me these last seven years. I don't forgive my parents for refusing to allow me to be anything other than their servant. I don't forgive Conal...

Perhaps that wasn't true. Conal had wounded her that day on the bridge, but likely not without reason. She could have tried harder to talk to him back then, could have expanded her social group beyond the popular kids, could have tried to see that being socially awkward was the kiss of death for a boy to whom no one had given a chance. And now she might have opened up to him, might have helped him more with the investigation.

He's been working himself into the ground to protect me and get us home and how have I responded? By not exactly making it easy for him, and for what reason? Because in high school he didn't show any interest in getting to know me. Because he didn't show up when we were supposed to go for a walk one night.

No, she wouldn't add Conal to the list of people who hadn't earned her forgiveness.

I'm at fault just as much as he is.

✳✳✳

Conal remained at the back of the Church. Maybe they should leave now. They were here, they could get the machine and go...but no. Mary had been good to them, it wouldn't be right to leave without telling her. Abby would never have it anyway.

Tomorrow it would be and no later. Whatever else happened, Conal promised himself that. Tomorrow they were going home.

Thirty-Six

This was the day. Conal knew it in his bones the moment he woke. The urgency grew in him all day. The Ripper would strike tonight, but with any luck, he and Abby would be long gone shortly after nightfall.

Abberline had called in extra men to search for Tumblety and to respond to all suspicious behavior.

When the night shift began, Abberline gathered the men closely around him.

"This is a big night for us. We believe the Ripper will strike again this night, or at least attempt to. We will thwart him in this effort. Every one of you must be alert, on your guard. We will stop him once and for all."

The station buzzed with activity. Abberline was briefing the constables about their duties as darkness crept over the city. A constable broke into the gathering, insisting on a word with Abberline.

Immediately after, he sought Conal. "James, I've just gotten word that Tumblety's been spotted. He was kicked out of a pub on Batty Street for exposing himself."

Conal's entire body stiffened in alert. "Who found him?"

Abberline pointed toward the man, who was now describing the scene to the other officers and briefing them on Tumblety's appearance.

Conal interrupted him.

"What direction was Tumblety headed, Constable? Was it toward Commercial? Near Miller's Court?"

"I believe so, sir."

"Right. Abberline, I'm going to Miller's Court. Pray I arrive there before he does."

Abberline's face was grave and drawn. If Tumblety was the murderer, this must end tonight. "James, take Smith with you."

"I'm faster by myself." Conal was already halfway out the door.

Smith caught up with him by the time he reached the street.

"I'm all right, Smith, go help Abberline."

"My orders are to accompany you."

What was the use in arguing? Soon enough it wouldn't matter anyway. "Fine. But you take orders from me out there and don't you dare slow me down."

Smith drove the carriage to Miller's Court. Conal leapt from the carriage before it had rolled to a stop. It was full dark now, and fog blanketed the streets. Night cloaked the Ripper's moves, but Conal sensed him. He was here.

"Smith, I want you patrolling these alleys."

"Sir..."

"You heard me. He could be watching us right now."

Adrenaline coursing through his body, Conal burst into the flat, where Abby had been tidying Mary's few possessions, a small act of gratitude before abandoning her.

"Conal? I thought we were supposed to meet later, at the bridge."

"Abby, we have to go now. There's no time for discussion. The Ripper will strike tonight and this was my one chance to get away from Abberline. The chance won't come again."

"What about Mary? We haven't told her we're leaving. I have to say goodbye. I have to warn her."

"Where is she?"

"She said she was going for a drink."

"Right now? It's not even six."

Abby spread her hands helplessly. "She's been under a lot of strain..."

"It doesn't matter. We have to leave."

Abby swallowed the lump in her throat.

"Please, Abby, we're wasting time. Smith is outside waiting for me. I sent him to check the alleys, but it's only a matter of time before he's poking his nose where it doesn't belong."

She refused to cry. Pressing her fingertips to her lips, she blew a silent kiss to her friend. *I'm so sorry, Mary. May angels protect you.*

There would be time for tears later.

Now it was time to run.

Together they sprinted through the streets, keeping to the shadows wherever possible. They cut through alleys, Abby following Conal, neither saying a word. He had carefully mapped out their route the night before, the one least likely to lead him back into Abberline's path. A twinge of pain had come at that. Conal would have liked to thank the man for all his help, but it was impossible. Abby wasn't the only one leaving a friend behind.

They neared a church when two men cut into their paths, running up an alley toward them. All four stood motionless in a standoff. The one was unfamiliar to Conal. The other was impossible to mistake. A mere ten yards away stood Francis Tumblety.

"There she is. Time for a cattle call. Did you miss me, little one?" Tumblety cackled, then whirled and ran in the distance. The other disappeared in the opposite direction.

Conal froze for a moment. He was right there. If Conal could overtake him, he could put an end to all of this for everyone, save Mary's life, and Abby's, too. But if he couldn't, they were both still vulnerable and Tumblety had reason to come after Conal, too. The smart thing to do would be to leave with Abby now, but Conal never was one for taking the easy way out.

"I'm sorry, Abby. I have to go after him. He's right there. If I can stop him..."

"Go! Hurry before he gets away." Abby knew it was a risk, but it needed to be done.

"Abby, keep walking straight. There will be a constable half a block to the right once the road curves. Wait for me there."

Conal's lungs burned to the point of bursting but he had to push on. He was younger than Tumblety and probably faster, but Tumblety knew the streets far more intimately.

Conal chased him through flats, diving through windows, swinging himself onto rooftops. There was no time for making apologies or wondering if the next leap would send him crashing to the ground. On and on they ran.

Then the sensations began.

Each time Conal leapt from one surface to another, his arms, right on cue, were turning red, his vision blurring slightly. He couldn't quite see the ground beneath him. It wasn't dizziness or vertigo. He just couldn't quite see.

Dammit! Not now!

But it wasn't blindness. His vision would refocus, and then the blur would set in again with the leaping motion. Maybe he had caught whatever Maybrick had. Could be anything. This town was rife with disease.

Conal flung himself across the next roof anyway, trusting his instincts over his failing eyesight. He crashed into a vegetable cart, which collapsed beneath his weight. Its foundation had already been weakened by Tumblety, who was already sprinting down the street. The last surge of adrenaline Conal had to give propelled him forward. Then they were a tangle of bodies. They rolled away from a horse as Tumblety bit at Conal's hands, his legs flailing wildly.

Two constables had been patrolling nearby. They jumped into the fray, throwing Tumblety to the ground and pinning him there with their boots and billy clubs. Tumblety's face was bloody and Conal's wasn't much better. His clothes were torn and his body throbbed.

But it was done. Tumblety would torture no one tonight.

Abby and the constable had heard the commotion. She screamed when she saw Conal.

They embraced, out of relief or fear or affection, it didn't matter. He clung to her as she had once held him, and she comforted him as he had her.

"You got him. It's over now. We can go home and Mary will be safe."

Abberline was there within minutes. "Well, James, you've done it. Got him just in time."

Conal coughed to catch his breath. "As long as he's the right guy."

Abberline patted him on the back. "You can take the night off, James. You've earned that much. But first you'll need to come down to the station for a report."

Conal looked to Abby. That could mean hours more before they were able to leave.

She nodded for him to go.

"Inspector, my sister saw the man as well before he ran from us."

Abberline turned to her. "Then we'll need you to come down as well."

Abby followed agreeably. What difference would a few more hours make, now that they were safe?

Thirty-Seven

M aybe it was meant to be that we were here. Maybe this was our purpose in life, to catch the Ripper, to save at least one person from dying."

Conal smiled at Abby beneath the yellowish lamplight. She was so optimistic when her life wasn't at risk.

"You don't think that's a little grandiose?"

She laughed. "Maybe. But don't you believe that we all have a purpose?"

"I do, but...if this was mine, why wasn't I able to save those other women?"

Abby grew quiet, but took his arm again.

"I don't know, Conal. But you can't blame yourself. You broke yourself trying to help them. You're not the one responsible for their deaths."

He didn't answer.

They walked slowly along the road to Miller's Court then looped back toward the church. If there were any officers still out tonight, Conal wanted to remain as inconspicuous as possible.

There would be no rest until they were home again and Whitechapel was truly behind them.

"Abby, have you been feeling all right? Have you felt...dizzy or disoriented or anything?"

"Not that I can remember. Why?"

He shook his head. "I've just been feeling a little out of sorts. Thought maybe a bug was going around."

"You haven't had a proper night's sleep since we got here. You must be exhausted, Conal."

"Yeah, that's probably it."

Abby giggled suddenly. "Look at what we're wearing."

She wore the red dress that Crooksie had given to her; he was still in his brown detective suit.

"Let's hope we land in a costume store when we get back because we're going to stick out like sore thumbs."

Conal laughed. "Somehow I think it will be easier to explain ourselves away in modern-day California than it was here."

"Abby, before we go back, there's something I wanted to tell you. Those things I said that day on the bridge, about high school and not wanting to know you when we're home...I didn't mean any of that."

"Conal, it's all right. I understand. I was kind of being way too emotional then. I just didn't want to hear it. I was upset that you thought so little of me, but it's...it's over now."

Conal paused a moment, then looked at Abby as he gathered his thoughts. *No, it's not. I think it's high time I tell you how I feel about you. I don't think I could bear the thought of going back to how things were.* "No, Abby, there's something I need to tell you. I should have just said it then, but if you let me explain..."

Abby whirled at the frantic sounds of a carriage behind them. The horses trotted ahead, then stopped short in front.

Walter Sickert, Sir William Gull, and Netley swept from the carriage.

"Uh, Abby, I'm going to need you to run."

"Wait, what?"

"Abby, go now. Run! Find Inspector Abberline and tell him I've been taken by Gull and Sickert. He'll know where to find me. Don't stop for anyone."

Netley was about to give chase but Abby was gone. Conal said a prayer of thanks that she had listened instead of arguing with him.

"Don't worry about the girl," Gull said. "We'll deal with her later."

Conal backed up as they gathered around him. "So what can I do for you ladies? How's that eye of yours, Sickert? Connected with a hard left, wasn't it? Or was it the right?" As they were about to grab Conal, he swung and connected once again. Sickert's knees gave out and once again he was out. You'd think this guy would have learned his lesson. Unfortunately, Conal soon followed. Conal felt Netley grab his arms, pull them behind his back, and then the sharp prick of a needle in his neck. Netley released Conal's arms. He and Gull watched Conal wobble a couple steps before collapsing to the ground, unconscious.

✳✳✳

Conal woke strapped to a table. It appeared to be some kind of rotating contraption. He struggled to lift his head just enough to see the room filled with several men that looked like doctors and at least three of the Royal Guard.

Sickert leered over him, his bruised, swollen eye hideous to behold. Gull was there, too.

As the haziness cleared, Conal saw that he was back in Colony Hatch Asylum where they kept Crooksie. He noticed there were others in the room as well, fifteen to twenty of them, all students observing whatever brand of torture was about to be doled out.

"What's your big plan, Gull? You going to put some balloons around me? Maybe put an apple on my head and throw knives at me?"

Gull simply chuckled. Conal wondered whether he was better or worse off than the victims who had come before. The men and women he'd seen himself dragged from their rooms, kicking and screaming. Knowing what was about to happen didn't make it any easier to take.

Gull flapped the lid of a hat in his hand, the grin never leaving his face.

"Mr. McWilliam, are you comfortable?" He asked it loudly enough for his students to hear.

Whatever happens, I won't die.

"We've been watching you, Detective. You may remember that the day you paid us a visit, one of our patients escaped from the hospital. That's very dangerous, for her, and for society."

"I thought you said it was a him."

"Mistakes can be made." The smile stayed on Gull's face and bloodlust was in his eyes.

"We had quite a difficult time not only finding her again, but determining how she got out. We can't have word about our experiments getting to the wrong people."

"Again? You found her? You have Annie Crook?"

Gull only laughed.

If Crooksie has been taken prisoner again, Mary might still be the one to leave with Alice. If Mary leaves with Alice and Crooksie is locked up, then the last body they find...

"Oh, Mr. McWilliam, how naïve. Did you really think you would get away with it, that you could help our patient escape and we wouldn't find her again? You're the amateur here, not us. Annie Crook is most desperately in need of our services."

"The only help she needs is getting away from you and that coward of a husband! Eddy, where are you? You coward! I know you're here. How can you stand by and let them do this?"

"Oh, I assure you it wasn't too difficult to figure out, with or without His Grace's consent. Miss Kelly has been frequenting Providence Row. Now what would a whore be doing in a convent?"

Conal closed his eyes.

Of course. Mary wasn't making arrangements for herself. She was visiting Crooksie.

"Miss Kelly led us right to Miss Crook. But now it's time to talk about you. I couldn't help but notice, Detective, what a lovely suit you're wearing. But I see you are without a hat. Now I ask myself, why would such a handsome suit come without a hat? Well, that made no sense, so we were gracious enough to find one for you." Gull began tapping the hat up and down the length of Conal's body.

A shiver ran down Conal's spine.

My own damned hat gave me away.

It was the exact one Abberline had given him when he donned the identity of Detective James McWilliam. And it was the exact one he had forgotten in a little utility closet in this very hospital, the day he had helped Crooksie escape.

Conal struggled to raise himself from the table. He could barely lift his head, but saw a figure at the door.

"Eddy! Get her out of here. Save her! Do one good thing with your goddamned life and save Crooksie!"

"Not another word, Detective."

"Sickert, is your only function to serve as Gull's thug?"

Gull raised a hand to silence Sickert.

"Now, Detective McWilliam, we begin. We'll send a series of electro-magnetic pulses to your brain. It's a test of your memory, of your brain's ability to stay intact under pressure."

Conal laughed. "Go ahead. It won't work. All your twisted experiments will prove to be a waste of time." *Anytime you want to show up, Abberline, I'm okay with it. Really!*

"Such confidence from a man strapped to a medical table. Put it in!" Gull ordered.

Someone grabbed Conal's jaw and he bit at them. He locked his jaw shut until they plugged his nose and he began gasping for air. He gagged on the block of wood they shoved into his mouth. For the first time, it wasn't Abby who seemed likely to die in London. It was him.

"Mr. Gull, sir, the Inspector is here and demands to see you immediately."

"Do it now," Gull ordered.

Conal's eyes widened as he tried to shout through the block of wood. *Inspector!*

Then he saw an assistant turn on the power lever and heard a loud hum as the contraption juiced up. The electricity began shooting into his body. Heat surged through Conal's body. Conal tensed, waiting for his memory to be erased and possibly worse, but the machine had no effect.

"Do it again!" Gull shouted.

Conal's arms began to glow but again, there was no effect.

"What? This can't be happening! Turn it up to maximum power!" Gull shouted.

Conal's hands shook and he fought off the spasms. Sparks shot out from the contraption and the overhead lights. Just as Conal began to smell smoke from the overheating machine, the power went out in the entire three story facility.

Conal didn't even breathe.

Hands moved over him in the pandemonium as voices screamed. Conal heard a desperate scramble in the darkness. The straps were loosened and Eddy's voice was in his ear.

"I will forever be ashamed for what I have done. Now go!"

Conal shoved past flailing, screaming bodies in the darkness. In the hall, someone grabbed his arm and dragged him away before he could shake himself free.

"James, it's me."

"Inspector, what the hell took you so long?"

"Tumblety has escaped!"

"What! We just got him."

"Would you like me to sit here and explain? He escaped, and now you must do the same, James. You must get to Mary and Julia."

"Thank you, Inspector."

By the time Conal reached the doors, a full-blown panic was ensuing and Abberline's men struggled to keep them at bay. The Royal Guard pushed past the officers only to be tangled up in P.C. Richins' grasp until he was eventually wrestled to the ground. Scotland Yard was no match for the Royal Guard.

✳✳✳

The silence had become more than Abby could bear. She had begun humming to herself to fill the flat with something cheerful but even the sound of her own voice frightened her.

Abberline had ordered her to stay inside after she told him where James had been taken. She'd heard nothing since then and Mary was still out doing God knows what.

Frightened, she hugged her knees to herself on the bed, rocking back and forth. That had always helped comfort her when she was a child.

She heard a scratching at the door. She tried to convince herself it was some kind of stray animal. Conal would be home soon. She'd not open the door for anyone else.

✳✳✳

Conal had run about three blocks, and his lungs were full to bursting when he saw an old farmer riding by on his horse and wagon.

"Hey! You, there. I need your wagon."

"'Who the hell are you? Bugger off." The farmer had a ruddy face and beady eyes, and from the looks of it, little enough respect for men of the law.

"I'm Detective James McWilliam of the City Police, and I'll have you thrown in the blackest hole I can find if you don't take me to Miller's Court right now."

"On what grounds?"

"Drive. Miller's Court or Scotland Yard, it's your choice."

The farmer glared at Conal but drove the carriage with a curse.

✳✳✳

Abby got up and put her ear against the door to see if she could hear anything. The scratches had stopped and it was silent for a minute. Abby's heart was pounding. She kept repeating to herself, "Please come home, Conal. Please come home, Conal." She prayed for even a constable to pass by. Then, with her ear pressed firmly up against the door, it was

298

as if someone was at the door the whole time, listening to her plea for Conal.

That's when she heard the laugh, low and menacing, dripping with malice.

"No, I'm just imagining things."

The laugh grew louder and suddenly glass shattered into the room. Abby dove to the bed, screaming. A gloved white hand pulled back out of the window.

The door had been unlocked and begin to open. A man stood in the doorway, large and looming. Abby couldn't see his face in the darkness but she knew it was him. She scrambled away, screaming. If she had promised herself not to become hysterical, that vow was broken. Tears streamed down her cheeks as she screamed Conal's name.

The silhouetted figure of a man in a deerstalker hat with a medical bag stood ominously in the doorway. With maniacal arrogance, he was toying with her. The more Abby feared him, the greater his pleasure.

Abby cried for help and scrambled around the fireplace, looking for anything in a hysteric attempt to find something to fend off her attacker. But she found nothing as she could hear the cold steel of a blade being drawn.

Conal's own shouting echoed down the street. He was out of the wagon and running now, screaming like a banshee.

The Ripper backed away, moving silently into the shadows.

Abby was nearly in shock when Conal reached her.

He dragged her off the floor and she collapsed against him.

"He was here, he was in the door, the window..."

Conal scanned the room and quickly looked around outside. "He's gone, Abby, and we have to go, too. Forget the Ripper, forget Mary, everything. The Queen's men are after me and they'll be here soon. We need to get the hell out of here now."

She whimpered against him.

Where the hell was the horse? Never mind. "Abby, we have to run. We're going home now, but I need you to stay with me."

He took her hand and they ran for their lives.

Thirty-Eight

The prostitutes were circling the church. Tonight they were out in full force since news of the Ripper's arrest had broken. Conal wanted to tell them he had escaped, that they weren't as safe as they thought they were, but there was no time.

He slowed to a walk when they approached St. Boltoph's and held Abby's hand tightly. "Act happy. We're less suspicious if we look like a happy couple."

Abby said nothing.

"Don't look anyone in the eye."

The Royal Guard were too good. Their humble lovers routine wasn't fooling anyone. A shout from one and they were on them, pushing through the prostitutes to accost Conal one final time.

A woman grabbed Abby. "Front doors are locked, lovey. The side's likely to be open."

Conal pulled Abby toward the side. *Keep up, keep up.* "The room at the back! That's where the machine should be. Go turn it on while I hold the door."

Conal scrambled to shove a pew in front of the door. "God, I'll do a thousand 'Our Fathers' if you get me out of this."

The blood rushed to his head and he had to clutch the pew to keep from falling. "Oh shit!" *Not now.*

✳✳✳

The voice in Abby's head kept her focused. *Keep it together. Only a few more feet, and were going home. So close...home...*

She raced through the church, yanking open the door to a long hallway. At the end of it, the time machine stood waiting for them.

"It's here," she sobbed. "Oh my God, Conal, it's here."

"Turn it on! I'm right behind you."

"What, Conal? What do I do?" Abby had run all the way back. The doors to the church came crashing open as Conal fell to the ground. There were six or seven guards climbing the pew.

"Run!"

Conal stood up and began to run, his surroundings beginning to blur again. When he looked down, it looked as though he was running his fingers across a still pond.

"No, no, not now." He slapped his face to shake it off.

The guards were right behind Conal. He could hear them yelling. Conal's arms once again lit up like glow sticks. He refused to submit to a heart attack or some strange stroke before he got Abby home.

"Conal, come on!"

He staggered down the hallways, following the sound of Abby's voice.

Abby reached for his hand, for a brief second in awe of his hands and arms, pulling him the last few steps. *So hot. Too much heat.*

"This is it," he yelled above the sound. "Think of home and don't let go."

The instant they grabbed the machine, it shook and vibrated as the world spun, just as it had the first time. Their entire bodies jolted and ripped with the force.

Conal struggled to hold on to the machine, let alone Abby. Whitechapel was gone and they were once again hurtling through time.

"Hold on tight!" he shouted above the noise. His voice was carried off.

"I'm losing it!"

"Hold on to me!"

One of Abby's hands lost its grip. It was as though an invisible force was dragging her away. Conal's grasp on Abby's other hand was the only thing keeping her connected. It felt like a hurricane. Abby was slipping away. Conal read the terror in her eyes.

She couldn't get a grasp. The force was too strong. Conal could feel the muscles in his arm pulling, nerves, tendons being torn and stretched and still he could not pull her back.

"Conal, please, don't leave me!"

Her final scream echoed as she was torn from Conal's hands and flung into time.

When Conal woke, he was lying in a field of marigolds, near present-day Santa Barbara. Alone.

✳✳✳

PRESENT DAY:

"So this is why you stay so secluded? You blame yourself?"

"It's my fault, Edie."

Edie kept her response to herself for the moment, simply shaking her head. "And this case of the Ripper...it was never solved?"

"No...no, there were many suspects but...that's another thing that kills me. That monster was allowed to go free."

Edie sat back with a comforting pat on Conal's hand.

"What did you say the inscription on that watch was?"

"*Tempus Omnia Revelat.* It's Latin. I believe it means 'Life Is Revealing.'"

Edie laughed and shook her head.

"What's wrong?" Conal rubbed his red eyes, trying to collect his emotions.

"Oh it's nothing. It's just, you have the translation wrong. It's Latin all right, but it means, 'Time Reveals All.'"

Conal laughed, a short, choked sound.

"Time Reveals All, huh? There's something cryptic about it when you read it like that."

Edie shifted in her seat. "Yes, well, it's time I headed home and left you with your thoughts. Thank you, Conal, for the gift of your story. I believe you'll find Abby and you will be together again someday."

"Me, too." Conal's chest felt as though it was made of lead. "Let me walk you home."

They crossed the street together arm in arm. The roads were slick and the air around them was damp. When they reached Edie's door, she embraced Conal, her hug strangely fierce for such a small body.

"You will see her again, Conal. I know you will."

Spilling his guts to Edie had done nothing to help Conal's nightmares. If anything, they were worse tonight, visions of a trapped and terrified Abby mingling with those of blood and corpses from so many centuries ago.

At 2 a.m. he gave up sleeping and headed for his study. Sparks of the old obsession prodded him, no matter how he willed them away, that crazy, driving desire to catch this bastard and put him away forever.

Conal turned Maybrick's watch over and over in his hands, mindlessly fondling the faded metal.

"*Tempus Omnia Revelat...*Time Reveals All..." He murmured the words to himself as he flipped the pages of books, hoping something would jump out, a clue that hadn't occurred to him the first three hundred times he had combed these pages.

One contained old photographs of all of the victims. His heart lurched as he recognized them, remembered the stories Mary and Abby had told of them. Living, breathing women who had had their lives stolen from them.

Then he turned his attention back to the suspects. One of these men had committed the murders. He was sure of it. But who?

It was 5:00 a.m. and Conal was banging on Edith's door. He knock for about ten minutes till she opened up.

"Good heavens what has gotten into you, Conal?"

"Can I come in?" Conal asked as a let himself in like a man with newfound purpose.

"Well, I'm up now, you might as well come in. Have you been up all night?

He started right in. "There was a time when I suspected Joseph Barnett, but I had seen enough of him to know he was a drunken coward. In his twisted way, he loved Mary, to an extreme, perhaps, but not the kind of extreme that forces a man to kill. Even if he had killed the women because of their so-called 'whorish influence' on Mary, why bother killing everyone to keep them away from Mary and when they're finally out of her life, kill Mary anyway? That makes no sense.

"And then there was George Chapman. This suspect is an odd one, because Abberline never spoke about this guy. He was just a leftover file on the table. Apparently, Abberline ended up pursuing this guy after Abby and I left. Chapman was definitely a murderer, this guy murdered his three wives. But he committed those killings with poison, not knives. He wasn't the gruesome killer the Ripper was. He did it cleanly. Abberline had acted so sure of this one in his old age, according to reports.

When Abberline was on his death bed, he said he knew it was Chapman. I'm not buying it, though. If Abberline had truly believed in Chapman's guilt, he would have said so long before he was on his deathbed." Conal felt sorry for Abberline. The Ripper had haunted him the rest of his life, too.

A pain surged in Conal's chest when he thought of Francis Tumblety. He remembered Tumblety's cruel eyes peering at him through the bars of his jail cell, the way disgust dripped from his voice when he spoke of women.

There were the uteruses, of course. There was every reason to believe Francis Tumblety had been the Ripper...but somehow, after all that, it felt wrong. It was too easy.

Any icy chill spread through his body as realization dawned.

"So that brings me to this watch. James Maybrick. Maybrick's wife, Flory, was having an affair and wasn't shy about it. Maybrick began an affair of his own. With how broken their relationship had been, he must have been humiliated, and beneath that, enraged.

"At Annie Chapman's body, the Ripper had left a note with the letter 'M.' He had removed Annie's wedding rings, the last tokens she carried of her dead husband.

"The scene of Kate Eddowes' murder had yielded a small tin containing a strand of cotton. Maybrick had been a cotton merchant. Coincidence? I don't think so.

"Son of a bitch." Conal muttered as the air whooshed from his lungs. He swallowed hard, recalling the images he'd seen of Mary Kelly's death. He knew now that Mary Kelly had truly been the last victim, since Abby, who history knew as Julia, had been swept back through time.

Mary Kelly had been left without a face, her smooth skin, dancing eyes, and lovely lips all gouged away by a cruel, purely evil, shattered monster.

Conal opened a book. "I found the image in one the books from my library." He steeled himself, forcing himself to look again.

"And then I saw it. In the background of one of the photographs, the initials FM were marked on the wall. FM! Flory Maybrick! Maybrick's wife!"

Mary's beauty had been torn away, destroyed, her heart cut from her chest. What Maybrick couldn't bring himself to do to the mother of his children, he did to the other women.

"Oh dear God." Edie was horrified.

"It all makes sense. He played games. The letter 'M,' the leather apron he left behind to incriminate Pizer, and he wrote of it as his game in his letter. The two V's were an upside down version of an 'M.' The word we thought was 'JUWES' written on the wall, wasn't the word 'JUWES' at all. He wrote 'JAMES.' We just read it wrong. He even referred to it as his little 'Jewish joke.'

"Lastly the watch. "Time Reveals All"—another play with words. He wanted us to know, he was telling us time reveals all of the victims and the truth. He wasn't speaking figuratively, he meant literally. I pried the back of this watch open with a knife. Inside, he'd scratched into the metal, 'I am Jack,' his signature James Maybrick, and the initials of every victim, including Mary Kelly, before he actually murdered her. He knew he was going to kill her before he did it. He was watching her the whole time. Even the name Jack was a clue: the first and last letters in his name. JAmes maybriCK. This was all one twisted puzzle he wanted us to figure out.

"I hope this brings you some peace of mind, Conal. After everything you went through, you need this closure."

Conal could rest easier now, but peace came with a heavy heart. He had lived to discover the identity, but all those women had known it long before he did. James Maybrick's had been the last face they had seen in this world, just before he killed them.

Thirty-Nine

"Well, Conal, you've solved one of the great mysteries of our time. What are you going to do about it?"

Was she being sarcastic? He couldn't tell. For a woman her age, Edie was sharp and her words could have a bite.

She smiled at him.

"I'm not teasing you, Conal. This discovery...it's very important to you, I know. But what are you going to do with it?"

Conal kneaded his hands together then tugged at the ends of the sleeves of his long gray hoodie. It was a nervous habit he had developed in grade school.

"I'm going to call Scotland Yard. Maybe someone there will still care."

"Do you think it's going to matter?" Edie asked quietly.

Conal held her gaze a moment.

"Maybe not to anyone now, no. It will probably just be some cheap tabloid story that gets picked up by the nightly news and forgotten in a few weeks. But...I have to believe it matters somehow. If they're out there somewhere, maybe it will put the souls of Mary Kelly, Annie Chapman, and all the others to rest."

Edie wrapped her blue cable-knit sweater about her as though she had a chill. Sunlight filtered through her kitchen window and framed her face. For a moment, Conal could see that Edie had once been beautiful.

"You're a good man, Conal Benjamin."

"Am I, Edie? I lost her. And I let all of those women down. I let them die. What difference will it really make? Even if I'm right...even if it is Maybrick that killed them...even if somewhere they can rest knowing that their murderer was revealed...they're still dead. They died because I wasn't fast enough or strong enough to stop him. And the worst part is, I'm not even sure it was worth it. I left Whitechapel behind so I could get Abby out of there and I lost her anyway. Yeah, I'm a hell of a guy."

Edie reached forward and gripped his arm tightly, with more strength than he would have expected. Her angelic expression from only moments earlier was now one of intensity, almost anger.

"You listen to me, Conal. You did what you could to save those women. Did it ever occur to you that maybe you weren't meant to save them? That they were dead before you arrived? You had already read the history books. You knew their fates by heart. If you want to beat yourself up over something, let it be that you couldn't accept that harsh truth, not that you didn't try to save them. Then turn your attention to right here and now, because this time, you can change the future."

Then she was hugging him, holding him the way his mother had done, once again he was helpless as a child.

"I've got to find her, Edie," he murmured into the old woman's hair.

As the month passed, Conal tore himself apart over Abby. He lay in bed at night, exhausted but terrified of sleep, when he saw her falling away from him, always into the same horrific place. He would wake drenched in sweat, sheets soaked through from his night terrors.

Conal kept the time machine and labored over it every spare moment. He took pieces apart and put them back together, never to any avail. He was heartsick, desperate. Abby filled his thoughts constantly.

Where was she? Was she even alive? Conal prayed that was the case, though he had no reason to believe she would be any safer lost in another decade, another century. Serial killers existed in all societies, and sometimes worse.

He had to bring her home.

Reclusive, Conal stopped seeing the few friends he claimed to have. It was his younger brother who prodded him out of the house, and then only to his parents' place. His brother Casey had a new girlfriend and insisted on getting his brother's seal of approval.

That dinner had been torturous. While Casey and his new girlfriend held hands and told stories, Conal fought the urge to scream or put a hole through the wall. If this was a preview of the rest of his life, grinning and bearing it through family get-togethers where he was the only one miserable and carrying the most twisted secret he could imagine, he wanted no part of it.

But for today, he would do it for Casey. Why shouldn't his brother be happy? He'd have to do the living for both of them, since Conal's world shrunk a little more each passing day.

If Casey noticed Conal's unhappiness, he said nothing about it. Nor did their father. The same couldn't be said for Conal's mom. She could always tell when something was bothering him. She knew Conal was distant, and before it put a damper on anyone's night, she let Casey and his girl visit with Dad. "Come on, Conal. I could really use some fresh air. Come and keep your mama company on the porch."

"All right, Mom, I'm coming." Conal excused himself from the table.

The two sat on the porch and right away she started in.

"Okay, Conal, what's going on? Hon, I can tell something's on your mind."

"Oh, Mom, I don't think you'd believe me if I told you. In fact, I wouldn't believe me if I told me! You're going to think I'm nuts."

"Conal, in case you forgot, you're my son. I know you wouldn't lie to me and I already know you're crazy, it's in the blood." She smiled and reminded him that she'd always been there for him.

So Conal told her. The moment he said the words time machine, she opened the screen door. "Hon, we'll be right back. We're going to walk our food off." She looked at Conal's Dad. "You going to be okay in here, honey?"

"We'll be fine."

"Walk with me, Conal. Your old mother misses you, you know. So tell me, does this have anything to do with why you haven't come to see us for months?"

She looped an arm through Conal's as they walked along the greenbelt that weaved through the neighborhood. Conal's heart lurched passing the familiar homes, mustering waves to faces from his childhood that had grown old, but remained sweet, comforting.

He spent the next few minutes telling Mom the short version about what happened with the time machine and Abby. The words poured from him then and he was a child again, desperate for his mother's reassurance. Adult Conal knew his mother couldn't change what had happened, couldn't make everything better, but what he wouldn't have given for that to be the case.

"She's gone, Mom, and it's my fault."

"Oh, Conal, it sounds to me like it's not your fault. It couldn't be helped."

"Yes it is, Mom. You don't understand. You don't know what it's like to lose someone. If I had done some things different, I..."

"Conal Benjamin, you stop right there. How do you know what my experience with loss is?"

Once, Conal had thought he'd settle down and marry someone, maybe move into a place in this same neighborhood as his folks so his children could be close to their grandparents.

"I'm sorry, Mom. You just don't get it. I don't deserve that. I'm not fit for any of that. I'm nothing more than a pathetic shell of a man.

His mother stopped him, took his shoulders, and turned him toward her.

"What's happened to you? My goodness, you require a lot of patience. You're not the only Benjamin with a crazy story, you know."

"What do you mean? I don't get it."

"Believe it or not, there is a story or two I haven't told you, and I think now is as fitting a time as any to tell you one in particular. Your Father and I were coming home from your grandparents, and it was pouring rain pretty hard. Well, your father was driving. The rain was so heavy we could barely see five feet in front of us. Your Dad must've hit a pot hole or something because we ended up getting a flat. Well, even though we were okay, we were still stuck. There we were in the middle of nowhere, in the rain with a flat tire.

"He told me to stay in the car, but I was stubborn and wouldn't listen. It was pitch dark except for the lightning. Certainly he couldn't hold a flashlight and change a tire. I was convinced that he needed me, and I wasn't going to be told otherwise. I grabbed the umbrella and flash light. When your father was finishing up, I closed up the umbrella was headed back into the car. Before I took one more step, I felt the most incredibly painful amount of energy surge through my body in a flash and then I blacked out."

"You're kidding, what happened?

"Well I didn't know it then, but we had been struck by lightning."

"You and Dad both?"

"No, Conal." She paused to take Conal's hand and looked seriously into his eyes. "You and I were. If I remember correctly, I was twenty weeks pregnant with you, Conal. Your poor father...he was brilliant. He got us back in the car and on the road, rode us right off the tire jack. When I came to, I was lying in a hospital bed, and your father's head was lying on my belly. When he saw that I was awake, we both started to cry."

"People think it may have been the umbrella or the flashlight being out in the open. I started to panic and asked him about you and what had happened. He told me, and the very second he said we had been struck by lightning, you kicked."

"You're kidding!"

"Nope, God's honest truth. Of course, I was already emotional because of the pregnancy anyway, so that didn't help matters much. Anyway, maybe it was only for a short time, but both your father and I know what it's like to have the fear of losing a loved one."

"Wow, Mom, I had no idea. Why didn't you ever tell me?"

"Well, I didn't want it to be anything to worry about unnecessarily."

As they arrived back at the house, she said, "You know, son, there are plenty of things in the world that we don't know about, and I'm no scientist, but you told me that time travel has something to do with light and energy. What if you've been spending all this time on that machine and it's not the machine that sent you back in time?"

"What are you saying, it's me?" I laughed at her.

"Well, I don't know, Conal. You're the scientist. I'll leave that to you to figure out. I'm just saying you see it all the time on TV. Psychics, horse whisperers, dog whisperers, I mean really... people talking to animals and contacting the dead, there's even stories of people lifting cars because of adrenaline. We all would have thought those were crazy until they happened. Conal, if what you did is true, and I believe it is, then why not?"

Conal's heart leapt, and his mind scrambled to calculate this information. "Were there any...effects...of us being struck that you're aware of, Mom?"

"Not obvious ones, no. But I always sensed there was something...lightning never frightened you, Conal. You were drawn to electricity."

"Okay, Mom, now you do sound crazy."

"Yeah, that's what your father says. I love you, son. Just be careful."

"I love you, too, Mom. Thanks."

They headed up the steps. "Don't you worry. I'm sure you'll figure this whole thing out. Come on, let's go inside and save that poor girl from your father's stories."

His head swam. Thoughts spun in his head, hysterical thoughts. He drove home in a daze that night, wondering about his own sanity.

Could it be true?

The blurred vision, the jolts of electricity, the red glowing in his hands and arms, the thrumming in his fingers.

Am I the time machine?

315

Forty

After Conal's visit back home, he began to think of the many memories he'd never thought twice about before. Things from the past that had even confused himself; things that seemed odd or coincidental. Electrical malfunctions like his alarm clock not going off, the car spontaneously dying, power outages. His hands glowing bright red with that burning sensation. He obsessed over books about Einstein and his time travel theories and then examined the time machine again and again, going through all the steps he had taken the first time he traveled. Conal didn't know if it was out of sheer desperation or maybe he just needed to have hope in something other than this damn time machine, but he decided to consider his mom's theory. As unrealistic as it was, Conal had to at least try. If nothing else, he wanted to be open to anything when it came to getting Abby back.

Conal sat down on a large tool bench in the garage and put his arms straight out in front of him, trying to put energy into his hands. He tried everything, growling and grunting, summoning up all the energy he had inside, and unleashing all of the energy he thought he had. He tried again and again to focus his energy. Then he tried making a fist and clenching it really tight. Still nothing.

Nothing! Nothing! Nothing! Frustrated, he shouted, threw tools and knocked books off the shelves. "WHY?" He walked into the bedroom and threw his shirt on the bed. "I just need to calm down before I destroy this house. Just calm down, take a shower, and go to bed!" He stared at himself in the mirror, trying to rationalize and calm down. He could feel his blood boiling. "How could you let her go? How?" With one enraged cry of, "WHY?!" he swung his right fist down as hard as he could. The lights in the entire house went out. He had created the blur. He saw the same type of blurry hands dragging on a still lake. He stood there in the dark, with both hands glowing red, shaking. He looked at them in amazement.

"Holy..." His hands and arms lit up to his elbows. It was like striking a match? It faded away pretty quickly and he didn't travel through time, but this gave him hope. "I don't believe it! Mom was right!" He now knew it could be done. This was the way.

Over the next few months he studied what he knew already in even deeper detail. Eventually Conal got to the point where he started controlling this energy. He discovered that the energy started within his gut and his heart. Literally, he felt his heart getting hotter and hotter, like putting logs on a fire, only his insides weren't baking, in fact, he was easily able to take it. "That's probably why Gull wasn't able to electrocute me."

However, unlike Conal, the cul-de- sac wasn't able to take the surge of energy very well. They had power outage after power outage, and somewhere over three hundred light bulbs had gone out. It got so serious the electric company and the fire department had to come out for safety inspections. He felt bad for ruining Edith's lights, so he always made sure to buy hers.

He went step by step, trying to do more each time. He would sit there all day and try to force the energy out through to his hands. It was the most incredible feeling. His next struggle was creating a circle with the energy. To create a wormhole in time to travel through, he would need to create a continuous circle of energy. Each time Conal tried to get the energy to go in a circular motion, his hands would go cold, like blowing out a candle. It felt like he was trying to pull start an old lawn mower.

He picked up books on yoga, breathing techniques, martial arts, and boxing. He needed to focus on relaxing, breathing, and hand speed. Conal worked at it around the clock. His newfound hope was like an addiction, he didn't go anywhere, do anything, or talk to anyone. Staying in, ordering delivery, staying up late, getting up early. He hadn't even spoken two words to Edith.

In the beginning, his arms and hands were sore and tired, but gradually his tolerance grew, and after months of hard work and determination, he did it. He created his first wormhole! "Finally!" It looked like a big five foot puddle of clear water on it's side, slowly turning, but this wasn't water, this was space and time.

Still he didn't go in. It wasn't that simple. Bringing Abby back was going to require a plan and he needed to know more about this, he couldn't just jump in aimlessly.

The more he studied, the more he learned. The wormhole gave him between fifteen and twenty-five seconds before it closed, and although the energy and heat seemed to protect his arms from damage, he still couldn't do this in succession. Conal had one shot at it a day, maybe two. He made as many preparations as he could to bring Abby back.

Weeks went by. Conal walked over to Edith's.

"Come on in, Conal."

"Thanks, Edie. Brought ya some more light bulbs."

"Thank you, dear. You don't have to keep doing that, you know."

Conal laughed. "I do, trust me. And it's no problem.

"Wait! You found a way to go back, didn't you?"

When Conal stopped speaking, he found that Edie was holding his hand. "I couldn't hold her." Sadness with a twinge of anger covered Conal's face. "I should have let go of the machine and went after her."

"Oh, Conal, dear," she murmured. Her wrinkled skin was warm and soothing to the touch, oddly comforting, though Conal felt an empty pit in his chest, as if his heart had been ripped out.

"That's the first time I've ever said it all out loud," he whispered. He was surprised to find himself short of breath.

"Do you have any idea where she is? "

Conal exhaled slowly. "I do."

"I think you'd better sit down and explain." Edie reached for the porcelain tea pot with the faded pink roses that had been painted on years ago. They had begun to wear away after decades of use. Edie had brewed a pot of good English tea when Conal had appeared on her doorstep at 6:30 in the morning, unable to keep the news of his discovery to himself a moment longer. Edie was his only friend, the only person he could share this with.

Conal almost refused the tea until he remembered how much Abby had loved tea, one of the small things he had learned about her in their short time together. Maybe it would give him luck, or something like that.

He accepted the cup as he took his seat again. "I saw her."

"You...what? How?"

"I've got to go get her."

Edie pulled back. "Go get her?" Her voice dropped to a whisper. "You know where Abby is?"

Edie backed her way toward a chair and allowed herself to drop into it.

"The weird thing about time traveling is bits of time pass in front of you, almost what you might think having your life flash before your eyes is like or watching a big movie reel, only it's all around you. Anyway, when she slipped, I saw where she went."

Edith just sat there with a worried look on her face.

"She's in Nazi Germany, Edith. I saw Nazi flags all around, and as soon as she let go, she became part of the picture, a part of time. A part of that time until it disappeared. I've had the same reoccurring nightmare about what I saw like I did when I crashed my truck into that pole. It's always the same thing and always just for a moment, bombs dropping, and there's a man—he has her—she was terrified of him."

"I hate to sound a little negative, Conal, but how are you going to find her? World War II covered a lot of places over a long period of time. How will you know where to find her?"

"It's okay, Edie, that's a good question. For over two years now, I've been digging up old periodicals and books, praying that somehow Abby was smart enough to get herself in a picture somehow, letting me know where she is." I scooted close beside Edie and slid a book from my lap to hers, WORLD WAR II IN PICTURES, page 214. "Holding the hands of the two children. That's her. She's in 1940. She's in Nazi Germany."

The color drained from Edie's face. "No," she whispered. "Conal, you can't go there. The risk is too great. What if you're wrong? What if she's already..."

320

"Dead?" Conal shook his head vehemently. "No. She's not. Even if she was, I owe it to her to bring her back here. But she's not dead. She is in danger, though, and I'm the only person who can get to her."

"How will you get there? I thought you didn't know how the time machine worked. Have you fixed it?"

Conal gnawed the inside of his lip. If Edie believed him up to this point, no reason not to trust her now. "Edie, it's me. I'm the time machine."

He slowly explained the story his mother had told him, and about the blurring vision, the heat in his hands.

Once he had realized it was him, not the hunk of scrap metal, he had done everything imaginable to harness the power. Seeing as he had no real reference for how to handle this, he had guessed his way along, using breathing exercises, yoga, anything to learn to control his thoughts.

Seeing Abby in the rainstorm put him over the edge. He couldn't wait any longer. It was time to find her.

"Conal, you can't go there. It's a horrible place. You don't know the loss and devastation you're getting yourself into. You may not make it back."

"I'll be safe, Edie. If I'm not, it's better than staying here and wondering what if and knowing she's in danger."

Edie's shoulders stiffened. "Then I guess there's nothing else to say." A tear slipped down Edie's cheek. "Won't even stay for a lonely old woman?"

Conal resolved to stay strong. He couldn't afford to fall apart.

"I'll be back, Edie. You can't get rid of me that easily."

Ripping the photo from the book, Conal hugged Edie once more. "I'll be all right Edie...you take care of yourself, all right?"

"I'm not going to die, Conal, if that's what you're worried about," she said with a teary smile. "I'm not going anywhere until you come back." Her face would be the image he held in his mind, his connection to the present, when he gave in to his power and slipped once more through time.

THE BENJAMIN CHRONICLES

ANGEL OF DEATH

Matthew DiConti

ONE

The burn spread through Conal's body, beginning in his heart and surging through his legs, arms, belly, chest. The balls of his feet stung as he stumbled forward as he landed.

He righted himself and waited for his vision to clear. *Looks like I'm getting the hang of this*, he thought wryly.

The red glow on Conal's hands and arms dissipated and the blurriness began to recede. He could see that he was in a field. To his left, a small herd of cows grazed lazily. One of them stared at him and let out a pretty loud moo. There was moisture in the air and the ground was soft where he walked. A rainstorm had passed through not too long ago. It couldn't have been more than a couple of degrees above freezing. At the edge of the field, a forest grew that crept up the base of a mountainside. Conal spotted a winding dirt road, smoke curling upward from the forest.

None of this was helpful. Cows and trees couldn't tell him when he had landed. A person, a newspaper, he'd take anything right now. He needed to be sure he had done this correctly.

He shook the dirt off of his clothes "Let's see how close I am to Germany, 1940." He tracked the smoke down about a half of a mile into the woods. It was a downed fighter plane. It was a British Spitfire. The Brits produced more of these than any other fighter plane.

The cockpit was empty. No pilot? "He's gotta be here somewhere."

Conal scanned the surrounding area. Whoever it was, he had likely ejected before the crash.

Sure enough, the second Conal looked up, there was the pilot's body caught in the trees, by his chute. "Hey, man! Are you okay? Don't move, I'm going to get you down. There was no response. Conal repeated a couple more times.

"Hey! Can you hear me? I'm coming up!"

Still there was no response. Branch by branch, Conal made his way up the tree and got a closer look. The pilot's face and hands were pale blue.

It made it easier that he was already dead. None of his blood had been shed, most likely his neck had broken upon impact.

The sounds of vehicles trembled in the distance. There wasn't much time. Conal cut the man down, said a quick prayer asking whoever was listening to show him some forgiveness as he stripped the body, and covered it with leaves beneath a fallen tree. "Sorry, pal, but this uniform is going to help me a lot more than it'll help you, now," he told the corpse. "I promise I'll wear it well. Rest in peace." The sounds of the vehicles went silent, signaling that whoever shot down that Spitfire was upon him. Conal quickly snatched the dog tags, hung them around his neck and headed out.

Conal moved quickly through the woods, staying low to the ground, attempting to cover his tracks as he went. Someone in the distance behind him began shouting, but Conal kept moving forward.

The shouting got closer. That's when the bullets began to fly.

Conal raced up the hill, shots zipping through the leaves and bushes, carving up the trees.

Zip! Zip! They passed by again and again. Not looking back, not pausing to breathe, running desperately for his life. Conal could hear the voices of Nazis. It was surreal. The fear of reality hadn't completely sunk in until he felt the clean air of a bullet toss up his hair.

Where the hell am I going? Everything looked the same. There were no paths, no clear ways out of the thick forest. Dense timber surrounded him and for a moment he wondered if perhaps he had made a mistake about coming when he did.

His feet flew from under him as the ground beneath him disappeared. Suddenly he was falling, rolling, tumbling down a hillside he would later estimate to be fifty feet high. The impact reverberated throughout his body. He stifled a groan as he rolled himself beneath the cliff, out of sight of his pursuers.

"*Hier! Hier! Denken Sie, dass ich ihn habe!*"

Conal closed his eyes, focusing on their words. "Over here! Over here! I think I got him!"

A couple of positives out of nearly taking a bullet or two is they were speaking German, so it was likely he was at least in Europe, and given the current circumstances, he had to be pretty close in his time travel, and most importantly, everything was translating. Among World War II warfare, maps, and basic survival skills, Conal had spent months on audio lessons and advanced books learning to speak Russian, French, and German, mostly German for obvious reasons, and he was pretty confident that any American accent would be undetectable, but he was in no hurry to find out.

"There's no one here, you idiot! For all we know, he's long gone and you have us chasing some animal.

"Remind me never to take you hunting for deer. You'll end up chasing rabbits the whole time! We must get back."

"I swear he was right here."

The soldiers were no more than five feet from Conal. One of the soldiers paused for a minute, turning in all directions, poking at leaves and branches, fishing for anything to prove he wasn't chasing forest animals.

"Let's go, you idiot!

"I swear, you're useless! I should shoot you instead."

Conal waited several minutes till the shouting receded to move again, until there was no sound from another living soul. He spent the next hour climbing back up the cliff, finding and slipping from footholds until he was back in the forest. Twilight was nearly upon him and he needed to find the main road before he spent the night in the dark.

When he found it, headlights cut through the dimness. Instinct told him to take cover in the woods until it got close enough for him to tell it wasn't a German military vehicle.

His chest deflated with relief when he saw the vehicle bore no military markings.

He waved his hands wildly.

"Stop! Stop! Please stop!"

The car slowed as it got closer. He saw it was a convertible black and white 1938 Mercedes-Benz 230 Cabriolet. Whoever these people were, they likely came from some wealth.

A man who looked to be in his fifties sat in the driver's seat. A woman sat next to him. Both eyed Conal warily.

He was about to approach when the woman said something inaudible to the man and he picked up speed, zooming past Conal.

Conal ran his hands through his hair, frustration building in his chest. Then he noticed the marks that riddled the back hood of the car. "Bullet holes." *Who could blame them for not giving me a lift?*

He began walking in the direction the car had gone, resigned to a hitchhiker's plight if that's what it took to find Abby.

For the first time since arriving, Conal's thoughts shifted from his own survival to his plan to get Abby back. At the moment, it was a bit thin. He was increasingly sure he was on the right continent and in the right time, but that was it. She could be anywhere.

When the first rain drops hit him, he laughed. "Wonderful! That's just what I need. It's not like I didn't know this wasn't going to be easy," he said aloud to no one in particular.

He kept walking and the rain kept coming. Hours passed and he forgot about the cars, the road, the suspicious sight he would make trudging along in this soldier's uniform, alone. He was shivering so hard and lost in thoughts of Abby that he barely heard the car that pulled up beside him.

He was on his fourth attempt to form a smoke ring with his breath in the cold when a man's voice startled him back to reality.

The old man spoke in a gruff British accent. "Are you RAF?"

Conal jumped at the sound. "RAF?" *What the hell is...oh, right. Remember yourself, Benjamin. Royal Air Force.* "Yes sir. My plane went down a few miles back."

Praying his imitation of a British accent would pass muster, Conal did his best to put on an innocent but valiant face. A woman and a young girl were also in the car, probably a wife and daughter. No need to give this guy the idea he was unsafe to have around the family.

"I don't think you'll find any bases out here, but you can ride in back to where we're going," the man said.

Conal accepted the offer gratefully. He made his way along the wooden side rails to the back of the pick up. There were three people already sitting there. Conal gave them a hesitant smile.

"Hi there. I really appreciate the lift."

No one would make eye contact with him. For a moment, sarcasm flared and he considered sharing his day with them. *Don't mind me people, I just traveled through time, walked five miles in the rain, outran gun-wielding Nazis and may or may not have gotten a dirty look from a cow.* He kept his thoughts to himself, remembering that they were likely scared and traumatized. He had been here a few hours and at least had the benefit of knowing how it all turned out on his side. War was their reality.

Conal surveyed his fellow passengers as discreetly as possible. One was a huge, hulking creature who looked like he could have been a heavyweight champion. The man's jaw was large and strong and he had a thick nose that looked as though it had been broken a few times. His hair was a close-cut cap of red flames, and from the looks of how his legs were curled up in the space, he was as tall fellow.

A woman curled against the giant man and Conal noticed that both wore rings on their left hands. Husband and wife, no doubt. A small, thin boy sat next to them. A son, perhaps. He looked the least skittish, so Conal decided to take his chances.

He drew the photo of Abby from a pocket where he had secured it in his stolen uniform and held it in front of the boy.

"Hey, kid, excuse me. Do you speak English? Can you ask your mom and dad if they've seen this woman? Do you know where this was taken?"

The boy tilted his face ever so slightly toward Conal, glanced at the picture and looked away.

"Was that a yes, no?" He shouldn't have been so impatient with the kid, he knew, but dammit, why couldn't anyone at least look at him?

"Has anyone...seen...this...woman?" Conal spoke slowly, hoping something would click since they didn't seem to speak English. He thrust the photo back toward the boy. It was a clipping from a *WWII IN PICTURES* book he had purchased in the bargain bin at the local bookshop. The photo was of Abby holding the hands of two little girls outside of a large brick building that resembled a church. The picture was quickly passed to the couple. How many hours had he spent searching for this, a photo of Abby somewhere in this awful mess?

The red-haired man remained expressionless and silent but the woman leaned over and whispered something in the boy's ear.

"No, sir. I'm sorry. I don't recognize her," the boy finally said. His voice was high and raspy.

Conal could finally see a bit more of the boy's face and took in the dark smudges on his cheeks. He looked as though he had been through a fire.

"So you do speak English."

The boy nodded.

Conal laughed in relief.

"That's great. Are you sure you don't recognize her? Can you look again? It's very important that I find her."

The boy shook his head and looked down again. "No, sir. I'm sorry."

Conal nodded. "Thanks anyway, kid."

Several moments passed before the boy looked up again. "D. Whistler, is it?"

"Excuse me?" Now the kid wanted to talk but not before, when Conal could have used his help getting his parents to look up from whatever fascinated them so deeply there on the floor of the truck.

"D. Whistler. That's your name, isn't it? That's what it says on your uniform."

Conal grabbed ahold of his dog tags and glanced down.

"Oh, right. Right, yeah, that's me. Daniel Whistler."

Assuming identities was becoming commonplace at this point.

The boy laughed. Bit of a pretty boy, Conal thought. He had laughing eyes and a certain soft, feminine quality about his face.

"This is Helen and that's her husband, George," the boy said. "And I'm Edie."

The boy shifted forward to offer Conal his hand and his cap slid askew. Giggling, he lifted it off his head, only to reveal this was no young boy at all.

Long, flowing sandy blond hair tumbled from beneath the cap. Edie. Not a teenage boy at all.

The shock must have registered on Conal's face because Edie's giggle became outright laughter.

"Nice to meet you all," Conal managed awkwardly. "Edie, I'm...I'm sorry. With the cap, I thought you were a...a..."

"I know what you thought. Just don't go getting sweet on me now that you know I'm a woman."

Conal coughed.

"Oh, no, it's just a surprise. I have a friend back home named Edie. You reminded me of her, that's all."

Suddenly it was Edie who was in his head, telling him a story. She had known a man named Daniel. Daniel...Daniel Whistler.

"Sorry, Edie, I didn't get your last name."

She looked at him, puzzled. "I don't think I gave it. But it's Clauson. Edith Clauson."

Conal's head began to ring. Yes, his Edie was Edith Clauson, too. Edith Clauson who had survived World War II, who had fallen in love with a man named Daniel Whistler, only Edie had lived her life alone because Daniel Whistler died in the war.

The real Daniel Whistler was already dead. But Conal wore his clothes. And it was Conal meeting young Edie Clauson.

"Are you all right, Daniel? May I call you Daniel?"

"Certainly...certainly, Edie. Daniel's fine."

"You look as though you've had a bit of a fright suddenly."

"Yeah, I suppose I have. Would you mind telling me where we are? I couldn't get my bearings after I crashed earlier and was just trying to keep moving. Nazi soldiers were nearby and if I had been captured, well, I was just trying to stay out of their range."

Edie nodded sympathetically. "We're just a few miles outside of Dunkirk, so that's not much of surprise. You're very lucky you weren't captured."

Before Conal could respond, the old woman in the front seat whipped around, motioning ahead.

"Jerrys!" Edie hissed.

The driver was heading directly toward a checkpoint manned by four armed German soldiers.

###

Principal Sources

Diary of Jack the Ripper: Shirley Harrison, 1993

Casebook: Jack the Ripper: Produced by Stephen P. Ryder

Jack the Ripper; The Casebook: Richard Jones

Jack the Ripper: Histories Mysteries

Jack the Ripper: A&E Biography

The Phantom of Death: History Channel Biography

Stalking the Ripper: Patricia Cornwell

The Whitechapel Murders: History Channel

Jack the Ripper: The Final Solution : Stephen Knight

Jack the Ripper: Mystery Quest

Jack the Ripper: Discovery Channel

Time Travel the Truth: National Geographic

How to Time Travel: National Geographic

Through the Wormhole: Science Channel

The Fabric of the Cosmos: NOVA

Time Travel: The History Channel